D0051614

MEET THE CHIEF . . .

DECORATED VIETNAM VET

"Tam handed me his knife and waited to see what I would do with it. I stripped down to my shorts and gave him my rifle. The guard never knew what hit him."

DRUG KINGPIN

"The heroin came back with soldiers returning from Vietnam. They would stop in Hawaii and my men would relieve them of their packages."

RUTHLESS KILLER

"I have a one-bedroom bungalow outside of town. It's private there—you can kill people in your livingroom without disturbing the neighbors."

Avon Books are available at special quantity discounts for bulk purchases for sales promotions, premiums, fund raising or educational use. Special books, or book excerpts, can also be created to fit specific needs.

For details write or telephone the office of the Director of Special Markets, Avon Books, Dept. FP, 105 Madison Avenue, New York, New York 10016, 212-481-5653.

JEFF RAINES

AVON BOOKS NEW YORK

For David Raines,
scholar and gentleman

I'd like to thank Alice Turner, Teresa Grosch, Jim Landis, Bonnie Nadell, Bruce Giffords, Mary Silver, Glenn Katz and Ray Seed for making this novel possible.

AVON BOOKS
A division of
The Hearst Corporation
105 Madison Avenue
New York, New York 10016

Copyright © 1987 by Jeffrey Riggan Raines
Published by arrangement with Beech Tree Books/William Morrow and Company, Inc.
Library of Congress Catalog Card Number: 87-1122
ISBN: 0-380-70552-4

All rights reserved, which includes the right to reproduce this book or portions thereof in any form whatsoever except as provided by the U.S. Copyright Law. For information address Permissions Department, Beech Tree Books, William Morrow and Company, Inc., 105 Madison Avenue, New York, New York 10016.

First Avon Books Printing: January 1989

AVON TRADEMARK REG. U.S. PAT. OFF. AND IN OTHER COUNTRIES, MARCA REGISTRADA, HECHO EN U.S.A.

Printed in the U.S.A.

K-R 10 9 8 7 6 5 4 3 2 1

CHAPTER ONE

□

HAWAII

The present

The Big Island is hot in September. The trades blow from the east, down from the volcano, melting the *haole* tourists like *'uki 'ukis* in a cheap lei.

If the heat bothered the big *haole* squinting at me from across my desk he didn't show it. He was dry and looked as cool as ice. I wondered if he had factory-installed A/C. He was wearing khaki hiking shorts and a white cotton button-down shirt, the kind favored by cowboys for Sunday afternoons.

"Afternoon, Sheriff," he said.

I was disappointed he didn't sound more like Gary Cooper. But these days all the tough guys try for Clint Eastwood.

"Sheriff's a fag politician in Hilo," I told him. "All he's good for is bringing in dangerous scofflaws and throwing old ladies out in the street. I'm chief of police. Get it straight."

"Sorry, Chief. It's all the same to me."

Back when I weighed 180 pounds and was an all-island linebacker for the Kohala Cougars I probably would have kicked his butt for being a wise guy. But I'm up to 260 now, and I haven't been lifting any weights recently. I let it pass.

I didn't say anything, letting the silence hang there. It's an old cop trick—folks with guilty consciences always have something they'd like to talk about and they're always rushing to talk about anything else. This one's conscience appeared to be clean. After he figured out that I wasn't going to say anything, he got on with his business.

"I'm going up in the hills to do some hiking," he told me. "I thought I'd check in with you in case something should happen."

He didn't look like the type who worried much about things happening. But smart hikers always have somebody waiting for them. Every five or ten years the boy scouts out on a Sunday walk find a solo hiker wedged in some rocks with a broken leg or two. Sometimes they even get there before the crabs.

"You can't get in much trouble up there less you shake hands with a centipede," I told him.

"Oh? I've heard bad things about marijuana growers: booby traps, machine guns and things like that."

I gave him my best world-weary shocked-by-it-all expression. Criminals engaged in felonious acts under my jurisdiction. Heavens, what's the world coming to?

"Last year we had four hikers disappear. We figured they'd stumbled into the cogs of the free-enterprise system and one of the local entrepreneurs had turned 'em into fertilizer. We spent two weeks up in the hills chasing our tails looking for 'em, but we didn't find shit.

"The only thing we did find was fifty thousand marijuana plants and a dozen or so slow growers. It was real bad for business. I don't think you'll have any problems."

"That's right," he said. "I remember. Mormons, weren't they? They drowned."

"Well," I told him, "we found their boots and two sets of clothes at Kaaha. We figure two of 'em went swimming and got into trouble. The other two jumped in to help and they all drowned. It's an old story."

"That's right, I remember being surprised. . . . Two of them were very strong swimmers, weren't they?"

Bells? Alarms? Red lights flashing? Nope, didn't hear a thing. I sure hope it's not because I'm getting stupid in middle age, cause it's sure as shit that I can't retire. It must be because at least ten times a year I give the same speech to dumb fucks from California. My brain just slides into neutral and my lips flap.

"Poor swimmers never drown, they never get far enough away from the shóre. It's always the strong swimmers who find they can't swim north as fast as the currents taking 'em south. If we know about 'em we go pick 'em up. If we don't, well—it's a long way to Tahiti.

"The real strong ones last two, three days. After the second day they have first-degree burns on their heads and shoulders and they ain't thinking too clearly. They all start to drink the water by the third day. Just a little at first, to moisten their lips. Eventually they take big gulps of that cool, cool water, though. And then the little fishies find them, and then the big fishies."

It never fails to scare the shit out of little blond pricks shivering in the police launch. This guy looked like I'd just given him the five-day forecast.

He handed me his business card, Joshua Smith. He sold farm equipment in Idaho.

"You enjoy hiking, Mr. Smith?"

"I'm an amateur geologist," he replied. "I'm looking for specimens."

I thought about telling him that the rocks were Pele's tears, and that it was bad luck to steal from the goddess. He didn't look like he'd be much interested in the quaint local folklore, though. So instead I told him to give a call in ten days, or maybe I'd send someone out looking for him.

Dumb? I guess so. But I'm really just a hick cop from a small town in the middle of nowhere. And really, what's one more tough guy? They're all tough guys now. Goddamn Clint Eastwood anyway.

Hawaii, the Big Island, was such a nice place when I was growing up. Everybody knew everybody else and they were always willing to lend a hand when times got rough. There wasn't any dope in the high school and hardly anybody ever got the shit kicked out of them on Saturday nights.

Judge Ohira thinks it was World War II: all those strangers seeing what a good deal we had and trying to get a slice of it for themselves. The Californians are certain it was the war that ruined California, especially the ones who turned their grandfathers' pecan orchards into industrial parks, assholes.

Personally I think it was the 707 that did it. The damned Boeing Company and fucking Pan American Airways sold Hawaii as the vacationer's paradise. In 1957 *Life* magazine did three features on Hawaii, happy snorkelers at Hanauma Bay and the whole nine yards.

But whatever the reason, the first millionaires started building their vacation hideaways on the west coast of Hawaii—the island, not the state—shortly after the war. Right behind the millionaires came the real-estate developers and right behind them came the tourists.

Worse than the millionaires and the tourists were the disabled vets who decided they might like to retire in paradise. The Army and Navy discharged thousands of maimed soldiers and Marines out of Tripler Hospital on Oahu. They'd been shot to pieces fighting for shitty little islands in the Pacific and didn't feel real good about the war. The government made up for their various missing arms and legs with full disability pensions, and they didn't feel real good about that either.

The ones who didn't have anyplace better to go, and the ones who did but didn't feel like going there in a wheelchair, settled in the islands. They tended to live far from the beaches in beat-up shacks where they could distill their own private painkillers and tend their secret herb gardens. I grew up with them.

I was born in 1941, nine months before Dad's cousins bombed Pearl Harbor. My father was pure Japanese, my mother half native and half *haole*. *Haoles* are Caucasians, which makes me one-quarter white, my secret shame.

Dad was a welder in the navy yard until December 10, 1941, after which his services were no longer required. Pretty ironic considering how much of the fleet was playing coral reef. He was thirty-four years old, too old to get his ass shot off in Italy and too brown to work for the Navy. He didn't even outlast the Greater Southeast Asian Co-prosperity Sphere: his liver gave out in 1945. Mom moved us to the Big Island the same year.

I had a happy childhood here, diving for fish and climbing the coconut palms. My friends and I hiked up the volcano one summer, sea level to over thirteen thousand feet. Took us three days and we damn near froze our asses when we got to the top.

The only trouble I was ever in was when Charlie Nianga, a fine example of Tongan manhood, called me "*haole* breath" to my face. I broke his nose with a sucker punch and he broke six of my ribs. Luckily the rest of the offensive line was there to stop him from breaking the rest of me. No hard feelings from it—Charlie does some work for me from time to time.

By the time I turned eighteen the islands were booming. Money was flooding into the state and the greatest real-estate boom in history was making millionaires out of the store owners in Waikiki. There was more than enough money at the University for poor boys who could play football. It was the best of times.

Hawaii almost got lucky. The Mafia had every nickel it owned tied up in Las Vegas and didn't have anything to spare for the Pacific. Unfortunately the Japanese *yakuza* gangs had American dollars coming out of their wazoos—remember the Korean War? They saw Hawaii as a golden opportunity to invest in the flagship of the free-enterprise system and they jumped at it. The gangs practically own Honolulu.

The *yakuza* gangs weren't interested in running Hawaii; well, actually they were but the Chinese convinced them that it wasn't such a good idea. What the *yakuza* wanted, and what they eventually got, was a toehold on the mainland. Which is what they had been after in the first place.

We could have outlasted the *yakuza*. The Vietnam War was the straw that broke the camel's back. Don't get me wrong—it was a popular war in Hawaii. It was a big boost to the local economy and not many of our boys had to go:

wrong color skin, wrong-shaped eyes. Just about the only ones who did go were the poor *haoles* and Hawaii's West Pointies, who were inevitably shot in the back the first time they got within fifteen miles of the Viet Cong.

The big problem with the war was that the World War II vets—the ones with the pounds of Mitsubishi steel in their craws—decided it was their patriotic duty to sell some of their private herbal painkillers to the boys in uniform. The boys in uniform were crazy to buy too, singing, "Oh no, ah don't give a damn, next stop is Vietnam."

The next group of boys discharged out of Tripler weren't interested in living in shacks and guiding tourists for pocket money. They remembered how much they'd paid for the local weed on their first trip through, back when they could still have sold their bodies to the med schools. A lot of them decided to go into business for themselves.

Maybe they'd seen how much Dow was making in the jellied-gasoline business and figured they deserved a piece of the pie. Or maybe they'd learned more than just how to smear shit on a punji stick in the great Vietnam finishing school. Whatever it was, they took the AK-47's they'd mailed home a piece at a time and headed straight for the hills in full-tilt pursuit of the American dream.

They pushed the World War II vets out real quick. Most of the old men weren't greedy and were pretty fast on the uptake as well; they retired quietly. What once had been a private hobby became big business overnight, and it brought all the evils of prohibition with it. Honest citizens stopped looking too closely at the money people were handing them, becoming silent partners. Scum from everywhere came to cash in on a sure thing and the creatures that live off scum weren't far behind.

And then people started dying. Don't be surprised that you didn't hear about the great Kona grass war. The town fathers made sure it never made the papers. A lot of people went swimming that year and never came back, no bodies ever recovered. Bones decompose fast in the tropics.

By 1969 I was the youngest police lieutenant in Hawaii. I was the first college graduate—University of Hawaii at

Manoa, A.B. criminal justice, 1963—our force had ever hired and I was up to my ass in the nastiest little war east of Quang Tri province.

The chief solved his problem by retiring.

After Hizzoner made me acting interim temporary chief of police, he pulled me aside and told me I had six months to solve our delicate little problem, less if it made the papers.

"The tourists are beginning to wonder if it's the Fourth of fucking July around here every day," he told me. "What's more, if one more fucking hiker who's too fucking cheap to stay in a fucking hotel disappears, the governor's fucking sending in the National Guard. And guess what that's going to do to for fucking business."

I just smiled and said, "Right away, sir." Privately I didn't think sending in the Guard was going to do much good. I doubted that any of them would be any more anxious to step on a punji stick than my men. One of my men already had. He was in the hospital for more than a month before they cut his foot off.

The next day we arrested three of the bigger growers on suspicion-of-loitering charges. Got them all into my office and told them straight out that this shit just had to stop.

"Look," I said. "I don't care what you clowns are doing up in the hills, and I'm not going to go up there to find out. What's more, as far as I'm concerned you boys are first-class, honest, law-abiding taxpayers, entitled to all the protection this office can afford you. But I swear, if one more fucking tourist gets his head blown off I'm going to start a brush fire that's going to clear off the entire fucking volcano, and me and my men are going to sit at the edge of it and shoot every fucking thing that the fire flushes and tell the newspapers we thought you were wild pigs."

We all shook hands and agreed that America was the greatest country in the world, that the business of America was business, that I was the greatest law enforcement agent in the history of America, and that peace was indeed at hand.

The next day two of them were dead and the third had a .30-caliber machine gun set up in his barn and was blasting away at passing cars. It seemed that word had gotten out on the street that they had made a deal with the heat to drive the other growers out of business and set up a cartel with them as the bosses.

That night someone emptied a riot gun into my house. Years later I remember sympathizing with Jimmy Carter over the Middle East. I wondered if anyone else in the country realized what a shitty job he had.

Salvation came from an unlikely source—California. Marty Stine was a refugee from the Santa Monica surf war where teenagers were killing each other to keep outsiders off the public beaches. Marty had long straw-blond hair and that boyish shit-eating grin that made men barf and women drop their bikini bottoms. He walked up to me on the street about a week after my aborted peace conference and dazzled me with his most brilliant smile.

"Pardon me, officer, but could you direct me to the most favorable location for marijuana cultivation?"

I couldn't think of an appropriately snappy reply, so I decided to knock out all his teeth instead—looking over my shoulder for a week had made me irritable. I was casually looking around to see if any of the local Brahmins were watching when he went on.

"You see, Chief, they told me down at the beach that you've lived here all your life and would be certain to know the best location."

That took all the wind out of my sails. It wasn't that I felt sorry for him because he was an imbecile—it was just that I didn't feel like being used in somebody else's practical joke. On the other hand, I didn't want him wandering around in my town either. After a little thought I sent him up to Mad Dog Magill's greenhouse. Which, as it turned out, was exactly what he wanted me to do.

He told me later that he had taken Pig Psychology 101 at the Berkeley Free School and had had a pretty good idea as to how I was likely to react. It would have been a real shame if I'd disappointed him: it would have ruined a beautiful relationship.

In any case, that meeting marked the end of the war. I didn't realize it at the time, of course. All I knew was that people stopped dying. Not only did people stop dying, they stopped getting wounded. Hikers started wandering into the station talking about big fields of pot and asking why I wasn't doing anything about it. I actually checked up on two of the stories. They were true: fields of marijuana ripening in the sun with no one watching.

I was so amazed that for thirty seconds I thought about investigating and maybe cracking down on the growers. Common sense won out, thank God. Ordinarily I don't care for puzzles, but since this one had job security written all over it, I decided that I could live with a little mystery in my life.

After the mayor took the "acting," "interim" and "temporary" out of my job title, he pulled me aside again and asked how I had done it. I could tell he was impressed because he hadn't let loose an obscenity all night.

"Mr. Mayor," I told him, "there are things that no man who has to face the electorate really wants to know."

He mulled that over for a few seconds, gave me a glassy-eyed smile, shook my hand, told me to keep up the good work and headed back to the bar. I spent the rest of the night wondering what I was going to do when the bodies started piling up again.

But they didn't. Six peaceful months went by, full of long afternoon naps and even longer-legged *wahines* from California, the reason I'd taken up napping in the afternoons. If I ever wondered what was going on in the hills, I managed to control myself. Eventually, I reasoned, I would find out, and I saw no reason to hurry the day.

And then, that long-haired son-of-Jesus surf freak from Santa Monica showed up at the station driving a brand-new candied-apple-red Porsche.

"Chief," he said sitting down next to my desk, "I need some more advice."

"How's Mad Dog?" I asked.

"Mr. Magill is fine. As a matter of fact, Mr. Magill has never been better."

"Oh?" I said. "And why is that homicidal maniac feeling so chipper these days?"

"Because, sir, since Mr. Magill joined our organization, his productivity has doubled and his net has more than tripled. He now has spare time in which he can enjoy the fruits of his labor: he can stop to smell the roses, so to speak."

The story on Mad Dog was that he had been section-eighted out of a front-line Marine battalion. They had wanted to keep him because he scared the shit out of the Cong, but a photographer had gotten a picture of his genitalia collection and he had had to go. The thought of him with spare time on his hands was not designed to cheer my every waking hour.

"What organization is that?" I asked.

I carry the card he gave me to this day, which is real stupid of me, but what the fuck. It read, "Affiliated Macadamia Nut Growers of Western Hawaii, Martin Stine, Pres."

I stared at the card for a while, considering the possibilities of the lowly macadamia.

"Tell me, Mr. Stine, how can I be of service to the Affiliated Growers?"

"Well, for one thing, Chief," he replied, "you can stop hikers from trampling through our macadamia groves."

"Oh, no problem, Mr. Stine. Next time you spot a trespasser in your orchard, you just give us a buzz and we'll have a squad car down there on the double. Hopefully we'll even get there before they can carve their initials on your trees."

He gave me a dazzling smile.

"You don't understand, Chief. Our organization is very young and is at a critical point in its development. This is the sort of issue that could destroy the AMN-GWH in its infancy.

"Just think back to the bad old days of ruthless price cutting, when every grower was at his neighbor's throat and oversupply was threatening to ruin the industry. We wouldn't want to bring back those days again, would we? Especially now that some discipline has been restored to the market."

I had to think about that for a second. I may be a little slow, but eventually I figured it out. The fact that he was alive, driving a Porsche and evidently on good terms with Mad Dog was just so strange that it took me a while. When I had sufficiently rearranged my world view I began to slowly shake my head, signifying that no indeed, I did not yearn for the bad old days.

"Excellent, Chief, I knew I could count on you to be a booster. We already have crop insurance, to shield our members against unexpected crop loss, which as you can imagine has made them more philosophic about life's slings and arrows. As nature lovers we're willing to finance a series of hiking trails that will take the serious hiker away from the temptation of the ripening macadamia. We feel that with a little help from the local police, we can keep western Hawaii a nice place to live and raise children."

"How can we be of assistance?" I asked.

"Well, Chief, it's simple. We feel that most of the macadamia thefts are committed by a small band of incorrigible local youths. A few words about the horrors of macadamia addiction from the chief of police may be enough to set these young men onto the straight and narrow."

"The Marines are always looking," I agreed. "What else?"

"We want you to make sure the hikers stay on the trails."

"If you make them nice enough," I pointed out, "they won't want to leave them."

"Yes, that's true, but there's always a few."

"Well," I said, "it would sure be a shame if they ran into any feral pigs."

"Pigs?"

"Mean bastards," I told him. "Weigh up to three hundred fifty pounds and they hate humans. Gore you to death quicker than you can say Kalanianaole."

"Some of them may even be rabid," he said, warming to the idea.

"Most likely."

"Chief," he said, getting up to leave, "I want you to know that you have the full support of the Affiliated Growers. As a matter of fact, I think the growers will be willing to authorize a substantial retainer for your services as a consultant."

I was pretty quick back then. Before he could move I had him by the throat. I bounced him off the wall a couple of times and then showed him a trick called riding the baton that a drill sergeant had taught me back at Parris Island.

"Listen, faggot, I don't give a shit how you got those crazy fuckers into line and I don't give a shit what you're doing out there either. But you offer me or any of my men a fucking nickel and I'll feed your balls to the crabs with you still attached to them.

"This is how it's gonna be. No little kids are gonna bring pot into show 'n' tell. No long-haired loser's gonna drive a fucking stretch limo through town or live in a fucking mansion on three hundred forty dollars a month . . . and no fucking hikers are going to turn up missing.

"I swear, if the FBI or the CIA or the IRS starts sniffing around here, you won't live thirty seconds. Do you understand?"

I guess I came pretty close to dying then. I saw the wheels turning behind his light-blue eyes. He had been computing the cost-benefit ratio: no payoffs versus lack of control. I don't think the fact that his balls were busy trying to hide somewhere in his lower belly even entered into the equation. Finally he smiled and said that he'd known I was going to be a booster.

I let him down and he left. I guess he decided that not having to pay off the local police won the day because I'm still breathing. Maybe he decided he needed a management consultant. Later I found out that he had painstakingly explained the benefits of paying taxes to his clients, at least on the money they were planning to spend.

Over the years I got the whole story. After getting my directions, he had walked straight up to Magill's, fifteen miles, and bought three kilos of Kona Gold, on credit. He told Mad Dog, "The chief sent me." Not only that, he bought twenty-seven more kilos from the other growers. He used Mad Dog as a reference and nobody was willing to say no.

Then he flew to California and sold the lot to a motorcycle gang for an incredible forty-five hundred dollars a kilo, five times what it would have fetched in Hawaii. He got back on a jet with two paper shopping bags full of money and returned to Hawaii, where he reimbursed the growers and, effectively, ended the war. Feeding his balls to the crabs would never have worked: crabs don't eat steel.

The growers loved Marty; they even started to love each other. They traded composting tips, for Christ's sake. It was disgusting.

But it was peaceful. God, was it peaceful. As Marty had predicted, what was good for the Affiliated Growers was good for Hawaii.

Besides his abundant managerial ability, Marty was a visionary. He had spent a summer on Martha's Vineyard and thought that western Hawaii was a great place to put a year-round Edgartown. He was right, but if any of us had ever been to Martha's Vineyard we would have shot the bastard.

He opened the town's first antique shop, gourmet ice cream parlor and aloha shirt factory. He had actually bought fifty mopeds at one point, before the town fathers made him see reason.

And the town grew; shit, did it grow. Marty laundered the Affiliated Growers' money through a bank in San Francisco and invested it through two Swiss corporations. Development money just poured in, faster than any of us would have believed. Anybody who owned any land started to get rich, so nobody was too fussy about what was going on in the hills. If one day a shiftless no-account was driving a Corvette and having his taxes done by Tsutsumi and Lane, well, that was the American dream, wasn't it? Small-town boy makes good.

We did have a few problems over the years. Five or six times a year a long-haired son of Jesus would hitchhike into town thinking it was his sacred right as an American to homestead a plot in the hills, and then be able to sell the fruits of his labor on the open market for all that the market would bear, assholes. Marty delegated that problem to his personnel director, Orville Magill.

We had other problems. In the late seventies the DEA started spraying weed killer on the state's number one agricultural product. Marty rose to the occasion, though: he simply harvested early and sold at a steep discount. He even came up with a new brand name for the stuff, Jamaican Blue. Californians will believe anything.

Ironically, the biggest problem we ever had was with the feral pigs, not that the pigs were a threat to anything but the environment, you understand. It was just that by the mid-seventies the rumor about vicious man-eating pigs had gotten so widespread that the assholes in the state legislature decided that they should do something about it.

They passed a bill, which thank God the governor vetoed, that offered a hundred-dollar bounty for dead pigs. That would have been great, two thousand drunks armed with shotguns tramping through the hills hunting wild pigs. Luckily the swine flu came around about then and essentially wiped out the herd. Where Marty found those dead pigs I'll never know.

But by and large the town was much the same as it had ever been, a sleepy fishing village, a nice place to raise your kids. There were hardly any drugs in the high school and prostitutes didn't hang out on Main Street. Scuzzball pornographers confined themselves to Hilo.

The only excitement we had was twice a year when the sport fishermen came to town for the million-dollar tournaments. Big happy-go-lucky rich kids who liked to kill thousand-pound fish and break things that didn't belong to them. They're easy, though. Their idea of fighting dirty is to kick a man in the crotch. Mine is to have four of my men hold someone down while I do amateur orthodontics with my nightstick.

Just a nice peaceful town, until four Mormon missionaries decided to go explore the volcano and neglected to come back. They had spent two years in Hawaii proselytizing the heathen and were just having a little fun before going home.

The Mormons are possibly the most boring people on the face of the earth. They don't drink, they don't smoke, they don't do drugs, they don't carouse and they don't cause trouble. Except that it would drive me crazy, I wish everyone was a Mormon. The only problem with the Mormons is that they're certain that they're on to the God-given truth and they aren't shy about letting you hear about it.

Every young Mormon male is expected to go out on a two-year mission to save the souls of us less fortunate gentiles. The church doesn't seem to mind much that the success rate of these missions hovers somewhere around zero because the main reason for them is to strengthen the missionaries' ties with their church. Returning missionaries are hailed as conquering heros on their return and made to feel like real disciples of Christ. I didn't think the church elders were going to be too pleased about losing four of them.

I knew it would be bad, but it should have occurred to me that their daddies must have been able to pull some heavy-duty strings to get them sent to Hawaii. I mean really: sending Mormons to Hawaii's like sending Jews to New York.

I got my first nasty surprise the first day of the search. I'd spent all day in the foothills burning pot fields and arresting longtime citizens. It was hot nasty work and all I could think about all day was punji sticks. When I got back to town I found the governor himfuckingself holding a press conference in my office.

I should have known that the strings those boys' daddies had pulled to get them to Hawaii in the first place wouldn't be anything compared to the strings that they'd pull to get them back. I could see His Excellency being jerked like a marionette.

Bastard was paying his first visit since the last time he'd run for reelection. He'd brought half the state police force with him and pledged he'd have those boys back safe and sound within the week. He was wrong. Five hundred volunteers from Brigham Young University's Oahu campus, hundreds of police officers and all of the park rangers couldn't find shit.

After a week it was national news. Ted Williams was right—pour hot water on a reporter and you get instant shit. Since there wasn't a story and the bastards were enjoying their all-expenses-paid vacation in paradise, they started writing color pieces. They dug up all the shit that had gone down in the sixties and wrote about Hawaii's Barbary Coast. They started asking me questions about the local criminal element, assholes.

The state police captain was having the time of his life. Fucker turned out to be a great counter. He was the one who came up with the fifty-thousand-plants number. Luckily he got arrested for drunk driving two months later or he would have made it an annual event.

After the initial shock, Marty was the calmest person on the island. He bailed out his growers, declared the crop a total loss and paid off all the insurance policies. Then he quintupled the local price, due to the emergency, and imported seventy tons of Mexican for the export market.

"Look," he told me, "it's all in their heads anyway."

He cleaned up.

After two weeks an idiot camper on his way out of the park mentioned that somebody had left some shoes down at Kaaha. The state police captain was the first man on the spot—after the park rangers, that is. With only a little help from me, he gave a really heartrending speech about the nobility of those who had sacrificed themselves for their comrades. Thirty seconds of it even made the national news.

I was relieved. For a while there it had looked like I was

going to have to send somebody down to Kaaha to find the boots, and that wouldn't have been clean. No, that wouldn't have been clean at all.

I had had an awful premonition of death as Marty and I had driven out to the Evans plantation. He wouldn't tell me why I had to go out there, just that it was out of his league. I wondered the whole way out what could possibly be out of Marty's league. I found out when we got out there. It was out of my league too.

All four bodies were lined up neatly by the drying racks. The first one had evidently taken a large hunting knife, the kind teenagers carry into the woods to protect themselves from deer, directly in the stomach. It was the oldest type of deadfall. Nobody who'd been in Vietnam for more than a week would have tripped it.

The other three had been shot once each in the back of the head. Their hands were tied behind their backs with baling wire. Two of them had struggled and cut their wrists on the wire, one more than the other. Nobody had to tell me what had happened. I wanted to throw up.

The Evans brothers were dancing around in the background, looking nervous and ready to go to pieces. White men really shouldn't live in the tropics, I reflected. It eventually parboils their brains. I looked over at Marty. He looked pretty sick too and I knew he didn't have to be told that this was going to be very bad for business. Once word got out—and I could just see the brothers giving a blow-by-blow description to their friends down at the Whale and Lion—the shit was certain to hit the fan. The state would have to land on us hard, and I wasn't that sure they wouldn't find something if they looked.

"See you caught some trespassers there, Jimbo," I finally said, talking to the older of the brothers. "Why don't you put that gun away and let's figure out what to do with the bodies."

He was dumb, he did it. I walked over to the bodies, took my service revolver out and shot Jimbo right in the chest, twice, just like the book says. His brother looked at the body with his mouth hanging open.

Marty said, "Sorry, Billy," and then clipped him behind the ear. He stood there over him, looking at me.

"Well," I said. "Partner."

"I don't carry a gun."

"Then improvise," I told him. "That's what you've always been good at."

He knelt down and put his hands around Billy's neck and started squeezing the life out of him.

"Did I ever tell you how I came to Hawaii?"

"No," I answered.

"There was this asshole from L.A. He just moved in one day and started surfing our beach like he owned it, hogging the killer waves."

"Bad form?" I asked.

"The worst. Finally I told him that jerks who couldn't surf should stick to inner tubes at the city swimming pool and the bastard pulled a knife on me. So I killed him with my board: it wasn't an accident."

Billy began to look pretty dead, but I told Marty to break his neck anyway, just to be sure. He stood up and went on with his story; he didn't appear to be very shaken up.

"I had to leave town pretty quickly after that."

"Police?"

"No, bastard's brother was a biker."

"Different club than your customers?"

"There's really only one club—they just have different names so the consumers won't catch on. But this is business, that was personal. You should have been there. I walked into a biker bar in East L.A. with thirty keys of Kona AA and offered it to the club president for two hundred thousand dollars."

"What'd he say?"

"Asshole just looked at me and asked where the fuck Kona was. I told him it was on Maui. He practically cried. 'You got da Maui Wowie!' Christ, it was like I'd offered him Laotian Deathweed."

"What about the guy's brother?"

Marty grinned. "Beats me, bra. Maybe he moved to Texas. Nothing was going to stand in the way of the club being the sole west coast distributor of 'da Maui Wowie.' What are we going to do about this shit?" he asked indicating the bodies.

"Don't worry," I told him, "I have a plan."

It didn't quite work out as I had foreseen it, but it did get the job done. We had gotten a lot of nasty publicity, but nobody in Honolulu was agitating for the quick extermination of the murderous pot growers. I even thought we had gotten away with it.

I had this terrible feeling of déjà vu, riding into the hills with Marty, him not saying a word. This time it was Dave Bellamy's camp. Dave was hanging by his feet from a tree branch; flies swarmed around the gaping hole in his throat. From the smell, I figured it had happened less than a day before.

"You hate to see it," I told Marty. I really did. The same thing had nearly happened to me once.

Marty swung him around to show me his hands. They were black where someone had held a cigarette lighter up to them. Evidently that someone had had a few questions for Dave.

The flies were very loud.

"You know, Marty," I said, "this is going to cause talk."

"Why," he asked, indicating Dave's hands, "would somebody want to go and do this?"

"Maybe the farm equipment game's gotten rough," I answered. Marty just stared at me. I told him about Mr. Smith on the way back to town.

It didn't really surprise me that Smith was waiting for me at home. My address is in the book, right next to my number. Maybe I'm expecting that big call from *Dialing for Dollars* or something.

"You haven't been playing with matches out in the rain forest, have you, Mr. Smith?" I asked him.

He didn't reply and his pistol never wavered from where he was pointing it: my stomach. I walked over to my bar and poured myself a port and sat down.

"Where are the bodies?" he finally asked.

"In about fifty feet of water off of Mana Kona Park, vicious undertow. I guess it doesn't carry much weight with you that the guys who did it are down there with them."

He shook his head. He'd come a long way to kill someone and it looked like I was his number one candidate.

"What tipped you off?" I asked.

"The shoes the alleged heroes kicked off during their mad dash to rescue their friends . . . one pair belonged to someone who didn't swim."

"Shit," I said. "Well, we were constrained by the bloodstains. You know how tough they are to get out. Why'd they only send one of you?'

"They were content with the coroner's report."

"Ah," I said, "I understand. The church can always use a few heroes. You must have a personal interest."

"My oldest son."

"Well," I said, "that certainly ties up all the loose ends."

That was supposed to have been Marty's cue, but no Marty. I sure hoped that he hadn't decided he could cut a better deal with my mentally retarded lieutenant. I regretted the stains remark and started to sweat for the first time since I'd seen Smith sitting in my best recliner.

"Tell me, Sheriff, how much does a decorated war hero cost?"

"A lot," I told him, ignoring the "Sheriff."

"Is that what's important to you, money? Do you ever think about the lives you ruin? Or do you think it doesn't matter because it happens somewhere else to people with different color skin?"

There was a lot of truth to that, but I didn't think that this was the time to discuss moral philosophy with him. On the other hand I figured as long as he was talking he wasn't going to shoot me.

"What use is honor to a half-breed?" I asked him.

He resisted the urge to perform psychoanalysis and delve deeply into my childhood—my luck to run into someone who'd been brought up correctly. He raised his gun until it pointed straight at my head, a real amateur's mistake, but I didn't think it was going to cost him.

"Good-bye, Sheriff," he said. And then he died.

Marty shot him in the back of the head about an inch behind his right ear. He was dead before his body reached the carpet. His trigger finger didn't twitch, but considering what had just happened to his brain's motor center, that wasn't very surprising.

"You know, Marty," I said, "you're getting to be a real asshole."

He hadn't lost anything on his smile over the years. It still made me want to barf.

"Remember that trick you showed me with your nightstick?"

He shut the window and came in through the kitchen door. He carefully picked up Smith's head and put an old copy of *Guns and Ammo* beneath it. It didn't look like Smith had leaked much on the carpet.

"Thanks, Marty," I told him. "That rug's a real bitch to get dry-cleaned."

He looked up at me and gave me an odd look. "God, some cop you are. Haven't you ever heard of evidence?"

I just shrugged and sipped at my port. Bits and pieces of Smith's occipital lobe were probably splattered on all four walls and the ceiling. It would take the FBI crime lab about two hours to determine someone had been murdered in my living room. They'd probably be able to tell Marty what color underwear he'd been wearing when he pulled the trigger.

"It doesn't make much difference," I told him. "If it ever gets to the point that somebody's looking, we'll be dead anyway."

"Do you think there'll be any more like him?" Marty asked.

"No," I said. "They know he went looking for trouble,

they won't be surprised that he found it. As long as they don't know anything concrete they won't come sniffing around."

I found out how wrong I was two weeks later. I was surf-casting down at Hapuna. It was before dawn and the beach was deserted, just the way I like it. I figured I had two hours before the first tourist showed up.

"Sheriff Yamasaki," someone called out.

I turned and found myself staring at two of Smith's cousins.

"Sheriff's a fag politician in Hilo," I told him.

The one on the left said, "I know."

His buddy shot me in the leg, about an inch above the kneecap. I fell awkwardly into the surf and flopped around like a freshly landed fish. My leg started sending all kinds of confused signals northward. It wasn't sure if it was burning or throbbing or what. The noisy one knelt down where I was lying.

"We've come for the bodies: Brother Joshua and the boys."

The other one knelt down and grabbed my shot leg and gave it a twist, which straightened out the signal it was trying to send. It was pain.

"And this Stine person," he asked, "where can we find this Stine person?"

CHAPTER TWO

□

QUANG NAM PROVINCE, REPUBLIC OF VIETNAM

December, 1965

My left leg had been numb for two hours and I just wished to God that my neck would get that way too: the mosquitoes were having a picnic on the back of it. I wasn't about to move, though. Under starlight everything is blurred; shapes blend together and individual objects can't be picked out against their background. But you can see motion, and I was waiting to see some out on the rice paddy. And when I did, I was gonna get to kill something.

Pfc. Washington, late of North Philadelphia, was about twenty-five feet down the dike. The local militiamen Kam and Suong—Suong was the militia commander—were somewhere off to his left. I hadn't heard a sound from that direction for hours. We didn't have VC pinned down in a rice paddy every night and none of us was willing to share the kill. We wanted it for ourselves.

The idea behind night patrols is to take the night away from Charlie. If you don't go out to meet him every night he gets bold and comes right up to the wire and leaves things for you to step on the next day. The assholes in the Americal Division were finding out the hard way that you can't depend on artillery to keep Charlie out in the jungle. You have to go out and kill him personally.

My squad and I are attached to the South Vietnamese Army in conjunction with a detachment of local militiamen. It's not a typical arrangement. Some bright boy at I Corps headquarters had noticed that no matter how often we kicked the shit out of the North Vietnamese Regulars, the backcountry villages stayed under VC control. At the same time the local militia, the PF's, were always asking for help on the ground. Putting two and two together the boys at headquarters decided to try sending a squad of Marines into one of the VC-controlled villages to see if they couldn't get any of those big red circles taken off their op-maps.

They asked for volunteers from the 3rd Marines and damn near every man in the division stepped forward. It didn't have anything to do with the heroic tradition of the Corps: village duty meant no first sergeants, no officers, no inspections and no ten-day patrols in the bush. It was a chance to meet the village girls and maybe even get lucky. You got to eat hot meals and sleep in the same bed every day. It promised violence every night.

The local militia really had needed help. Before we had arrived their situation had been described as "precarious" by an optimistic asshole in Army Intelligence. They could move freely in the village during daylight hours, the VC weren't that strong; but at night, the VC owned the night. Every day at sunset the PF's would retreat out into the jungle to a hilltop that they had fortified with concrete blocks cast off from the South Vietnamese Army. They spent every night there, shooting at shadows and waiting for the ax to fall.

The villagers watched the militia tuck their tails between their legs and run every night and it wasn't any wonder they weren't flying the national flag in the marketplace; who wanted to back a sure loser? The villagers were certain that the VC would eliminate the PF's when the time was ripe—it just hadn't seemed worth the effort as yet.

That all changed when we arrived. With twelve Marines and twenty provincial policemen, Suong didn't think he had to hide in the jungle anymore. We took over an abandoned French fort and repaired its crumbling walls.

Suong told me later that it had been abandoned after the original garrison had been massacred by the Viet Minh.

I wasn't thrilled by the thought of all those dead Frenchies. It's not that I believe in ghosts, it's just that I didn't want to see history repeating itself. Suong told me not to worry.

"Don't sweat, Jim," he said. "Since I already in here, I can't sneak in and slit own throat."

He chuckled really nastily and walked off. For weeks afterward, whenever he saw me, he would pantomime throat slitting and make gargling noises. The other militiamen told me that he had been King Shit in the Viet Minh.

The first month had been hairy—nearly every patrol made contact. Two Marines went home in boxes and three others paid for their plane tickets home the hard way. A lot of men died on both sides, but the VC got by far the worst of it. They hadn't been willing to admit defeat and lose face in front of the villagers, but eventually they learned who owned the night. Things had been relatively peaceful ever since. We aren't winning the war, mind you: we never cross the river, not even in broad daylight. The other bank belongs to Charlie.

But after we had killed enough guerrillas to teach them not to fuck with us, life on our side of the river settled down to a dull routine. My squad and the locals sit around the fort all day and drink beer or play cards or try to sleep in the 107-degree heat. Some days we go into the village to practice Vietnamese and chase local girls. But whatever we do during the day, after the sun sets we go back to the village or into the dunes or out on the paddies, and we wait; some nights we get lucky, and tonight we had been real lucky.

The village is actually six loosely connected hamlets that share a central marketplace. It covers about twelve square miles along the coast where the Tra Bong River flows into the South China Sea. There are five thousand people living in the village, more or less. When times are good they support themselves through farming and fishing. When times are bad, like they have been since 1957, the village survives by sending men to the provincial capital to hire themselves out as laborers. Some men earn money by serving in the local militia, but you have to be real hungry before you get desperate enough to do that.

But then again, there are a lot of desperate people in South Vietnam. The village is poor, the signs of abject poverty are everywhere: farmers dressed in rags and their children not dressed at all, huts so dilapidated that you have to wonder what's holding them up. The apathetic stares of the poorest villagers are what kill me. They work all morning scratching a living out of the dirt, rest in the afternoon and then work until long after the sun sets.

When the sun gets too hot they collapse in the shade. Weakened by amoebic dysentery and intestinal worms, they lie panting under the palm trees watching the big healthy Americans walk by with the shiny tools of their trade slung casually over one shoulder. I wonder sometimes if they have enough energy to work up a good hate.

The villagers walk a tightrope with the government before them, the VC behind and certain death just below. To support either side is a death warrant if you've picked a loser. And if you back a winner, so what? The village has always been poor, and it always will be; the winner won't change that. The village is a long way from Saigon, or Hanoi.

Some have chosen sides anyway, and once they've openly backed one side or the other, there's no turning back. The guerrillas out in the jungle know that the only way they're coming home is as victors, and the local militia know that they'll be dead when the VC come home.

Most of the villagers are too smart to openly back one side or the other. If they have an opinion, they keep it to themselves. Even the ones who have chosen sides aren't willing to burn all their bridges—a VC stalwart had whispered to one of Suong's spies where the guerrillas would be crossing the river tonight.

The informer had told Suong's spy that it would be a large band. It seemed that the village chief had been holding back on the village's rice quota and the VC were coming to teach him a lesson. That was a good sign. If people were hungry enough to be holding out on the VC, we knew the guerrillas would be starving in the jungle. It was also a vote of confidence in Suong. The villagers thought that he could protect them.

Sending a large party into the village was a sure sign that the Cong were in trouble. They'd never had to display much force to keep the villagers in line before we arrived. And to send a lot of men at one time was very dangerous. I wasn't expecting them to surrender, though. The VC are like roaches—they can survive for a week on a mouthful of dirty water and an old taro root.

Suong had been really anxious to get these ones. He figured that if we hurt the VC bad enough, the chief might decide it was safe to cut them off altogether. I told him not to count on it. Vietnamese politicians are a lot more careful than their American counterparts; they have to be, the stakes are higher here.

I was pretty anxious myself though, so we were extra careful on the way out. None of the VC spies knew we were still in the village. Twelve men had gone out of the fort on the midnight patrol, but only eight returned. I was counting on the VC being cocky too. As long as they aren't actually looking for trouble, they're confident that they can avoid the noisy Marines.

They're wrong. We've learned a lot in the three months we've been in the village. We wear skin-tight fatigues that don't swish when we walk or tangle branches as we pass. We wrap our spare magazines in burlap and fix rubber bands around our hand grenades. We don't wear insect repellent anymore. You can smell it for a hundred meters.

We dropped off from the main patrol on the way home and dug in on the dike. We waited a long time for the Cong. We would've waited all night if it had taken that long, but it didn't. A VC scout appeared at about three A.M. He was so intent on not making any noise himself that he never even saw Washington. Washington loves to use his knife. He says he's had it since he was twelve and they didn't teach him nothing at boot camp that he didn't already know. I believe him.

The main party followed soon after, between five and eight shadows wearing black pajamas and carrying things that didn't look like farming tools. They were about halfway across the paddy when their point man froze. Maybe he heard something, or maybe he had a finely tuned sixth sense. He wasn't bulletproof, that was for sure.

I think it was Washington who fired first, but it could have been me. Regardless, the four of us opened up within a second of each other, Washington and me spraying automatic weapon fire across the paddy with Kam and Suong firing their carbines as fast as they could. I was sure we got most of them in the first fusillade, but I was pretty sure we hadn't gotten them all, so we settled in to wait. We were very patient; we could afford to be. Charlie, frozen out in the paddy, wasn't so fortunate.

The rice paddies, where we had set tonight's ambush, run all along the riverbank between the hamlets. They're by far the most important things in the village, and the villagers treat them that way. But they stink. I wouldn't want to have to crouch down in one waiting for an invisible assassin to leave me face down and floating.

I had my eye on a likely looking hump; I thought it was moving, but it wasn't moving very fast and I wanted to be sure. As soon as I fired, the tracer rounds in my magazine would look like a fucking neon sign saying "Shoot here." It would take a pretty good shot to get me, but I've known a lot of pretty good shots. Besides, it would be light in a few hours and then it'd be like fucking ducks on a pond.

Evidently my hump figured that out too, because just then it straightened out and started moving. I dropped it with one shot and lucked out when it wasn't a tracer. I heard Washington whisper, "Bastard," from down the dike. After that we waited till first light.

Dawn in Vietnam is just like dawn back home. One minute it was dark and the next it was like someone had flicked a switch. Suddenly I could see Washington and the others as well as our handiwork floating out in the paddy.

There was just one left—he slowly stood up with his

hands high in the air. He was just a kid and he looked scared to death. Six of his friends were scattered around him looking very dead. I climbed up on the dike and started pounding on my leg, trying to get some feeling back into it, hurt like a bastard. I was pleased; including the one Washington had gotten with his knife the kid made eight.

"Think he worth talkin' to?" Washington asked.

It was a rhetorical question. Suong's carbine barked once and the kid fell over in the paddy. I lined up my M-14 and started pumping shots into heads. You learned real quick that it really didn't pay to take chances.

"They find out you goin' foh head shots back at Pah-is Island and they gonna kick yoh butt right outta da Corps."

I looked over at Washington, who was taking his boots off, and asked him what the fuck difference it made if they weren't shooting back. I noticed that he had had a dysentery attack sometime during the night. His fatigues were stained brown from diarrhea. You really had to be anxious to kill people to shit in your pants and then lie in it all night. Washington was what you would call real steady.

Kam went off to the village to round up some villagers to cart our prizes into the marketplace while Suong and I went to collect weapons. Suong looked as happy as a teenage boy with his first real tit in his hand. Every time he recognized one of the dead men he would grin from ear to ear, carefully spit in the corpse's face and then kick it a few times.

I could understand why he was happy. Dead VC had a direct and positive impact on his life expectancy. Village politics being the way they were, Suong's ability to stay alive was directly related to the prestige of the government forces as compared to that of the NLF. If the VC thought they could sneak an assassination squad into the village to get him, they would. The only thing that stopped them was the certainty that one of Suong's spies was sure to betray the killers before they could do their job. If it began to look like the government was going to lose, all of Suong's sources would dry up and he would end up sleeping in the jungle again.

Since we had been there, Suong hadn't been afraid to sleep in the ville. Government prestige was at an all-time high and people who had been openly sympathetic to the NLF were regretting it. On the other hand not many people were willing to wave the national flag either; the tide ebbs and flows and who knew what the situation would be like next year. But for the time being Suong was riding the crest. Having eight corpses to hang up in the marketplace was sure to boost his prestige, and it wouldn't hurt his image any at the provincial capital either.

By the time we finished rounding up the usual assortment of Chinese carbines, Russian land mines and our very own government-issue M-17 hand grenades, Kam had come back leading a party of villagers. I knew they would all be from VC families—that was the way their nasty little war went. Each side was allowed to harass the other side's civilians up to a point, but no one would actually harm one. There were too many hostages: everyone in the village. If a vendetta started no one could say where it would end—ten of yours for every one of mine adds up in a hurry. Who would risk that?

But whenever there was a dirty communal task that had to be done, it was the VC families that ended up doing it. The year before it had been the militia families; the VC families had been untouchable. And in the four northernmost provinces of South Vietnam, where life had been precarious long before the first punji stick was planted, a day away from the rice fields could be much more than a day wasted: it could be the difference between eating and not.

The people Kam had rounded up looked sick. They were all expecting to find a son or a brother out in the paddy. They filed past me in silence, not daring to look up at me lest their faces betray some emotion. I could feel their hatred, though. Suong laughed.

"Sheet, no muthafuckin' pistols."

That was Washington's only comment. Pistols were

worth their weight in gold. They made the best souvenirs and there was intense competition between the Seabees and the Corps of Engineers to obtain them. Most of the creature comforts at the fort had been obtained by trading captured weapons with support troops, people who never heard a shot fired in anger but still wanted to have war stories to tell their grandchildren. There was a standing offer from the Corps of Engineers: three pistols bought a two-kilowatt generator. The only problem was that pistols were real prestige items on both sides, and hence, rare as shit.

"Tell you what, Washington, next time some NVA major comes down this way with his battalion, you got first dibs on the bastard's pistol."

"Why, thank you, Sergeant," he replied, using his best upper-crust Philadelphia accent. "That's mighty white of you."

One thing I'll say for Washington, he really knows how to piss me off. He hadn't bothered to put his pants back on and his shorts were somewhere out in the paddy. He was quite a sight standing there in his combat boots and olive-drab T-shirt. I didn't think anyone was likely to laugh, though. First of all, he was hung like a racehorse, and second, there was enough ordnance strapped to him to fight off a VC company.

Washington took the carbines that Suong had gathered and slung a sack of grenades over one shoulder and we started staggering back to the fort. Behind us we heard the sobbing of women and Suong's laughter as he gleefully gave orders and related how we had killed their children.

It was two clicks back to the fort, our home away from home. Even though the sun hadn't even cleared the horizon it was already in the mid-eighties. By the time we staggered home we were both gasping and soaked in sweat.

The helicopter was there waiting for me.

CHAPTER THREE

□

REPUBLIC OF VIETNAM

December, 1965

I never cease to wonder where the fucking Army gets its officers. The lieutenant who was waiting for me at the fort looked like something out of a John Wayne wet dream. He was dressed in jungle camouflage fatigues, the pants freshly ironed and tucked into spit-polished boots so that they flared out at the shins. There was a .45 automatic hanging from his Sam Browne belt, along with a canteen, six hand grenades and a fucking bowie knife. I could just imagine what he sounded like when he moved. The best parts, though, were the Anzac bush hat and the mirrored sunglasses. I could smell his cologne, quite a feat considering how close I was to Washington.

God knows what he thought of me, let alone Washington. We just stood there staring at each other for maybe a minute. Finally I guess he figured that as the senior officer present he should say something.

"Well, Sergeant, why aren't you saluting your superior officer?"

"Because we haven't had any sniper fire for weeks," I told him. Viet Cong snipers have been known to sit in the bush for days waiting for someone to look like an officer. The lieutenant didn't look like he got my point. But I didn't feel like explaining it so I just trudged by him into the fort. Washington walked by on his other side, pausing long enough to lick a finger and touch the lieutenant with it. He made sizzling noises and pulled his finger back real quick. The helicopter pilot looked like he was dying he was trying so hard not to laugh.

The lieutenant hurried after me. He really did sound like a walking junkyard. I made a mental note not to go on patrol with him no matter how much he begged; he'd probably insist on wearing his sunglasses.

"Hold on one second, Sergeant," he said. "You can't talk to me that way."

I stopped short and spun around on one heel. He had to pull up suddenly to avoid running into me. Worried about staining himself, no doubt. So I reached out and put my hand on his shoulder and told him, "No, you're right, Lieutenant, I can't possibly talk to you that way. I could really get myself into trouble." Then I turned around again and headed into the mess hall.

The mess hall doubled as our sleeping area, Fort Beau Geste being cozy. I could tell the looey didn't appreciate our taste in home furnishings. We had a .30-caliber machine gun mounted on one of the mess tables so that it covered the door. Probably not the kind of decor his mother had gone in for. He stopped dead in his tracks when he saw it and sort of edged into the room.

Our cots were set up around the perimeter. Next to every cot was a rifle cradle—no one wanted to have to fumble for his rifle in the dark. I leaned my M-14 into its rack and made a mental note to clean it before going out that night.

I walked down into the ammo locker to unload. It had been the wine cellar back when the fort had been French but the wine racks were long gone. I put the three carbines into the carbine stack and carefully put the land mines and grenades into the disposal crate. One of Charlie's favorite tricks is to take the delay fuses out of grenades and leave them around for idiots who've been brought up to believe in "waste not, want not." When the idiots get around to using them they detonate as soon as the pin is pulled. Generally this kills the idiot and anyone unlucky enough to be near him. We had left the rifle cartridges with Suong: he likes using VC bullets.

The lieutenant had followed me down into the locker and was standing behind me, greedily eying the AK-47 hanging from the rafters.

"Don't even think about it," I told him. It was the only automatic weapon I'd ever seen a VC carrying and I couldn't even imagine how much it was worth on the black market. I knew I wasn't going to settle for anything less than a jeep. I picked up my .38 Smith and Wesson and went back upstairs passing Washington, who still hadn't put on any clothes, on the way down. The lieutenant gave the AK one last glance and followed.

"Get your stuff," he said. "You're wanted at I Corps."

"Jeez," I said. "God, I'm wanted at I Corps. And they even sent me a real live officer to show me how to find the place. Boy, I wish you'd have told me that right off." I checked the safety on the .38 and that there wasn't a slug in the chamber and then collapsed onto my cot and was asleep almost instantly. The last thing I heard was Kelly saying, "I wouldn't do that if I were you." Followed shortly by "Because he's been known to come up shooting."

The heat woke me up three hours later. It was more than a hundred in the mess room. The lieutenant was still there, looking considerably more rumpled, and pissed off, than he had that morning. He was drenched in sweat and all the starch had come out of his blouse, not to mention his backbone.

"Look, Lieutenant," I told him, "you don't tell anybody about my nap, and I won't tell anyone what a useless leader of men you are." That didn't seem to cheer him up any. I stripped and went to take a shower. God only knew what they wanted me for at I Corps, but I hadn't been about to go there on zero sleep. After my shower I felt a lot better. I still felt like dried-up shit, but better is a relative kind of thing.

I found a reasonable-looking uniform and put it on. I got my AR-15 out of the ammo locker, making sure that the AK was still there, and reported back to the lieutenant.

"All ready, sir," I reported, executing a snappy salute.

He eyed my rifle. "Where'd you get that?" he barked, pointing at the AR-15. "That's not Marine issue."

"Don't get your dander up, Lieutenant," I told him. "The guerrilla who used to own it didn't need it anymore and he insisted on my taking it. And you know," I went on, affecting a confidential air, "I think he may have stolen it."

The AR-15 is a very nice weapon. It weighs three pounds less than the M-14, fires faster and uses a smaller-caliber bullet, which tumbles and does more damage. I've seen bodies where the bullet entered the leg and came out the shoulder, thoroughly fucking up everything in between. As far as I know the only outfit that gets them on a regular basis is the Green Beanies. I only use mine for special occasions like visiting I Corps headquarters. I wasn't real worried about the Army asking for it back since it had lost its serial number somewhere along the way.

I told Kelly to mind the fort, piled into the back of the helicopter and pretended to fall asleep. Even with headsets, nobody falls asleep in the back of one of those fucking birds, but I had things to think about. It was a ninety-mile flight and I spent the whole trip wondering what those assholes had planned for me.

The lieutenant commandeered a jeep when we arrived and hauled off for a building near the center of the compound. He'd given me a "Watch your step here, buster" look when we'd gotten off the helicopter so I was in my special good-behavior mode. The building we pulled up to had a sign out front that read INTELLIGENCE SECTION.

"Shit" was all I could think to say.

The office he led me to had COLONEL HORUS inscribed on the door, and whoever Horus was, he must have really rated because his secretary was the prettiest thing I'd seen since my layover in Hawaii. She eyed Wonder Boy like he was some sort of trained dog and told him that the colonel was in a meeting and that we could wait for him here. That was fine by me. I crashed on the floor and was out like a light, only to have Miss Blue Eyes shake me awake and tell me I couldn't do that here.

So I leaned a chair back against a wall and slept with my rifle cradled in my arms; I've found that people are really reluctant to bother you if you're holding an automatic weapon. Colonel Horus showed up around one and immediately proved himself to be a typical Army asshole.

"On your feet, Marine!" he bellowed. "We've got work to do." I stood up and shucked and jived for the man. I really didn't want to spend the next two weeks in the stockade for insubordination, even if the food was better than what I was used to.

"Sir," I said, "would it be possible to get something to eat before we begin? I haven't eaten since yesterday."

"Comstock!" he bellowed, looking at Wonder Boy. "Is this how the intelligence section treats its guests?"

For a minute I thought Horus was going to launch into a Napoleonic tirade on the importance of food to the enlisted ranks. Instead he just ordered Comstock to get some lunch for me. Comstock looked about as miserable as a human being can get. Getting ordered to fetch for a noncom wasn't scoring him any points with Miss Blue Eyes.

The colonel took another look at me and said, "You out chasing women all night, Sergeant?" From the way he said it I gathered that he was trying to be chummy: so as to win my loyalty, etc., etc. What an asshole.

"No, sir," I replied. "We had eight VC pinned down in a rice paddy all night and I didn't get much sleep."

"Excellent!" he roared. "Did you get them all?"

"Yes, sir, but we had to wait for dawn to get the last of them. If we had some of those starlight scopes you people have, I could have gotten some sleep last night."

"Well, I'll see what I can do for you, Sergeant. Step into my office."

His office was plush. We might have been in the fucking Pentagon instead of three hundred-odd miles from Saigon. The walls had hardwood paneling and the carpet felt like it might have been an inch thick. There was a Dali print hanging on the wall over a full-length leather couch.

His desk was about seven feet long. Its surface was covered with reports, most of them flagged CLASSIFIED. That had to be a security violation but evidently he didn't give a shit. Judging by the furniture Horus rated higher than most generals, let alone other colonels.

He sat on the couch and started asking me questions about the combined action team. He was very patient and had a knack for asking the right questions. He wanted to know everything about the village and the Vietnamese militiamen. He was the first officer I'd ever talked to who thought that eventually the Vietnamese would be able to handle the job by themselves. I was relieved that all they wanted was a firsthand report on the village. Some days I'm smarter than others; this just wasn't my day.

"You've got a tough opponent there, Sergeant," he lectured. I gathered he'd given the talk before. "The Viet Cong are ten times tougher than anything we've ever faced. They're tough physically, and worse than that, they're tough mentally. They've been fighting invaders for more than a thousand years in this stinking country, and it's given them a fierce sense of patriotism and a determination to be free of foreign domination. They threw the Chinese out, they threw the French out, they fought the Japanese for ten years. The Americans are just another foreign army to them.

"Besides being morally correct, as far as they're concerned anyway, the way their combat units are structured makes them particularly dangerous. The typical Viet Cong unit is between twelve and twenty guerrillas led by a political/tactical official known as a cadre. They train together, they eat together, they sleep together and they fight together. It's the same system the Nazis used and it's very effective. The unit becomes almost like a family with the cadre acting like a wiser older brother.

"Long after a man loses his will to fight for things like God and country, he'll still fight for his family. Don't count on any of them ever surrendering while there's still hope left. We'll have to kill them all."

"They don't like to leave their dead behind," I said.

"I'd always assumed it was because they didn't want us to know how bad we'd hurt them."

He just nodded his head. About that time Comstock came back with my lunch. He even brought me a tray to eat it on; they do teach them some useful skills at those wacko military academies. I thought about congratulating him on his skills as a lackey but thought better of it. Comstock stood in the doorway looking like a schoolboy eavesdropping on his betters. Horus looked up and saw him standing there and roared.

"What's the matter, Comstock? Don't you have enough work to do?"

I stopped chewing and fought back the urge to spit my food all over the carpet. I couldn't think of any reason that Comstock shouldn't hear about the village. Evidently Horus had things to tell me that he didn't want Wonder Boy to hear. I guessed that I probably wouldn't want to hear them either.

"All right, Yamasaki," he went on, "enough chitchat. As you've probably noticed, we ain't winning this fucking war. We're not losing it either, but the brass figures—and for once those assholes are right—that the VC are a hell of a lot more patient than Congress. So we've decided we're going to win this thing in the next two years or we ain't gonna win it at all.

"By this time next year there'll be close to a half-million U.S. soldiers in South Vietnam, and we are going to kick some ass."

I looked at him in amazement. If that was true—and I didn't believe him for a second—we'd be asshole-deep in Army boys by the spring. It wasn't just that what he was telling me was so crazy, I just couldn't believe he would tell something like that to a Marine Corps noncom, especially if it was true.

"The commander of U.S. forces in Southeast Asia, bless his heart, is concerned about the effect that so many of our boys will have on the cities in Vietnam and he's even more concerned about the effect the cities will have on our boys. Not all of the boys who'll be coming over will have college degrees."

He said that last bit with some sort of emphasis. I knew what he was driving at: he wanted me to know that he knew everything there was to know about me. He gave me a chance to say something but I pretended to be interested in my Jell-O.

"The general is concerned that being so far from home and family may leave many of our boys susceptible to the cheap drugs in Saigon. He isn't interested in exporting a generation of heroin addicts back to the States."

What had probably happened was a military courier had just been caught with a hundred grams of pure heroin on his way back from Saigon, or some such shit, and the Joint Chiefs were screaming for heads. Somebody wanted some action and it looked like the shit wasn't going to stop moving downhill until it got to me. I decided that it was about time to be calculatedly dumb. He obviously had something in mind for me and there was no way I was going to talk him out of it. My best chance was to make him decide that maybe I wasn't suitable after all. I sure hoped he wasn't going to ask me to play narc; it was all I could manage to keep the VC from killing me.

"Well, sir," I said, "you can count on me to keep my outfit clean; if I even catch a man with hard liquor he's in big trouble."

His eyes narrowed and I thought for a second that it might have worked, but I had worked too hard impressing the guy with what a fine leader of men I was and how well the combined platoon was doing. Someday I'll learn.

"That's fine, Sergeant, but the problem is just a little bit bigger than your squad. We've determined that the most effective way to keep heroin away from our boys is to keep it out of the country, so we've decided to cut off the source."

Suddenly it hit me why they wanted me and I damn near died. They were going to fucking Laos and they wanted me for a guide. God, fucking Laos, there was no way I was going back to Laos. Once had been enough.

"All of the heroin in South Vietnam comes from one source, the Golden Triangle of northern Laos, northern Thailand and southern China. There's not a damn thing we can do about the growers, so we've decided to go after the exporters. We've closed off the ocean route from Bangkok and the river route through Phnom Penh. There's only one more major route, and that's overland through Laos."

Fuck, there, he'd said it. When I'd first gotten to Vietnam, I'd been assigned to the 63rd Marine Battalion, commanded by Colonel John Henry McClanahan. The CIA borrowed twenty-five of John Henry's boys for a trip to Laos and then lost them somewhere. They told John Henry that his boys were dead and that he should write them off and send out letters to their next of kin, assholes.

Well, John Henry, being a Marine and twice the man of any motherfucker in the CIA, wasn't about to just "write off" twenty-five of his boys. He used some gentle persuasion—a knife actually, but time is money as they say—to get an operative to tell him where his boys had been, and then he invaded Laos on the sly.

He requisitioned fifty AR-15's from the Army—I still have mine—and led fifty of his Marines into Laos. He was risking a certain court martial and disgrace if anyone outside of the Marines ever found out, but I doubt seriously if he even considered it. Only God knows how he talked the Army pilots into giving us a ride to where we wanted to go. They said we were walking back.

The Air America cargo plane with John Henry's boys on it had crashed on a hillside deep in the rain forest in southern Laos. We didn't have much trouble finding it: it had left a big hole in the jungle. Most, but not all, of the passengers had been killed on impact. The Pathet Lao had taken the survivors to a nearby clearing and beheaded them.

John Henry, who looked like a pirate if he'd been more than fifteen minutes away from a razor, cried like a baby when he saw the headless corpses of his boys. He decided that we were going to have to do something, something drastic. We found the Pathet Lao camp that night. It was easy: we just followed the trail of heads that they had hung in the trees along the way. It was real stupid of them, but they hadn't been expecting any visitors.

When the Pathet Lao commander woke up the next morning, he woke up alone. We'd used bayonets and nobody heard a thing. We strung the bastard up by his ankles and then used him for target practice for an hour. The fun ended when somebody tried a particularly difficult shot, aiming for what was left of his right ear, and killed him. It turned out we should have just shot the bastard and then run like hell.

The trip home was a nightmare. The jungle was impenetrable. So we had to stay on the trails, the Pathet Lao trails. It was the monsoon, and it rained constantly for six days. The rain would stop for maybe fifteen minutes every afternoon and the jungle would look like a steam bath. The steam from the rain mixed with the smell of rotting vegetation, reminding me of death every step of the way home. Every man in the company had jungle rot on some part of his body and most didn't get any sleep during the two or three hours we stopped to rest every night.

We tried to move faster than the news and we killed everything that crossed our path, but they knew we were there. We broke out of five ambushes and lost men at every one. On the last day, though, there was nothing. I think they finally realized we were trying to get out and they didn't really want to fight us anymore. The Laotians aren't cut out to fight madmen. Seventeen men made it back to Vietnam.

No, I didn't want to go back to Laos, not for anything, and especially not so some asshole could score points with a fucking general.

"Intelligence," he went on, "has determined that a major center of heroin activity is the village of Tiehereaux in southern Laos. Large shipments come in from Thailand and are broken up there for transport here. We believe that the network is controlled by a French expatriate, first name Pascal, last name unknown.

"We have assembled a team of Army Special Forces for

a covert mission into Laos to find this Pascal and eliminate him. We also want to make sure that no one in Tiehereaux ever abets the heroin trade again."

"Where do I," I asked him, "fit into this mission, sir?"

He looked at me for a minute; I couldn't read him at all. He picked up a pencil and started drumming it on his desktop. Finally he decided he didn't have to play games with me.

"Don't fuck with me, Yamasaki, you'll never know what hit you. Technically that little stunt you pulled in Laos was desertion, and even if I can't make that stick, I'll find something else." He tapped one of his folders. "I have Colonel McClanahan's report here. You could be doing ten years at Pendleton starting tomorrow."

What a jerk: he could have cut off John Henry's balls with a broken Coke bottle and John Henry wouldn't have given him the time of day, let alone the names of any of his boys. As for threatening to send me some place where nobody was trying to shoot me, that was pretty rich.

"I'm sorry, sir," I told him. "There must be some mistake. If I'd ever been to Laos and Colonel McClanahan found out about it, he would have court-martialed me himself."

He looked at me, he sized me up like a side of beef and then he smiled. He dropped his pencil on the desk.

"Ah, Marine, you're so fucking smart. You belong to the least exclusive club in the whole fucking world and you're proud of it. Death and glory, Marine, that's what you want. Well, let me tell you something. You're going with those Green Beanies and you're going to be fucking properly grateful for the opportunity.

"You're right about McClanahan, he's as pigheaded as you are and I don't have shit on you. But I've got your pecker in my pocket just the same because I've got McClanahan. He went on an unauthorized killing spree in a neutral nation and got thirty-three Marines killed doing it, and I can prove that. How's it going to look in the papers, thirty-three dead Marines, killed for nothing? He'll be lucky to get a job washing dishes. Now why don't you go find Comstock and ask him to get you a ride to Firebase Romeo. That's where you'll find Captain Lucas. He's expecting you."

I got up to go. He was right: he did have my pecker in his pocket.

"What about the village?" I asked him.

"Your replacement's there already." I turned at the door and looked back at him. He eyed me coolly, waiting to see what I'd do.

"It wasn't just for nothing," I told him. He didn't reply.

CHAPTER FOUR

□

REPUBLIC OF VIETNAM

December, 1965

The Army had been ordered to cut off the Viet Cong's infiltration routes into the south and had built a string of outposts along the northern border to do it. They were all pretty typical: a fortified hill in the jungle covered with 155-millimeter howitzers and manned by chickenshit Army boys afraid of the dark, who liked to call in air strikes on water buffalo.

Firebase Romeo looked pretty typical from the air. It wasn't till you were on the ground and saw all the Green Berets that you realized it was different. It was located in the far northwest and was the closest American base to North Vietnam . . . and Laos.

Whoever was in charge seemed to have taken a more active interest in staying alive than was typical for Army commanders. The entire hillside had been cleaned off with flamethrowers, providing a clear field of fire for six hundred meters around the camp; I couldn't even see a blade of grass. There were claymores planted out along the perimeter, and somehow I didn't think guerrillas were sneaking in at night to pick them up and turn them around.

Turning around claymores is another of the Viet Cong's favorite tricks. A claymore is a surface mine that sprays shrapnel in one direction. We use them to blunt frontal attacks. If you have very cool nerves you can pick a claymore up and turn it so it faces inward. Then if you make a noise and the sentry sets off the claymore—well, if he was looking to see if he got you, surprise.

The machine gun bunkers were solid concrete with ports facing into and out of the camp. The barbed wire was strung tight as a moneylender's heart. You couldn't push it apart to get through and cutting it would sound like a string snapping on God's own guitar. Something else was missing and it took me a while to figure it out: there were no Vietnamese peasants, none. Evidently the Army boys at this base were doing their own laundry. It just wasn't typical.

The Green Beanies have a reputation for being casual about regs, and the ones at Firebase Romeo were no exception. No one appeared to have ironed anything since the last time McNamara came over and my helmet made me stand out like a sore thumb. But no one carried his rifle like a sack of potatoes, which is standard in the Army. And it was over a hundred in the shade, but I didn't see anyone without at least ten magazines clipped to his uniform.

The official greeting committee consisted of one man who was naked to the waist except for an ammo belt strung over one shoulder. He had on the requisite beret and carried an M-16, which was the new standard infantry rifle we'd heard so much about, all bad. He stuck out his hand and said, "Welcome to the asshole of the universe, Yamasaki. My name's John Lucas."

He was on the opposite end of the spectrum from Comstock. His fatigue pants were tucked in to his boots too, but I suspect that was only to make it easier to get the knives that were built in to them. His grip was firm and gave me a close look at his signet ring, which was from West Point, about four hundred miles north of the school Comstock had attended.

"I don't know how Horus got you to volunteer for this mission," he went on, "but we're might glad to have somebody who's been there coming along."

He led me to a sandbag-reinforced bunker to meet the rest of his team. There were thirty of them, two sergeants, both of them senior to me, and twenty-eight riflemen. The conversations died when we entered, but no one seemed to display any urge to jump to attention. Nonetheless, I could see that every man in the room was focused on Lucas.

"OK, people," he said, "listen up. This is Sergeant James Yamasaki, USMC. He runs that sweet little operation in Quang Nam that we've all heard so much about. He has kindly consented to come along with us tomorrow morning on our trip to beautiful Laos.

"It turns out that Sergeant Yamasaki's been to Laos before, although I'm led to believe by the powers that be that we're not supposed to ask him what the fuck he was doing there." He turned to me. "What the fuck were you doing there?"

I gathered that that was my cue, so I rose to tell them about my adventures in Laos. I knew it would be fucking stupid to jerk Lucas around. (A), I was pretty sure he would cut my heart out if I did. And (B), the more Lucas and his men knew about Laos, the better my odds of coming back were. There was also the outside chance that I could talk them out of going.

So I told them about the Laos. I described the jungle from the point of view of a foot soldier, the constant rain, the mud, the heat and the friendly natives, the ones who'd be trying so hard to kill them. I described the ambushes we had walked into, all five of them: at the river crossing, in the deserted village, the two at random points on the trails and the one in the clearing. I told them about the snake that got Havazanjian, and what a bitch it had been to carry the big Armenian until he died.

I talked for about an hour, and then I answered questions for at least that long. I had everyone's complete attention for the entire time. These were not typical Army assholes. No one fell asleep or even yawned and the questions they asked were probing. They wanted to know about Pathet Lao tactics: could they expect multiple ambushes, what sorts of weapons did the Pathet Lao typically use, and would the Communists run if the action got hot?

When I was through Lucas dismissed his troops and told me to follow him. He gave me a tour of the base. He pointed out how the 155's could be used as antipersonnel weapons in a tight spot and how each machine gun bunker could cover at least two others. He was as proud as a new father.

"If you'd like," he told me, "you can trade in your weapon for an M-16." From the way he said it, I gathered that it wouldn't be a very clever thing to do.

"No thanks," I told him. "I think I'll stick with what I've got."

"Wise choice: we'd heard about all those Marines who got dead trying to clean their M-16's during fire fights, so we weren't real anxious to trade in our AR's when the time came." He grinned at me, but didn't seem very amused. "They met our transport at Hamilton and confiscated the hundred or so AR's we'd reported missing."

He shook his head. "As it is, we can't ever get enough rifle-cleaning supplies. You should see my toothbrush—it's black." He paused for a second to admire my weapon, and then continued. "So, where'd you get yours over here?"

"Stole it from the Army."

"Typical fucking Marine, remind me to search you before you leave. You never did say what you were doing in Laos."

Since everyone else in the world apparently knew, I didn't figure it would hurt much to let him in on it too.

"Fucking CIA lost some Marines and we went looking for them."

"Somehow I don't see the brass sanctioning a mission like that," he said.

"They didn't."

He thought that through for a few seconds and then said, "Have to admire your guts for going in there without air support."

"We have air cover for tomorrow?" I asked him.

He grinned at me and held one hand up with its fingers crossed.

It was dusk and we stopped to watch the first of the patrols going out. They had darkened their faces with carbon black and were just shadows as they passed. I didn't hear any jingling of equipment and I noticed they were all wearing black sneakers.

"Sneakers?"

"The government evacuated all of the civilians for twenty miles south of the border. If anything moves out there we kill it, and we haven't had to kill anything for a long time. You won't step on anything more dangerous than tiger shit out there. Come on, I'll buy you dinner and you can tell me about John Henry, the steel-driving man."

Dinner was good, but I didn't remember ever having mentioned John Henry's name to Lucas. Wheels within wheels: I reminded myself that Lucas was Army, and hence not to be trusted.

I slept in Lucas's bunker that night. I dreamed that a giant was chasing me; I could hear his footsteps pounding behind me, getting closer. Then I was awake and it wasn't a dream. I sat up and listened. It was a long way off, but it felt like the earth was vibrating like an anvil under a sledge.

"It's the B-52's." Lucas was awake too. He was sitting crosslegged on his cot. "They pound the shit out of the provinces on the other side of the border every day about this time." He shivered. "It wakes me up at oh four hundred every morning. I can just imagine what it does for them over there."

He threw me an army field cap. "You better wear it, nothing like standing out in a crowd to draw sniper fire."

By 0430 his men were assembled. I felt naked without my helmet, and knew I was going to feel mighty foolish if I was to get shot in the head. Lucas checked everybody. I didn't think he was going to find anything, and I don't think he thought he was going to find anything, but I've seen DI's who were casual in comparison. After he finished inspecting his troops Lucas led the way to the choppers. Vietnam was just a pleasant memory even before the sun came up.

Laos was just like I remembered it, hot, wet and stinking. Lucas had wanted to put down twenty miles from Tiehereaux, so his men could get acclimated to the local conditions before going into action. I told him that it's damn near impossible to get acclimated to bullet holes and he'd be lucky to have any men left by the time he got where he was going. We compromised and settled for ten kilometers.

Lucas had some infrared aerial photographs of the area that seemed to indicate a trail, and wonder of wonders, there really was a trail. He sent two men out on point and had ten men trailing, in case we walked into an ambush. We weren't expecting an ambush, but Lucas seemed to have ambitions of collecting his government pension. I felt I was in good hands. So I was wrong, sue me.

The plan Lucas had explained to me the night before was that we would go in as fast as possible and overrun a gang of disorganized smugglers, who would be devastated by the surprise. We'd waste everybody in sight, leave the village in ruins and be back at Firebase Romeo before sunset. I thought it was a great plan up until I saw Lucas with the camera.

"What the fuck is that for?" I asked him pointing at the camera.

"Plan B," he replied.

"Trotting down a fucking goat trail in the middle of fucking Laos may not be the right time to ask this, but what the fuck is Plan B?"

"Well," he said, "ever since we cut off the infiltration routes through Vietnam, the North Vietnamese have been supplying their troops through Laos. And we're just a tad concerned that we may run into a few in Tiehereaux."

"How many's a few?"

"What a good question."

I mulled that over for a while, regretting that we hadn't put down a hundred miles from this fucking place. "You think the North Vietnamese are involved in the heroin trade, don't you?"

He looked over at me and grinned. I was beginning to get tired of seeing him grin every time it looked like we were going to get ourselves killed. "The CIA's convinced that that's how they're paying for their operations in Saigon. Also we don't think that it's very likely that you could move traffic through this area without the NVA's consent and I personally don't think the North Vietnamese would mind if the U.S. Army had a drug problem."

"So if we get there and find three battalions of the North Vietnamese Army reinforced with a regiment of VC along with some heavy artillery, you're just going to take pictures and then we're going home."

"Right," he said. "And then they send in the Marines."

"Anything else you think I might want to know about?" I asked him. "Chinese warlords? Russian spies? A missing USO troop?"

Lucas told me to shut up and try to at least pretend like he outranked me.

I felt like a first-class sap. I should have known that Horus would never have told me the truth, if for no other reason than to practice lying. He didn't care if every dogface in Asia was shooting up three times a day and paying for it with stolen ordnance. All he wanted was proof that the North Vietnamese were involved in the heroin trade so that his superiors could go to Congress and prove what inhuman monsters the enemy were. How else were they going to get a half-million GI's over here by next Christmas, assholes.

I knew we had arrived when one of the point men came back on the trail to meet us. Lucas sent another man back to warn the trailing party and we crept up the trail until we could see the village.

Tiehereaux had been the center of the provincial rubber industry back when Indochina had been French. The buildings were neatly laid out like a small village in the countryside of France, except they don't use a lot of bamboo in France and the center of town wasn't a cathedral, it was the headquarters of some long-forgotten rubber company. There was only one thing spoiling the picture-postcard perfectness: the village was empty. But it didn't appear uninhabited; something was keeping the jungle at bay.

"I don't like this," I said.

"Great, so you're a fucking psychic. Where is everybody?"

"I don't know how to tell you this," I said, "but they're apparently waiting for us."

"Now how would they know we were coming?" he asked sarcastically.

"Maybe your buddy Horus told them. If you're so fucking smart, where do you think they are?"

"Maybe they're out celebrating."

"Chinese New Year's next month and I doubt there's anyone here who cares that there's only six shopping days left before Christmas."

He didn't have anything to say to that. I was sort of hoping that he would decide that we'd had enough action for one day and go home, but he just had to know. He signaled two of his men forward and the others went prone to cover them. I squatted down on my heels and watched them as they carefully crept forward into the village.

They had gone about twenty feet forward when I saw the hole. It wasn't much of a hole, and someone had sort of almost filled it in, but it sent a surge of adrenaline through me that raised the hairs on the back of my neck. I had seen holes just like it. As a matter of fact, I had made a bunch of holes just like it.

It's one thing to read the shit that comes in the mortar manual, and it's another thing to trust your life with it. Back at the village we had spent an entire afternoon firing dud mortar rounds into the jungle to get the range of places we felt snipers might like to hide. When we had dug the duds up the holes looked just like the one Lucas was sitting on. It didn't take me very long to find six more just like it.

"Lucas," I whispered, "get those guys back here, now."

He looked over at me quizzically.

"Why?"

I'd of told him, but just then I heard the *chummmp* I'd been expecting to hear, followed immediately by *chummmp, chummmp*.

"Incoming!" I screamed and took off down the trail

like a jackrabbit, or at least what I assume a jackrabbit runs like. I looked over my shoulder and saw Lucas ducking behind a tree. From the expression on his face, I gathered he thought I had panicked. I was too busy counting to let that bother me; when I got to three I dove head first into the brush.

The barrage lasted more than a minute. When it ended I rolled back onto the trail and looked toward the village. The tree Lucas had sheltered behind was canted over at a thirty-degree angle and it didn't look like he was going to make major after all.

As Lucas had suspected, there were NVA in the village, and about fifty of them had used the cover of the mortar fire to get halfway to the trees. No one was shooting at them. They were wearing the typical NVA field uniform, khaki pants and shirts, brown belts and boots, topped with a safari hat. They looked a lot like the character that Johnny Weissmuller played after he got too fat to run around the Hollywood back lots in his jockstrap. Jungle Jim never carried an AK-47, though.

I emptied a clip in their general direction, hoping it would slow them down a tad, and then ran like hell. The man with the radio was in the rear guard, and I figured that with any luck, we could call in an air strike and get back to the rendezvous while the bad guys were still picking the bits and pieces of their buddies out of the trees. I was running so hard that I didn't see the rifle butt until it was about an inch in front of my face, and after that I didn't see anything for quite a while.

The first thing I noticed when I woke up was that my throat was sore. I was groggy as shit and spent my first five minutes of consciousness trying to figure out why. It finally occurred to me that I was breathing through my mouth and that that might explain it. So I tried breathing through my nose, and of course I couldn't breathe through my nose because it was broken. I was relieved. That cleared it up—my throat was sore because I was breathing through my mouth because my nose was broken.

I lay there for another twenty minutes before I started wondering why my nose was broken. Once I got started on that, it didn't take me very long to conjure up that rifle floating there in front of my face. After that it all came back in a rush.

I sat up and watched the world spin around for a bit. When it wouldn't stop I fell on my side and retched; I was only mildly surprised when nothing came up. Someone straightened me up and said, "Drink this, Marine." Whoever it was held something up to my lips and I managed to get some of it down. It tasted like blood, but that was only because there was a ton of dried blood in my mouth. The last thing I remember thinking before I passed out again was that my throat didn't hurt because I was breathing through my mouth after all, it was because of all the blood that had dried in it.

When I woke up the next time I decided to approach things more cautiously. I opened one eye at a time and looked things over. I was in a bamboo hut, and from the light filtering in, I guessed it was late afternoon. I put one hand beneath myself and managed to sit up. This time the world stayed refreshingly constant, but somehow I couldn't find any cheer in its stability. There were four other guys in the hut with me. They had all been up front with Lucas. There wasn't anyone from the rear guard. Somehow I didn't think that was because anyone in the rear guard had gotten away.

I looked around for the water bucket and crawled over to it. I was dehydrated, but I didn't drink very much; I wanted to see if any of it would stay down.

"You must be pretty tough, Marine."

It was the same voice I'd heard last time, the one that had given me the water.

"Thanks for the water," I told him. "What's the situation?"

"Lucas is dead. We're prisoners. They're going to kill us. How's your head?"

He must have been the optimist of the group. The other three guys just sat there with their backs to the wall—they were totally apathetic. I took a closer look and saw that two of them must have been heavily concussed by the mortar fire. The third appeared to be unharmed, but was just staring off into space. I'd seen men staring off into the distance like that before. They were seeing something back home, and that's where you had to send them. Sometimes they recovered, sometimes they didn't.

"It feels like I spent the weekend drinking a case of coconut rum and breaking the empties over my head," I told him. "Why do you think they're going to kill us?"

"Because it's standard operating procedure over here. They can't even feed their own troops. We've been here thirty-six hours and we haven't been fed. When it gets to seventy-two they'll waste us. They'll look on it as doing us a favor. How'd you know we were about to get blasted?"

I explained about the mortar holes and that seemed to satisfy him. Maybe he thought he could use the info the next time he invaded Laos. Probably not, though. They came to get us at dusk.

The six Pathet Lao guerrillas who came for us were brusque but not unkind. When they saw that the two wounded men and the head case weren't going to make it, they found villagers to carry them. They kept a close eye on me and the other guy who could walk, although in my case it was just so much wasted zeal; I couldn't have outrun a six-year-old.

The North Vietnamese troops I'd seen the other day were nowhere in sight. All we saw were a ragtag group of armed Laotian guerrillas. The NVA regulars hadn't been a figment of my imagination, though: there should have been thirty-one M-16's in the crowd, and all I saw were ancient carbines and one AR-15.

The guerrilla with my rifle smiled and waved when he saw me. I probably looked like a raccoon so he didn't have much difficulty picking me out of the crowd. I put him down on my list of people to be taken care of later and then thought what a shame it was that I didn't believe in reincarnation.

They led us into the center of the village and had us sit

on the ground in front of the rubber company headquarters. A guerrilla came out of the building and put a straight-backed wooden chair down in front of us, and then we waited.

After a bit, an old Caucasian walked slowly out of the building, wiping his mouth on a stained linen napkin. He wore an old white suit with no tie, and a straw boater that had seen better days. He sat down on the chair, crossed his legs and rested his chin on his fist. He sat there considering us for several moments and then spoke.

"Good evening, gentlemen. I am Pascal Fourier, late of Paris. You gentlemen would be?"

"Hansen, Donald J., corporal, United States Army, nine five . . ." That was as far as he got before the old man cut him off.

"Please, we are among friends here. There is no need for all these formalities, yes? Donald will do just fine, and of course you must call me Pascal."

He turned to me expectantly.

"James Yamasaki," I told him, and then, not to be outdone in courtesy, "late of Parris Island."

"I am so very pleased to meet you, James," he returned.

Then he turned to the other three and waited. One of them tried to say something, but he was too far gone. A second was totally blank. And the third was still dreaming of home.

"Such a pity," he said and then waved his hand.

I was still groggy, and probably had a concussion myself. Or maybe I'd seen too many killings and they just didn't affect me anymore. I watched the three men being beheaded as if it was something happening on TV. Hansen went for the man with the machete and was clubbed down for his trouble.

The first man never knew what hit him. The second tried to get out of the way, but it was like he was moving in slow motion. The third man was even more detached than I was. He never blinked as the knife fell. I doubt if it was even much of a transition for him.

"Please, Donald," Fourier said, "it is necessary and

really very kind." It looked like genuine concern in his eyes. I realized in a detached sort of way that Fourier was crazy as a loon.

"Fuck you," Hansen growled. I could hear the hatred and pain in his voice. Not *smart,* I thought to myself as the machete came down again, not *smart at all.*

The old man turned to me.

"Well, James, I certainly hope that you will be more reasonable than Donald." He sounded just like a playground monitor I'd had in third grade. Mr. Takada spent his entire life trying to get children to play together and love each other instead of fight and call each other names. He made a career out of getting four-eyed geeks into our kickball games. We all thought that he was a dork . . .. If only he'd had a machete.

"I'm always happy to do what I can to improve Franco-American relations," I told him.

"Very good, James. So explain for me, please, what you have wanted with us here in Tiehereaux."

"Ah, you know," I told him, "the usual. Go in quick, waste the heroin dealers, waste everyone else in the village to teach them a lesson, get out quick. It was a pretty typical mission."

He tapped his teeth with his thumbnail and looked at me thoughtfully.

"I just wonder where the rest of the battalion is. They should have been here by now." That didn't seem to put him out any, so I went on. "You aren't the Mr. Pascal who runs this organization, are you? We had special instructions for him."

"Ah, James, please to not tell me the fairy stories. Your government is not to the point where they will be sending battalions into Laos. Who was your briefing officer?"

That was an easy one. "A civilian from Saigon, I think he must have been CIA. He said his name was Clancy, tall stringy guy with red hair and big ears. He said he had an office in the embassy in Saigon." Clancy was the shithead who had gotten John Henry's boys killed, and it was beginning to look like he was going to get me indirectly.

Anything I could do for him would just be one less regret I would be taking into the great void.

"Where were you to be picked up?"

"Beats me," I told him. "If you really wanted to know you shouldn't have wasted Hansen. I'm just a dumb Marine who was along for the ride."

"And why the United States Army is taking Marines for the ride?"

"Funny you should put it that way," I told him. "They were looking for a trusty Indian scout to hold their hands and I was the closest thing they could find."

"You have been to Laos before, yes?"

"Just once."

"You should not have come back."

He sat there for a few minutes longer, contemplating me, or maybe he was just tired. Finally he sighed, uncrossed his legs and stood up.

"Thank you very much, James. You have been very helpful." I tensed, waiting for the cut, but it didn't come. Fourier saw me stiffen and smiled. "Please, James, cannot you see that you are just another Asian who has been cruelly used by the generals in your army? You have nothing to fear here in the bosom of your brothers." Then he turned to the crowd and said something in French. It didn't take a genius to figure out what he'd said, either: he'd told them I was Japanese.

The mob gave a guttural roar of animal hatred and came at me as one.

CHAPTER FIVE

□

HAWAII
The present

Most folks go through life completely unprepared to deal with emergencies. Most people, upon finding themselves flopping around in the Pacific after being kneecapped by a couple of yahoos from Utah who are apparently intent on torture, would probably panic. There aren't things in life that can prepare you to deal with situations like that. But, luckily for me, being strung up by your ankles over a slow fire in Laos is one of them.

I must have been a sight, a fat Japanese-Polynesian-Caucasian blubbering and rolling around in the surf while his life's blood seeped into the Pacific. I couldn't have inspired any fear in the two yahoos because they came real close and the second one hadn't even taken out his gun. They didn't have anything to be afraid of, two big strong men against one fat blubbering fool.

"And this Stine person, where can we find this Stine person?" What an asshole—he'd been watching too many Peter Lorre movies. I had been holding on to my leg and making whimpering noises as they got closer. When the idiot grabbed ahold of my leg to give it a twist, I caught his gun hand at the wrist and forced it down.

The second one realized that he should have been fifteen feet away covering me with his pistol, but he was too late. I grabbed his shirt and pulled him toward me, at the same time rising out of the water. Our heads met with a thud, but I'd been expecting it. He fell away and landed face down in the surf, motionless. I continued my upward motion and rolled, landing on top of the other one. All 260 pounds came down on his wrist and it snapped like a rotten twig.

His mouth opened to scream, but I had him by the throat and forced his head under the water. He thrashed around with his good hand, but he might as well have been a child.

He must have realized what I was going to do; I could see the fear in his eyes. The ocean receded for a moment and his face came out of the water, an expression of profound relief replacing the fear. He let his breath out in one explosive burst. I slapped my hand over his mouth and nostrils and waited for the next wave to roll in.

The bullet hole in my leg sent waves of agony up and down my entire body. I could feel the pain build up in my leg and rush back and forth across my body as the salt water washed in and out of the holes. I was glad, though. It was only the agony that gave me the strength to do what I was doing.

After maybe a minute, blood vessels burst in his eyes. He looked up at me through the water. His eyes were wide open, terrified and demon-red. I watched his face, but I felt more than saw the sudden intake of water as his lungs finally overruled his brain and sucked in the Pacific. A few seconds later his eyes rolled up in his head, leaving two solid red orbs staring up at me. He died soon after.

My body must have produced a year's supply of adrenaline in five minutes because I was shaking like a leaf. When the reaction came I vomited uncontrollably into the surf. I closed my eyes and told myself over and over again that I had seen worse, much worse. I knelt in the water for another five minutes while the ocean whipped my breakfast and the contents of the two men's bladders back and forth around my legs. Even if blood poisoning had been a certainty I couldn't have moved.

Eventually, I stood up. I looked around expecting to see

a crowd of marathoners training for the Ironman, but the beach was empty. Just as well: it would have been tough to explain my arrest tactics.

As my blood pressure returned to something close to normal, whatever that is, the pain in my leg became almost bearable. I waded down the beach and let the ocean wash out the wound.

I'd been shot before; this wasn't any worse. The bullet had gone clean through the leg, taking some fat and muscle with it. It had missed everything important—well, everything important except me. I wrapped my shirt around the openings.

I went back to the two bodies and dragged them up onto the shore. Dead bodies don't weigh any more than live ones; it just seems that way. It was three hundred yards to my cruiser and I didn't want to leave one of them behind for some fucking jogger—who didn't realize that you were supposed to take it easy on your vacation—to trip over. I got one of them up over my shoulder and took the other one by the collar and started back to the parking lot.

Limping and staggering under the weight of my cargo I must have looked like a grave robber from a grade B horror movie. "Just a bit further, Igor," I kept telling myself. I thanked Christ that the sun was busy rising on the other side of the island. No one gets up early to take pictures on the west coast of Hawaii.

By the time I got to my car my shirt had soaked through and I was leaving a bright crimson trail through the parking lot. My leg felt like it was on fire again and I wondered what people would think if I had a coronary and died on the spot. Tongues were sure to wag. "Did you hear about the chief and all those dead bodies? Isn't it terrible? My, what's the world coming to?"

I let go of the collar and did a tricky balancing act while I tried to get my keys out. I'd done it before with sacks of groceries; everybody has. I was afraid if I dropped the one on my shoulder I'd never get him into the car. After I got the trunk open, I dumped the body on top of the spare.

Then I levered the other one on top of him and got the first-aid kit.

The kits we'd had in Nam had morphine in them; this one had aspirin. I took two. I threw the blood-soaked shirt in with the bodies and wrapped an Ace bandage around my leg. I thought about going back for my rod and reel, but it just wasn't worth it. I got in the car and went to find Dr. Chen.

Luckily I keep a spare shirt in my cruiser, so I didn't scare the shit out of the good doctor's housekeeper when I pounded on his door at five A.M. It didn't look like she approved of the shorts and bare feet but she didn't say anything. When she saw who I was she fetched the doctor.

Dr. Chen had arrived in Hawaii in 1950, fresh from the recent triumph of democracy on Formosa and without a penny to his name. His English had always been excellent, though. And he was in tight with the local Chinese establishment. He hadn't had any trouble getting licensed to practice here. He had worked very hard and invested very wisely in local real estate and was rumored to be very rich. It didn't surprise me that he didn't have to be woken.

"Good morning, Chief. To what do I owe the honor of this early morning visit from the head of our local law-enforcement establishment?"

Of course he had seen the blood-soaked bandage on my leg. And the fact that I was soaked, barefoot and not looking like my usual chipper self must have crossed his mind as well. But he was much too polite to mention any of that unless I was to bring it up myself. Maybe I had come for breakfast.

"Good morning yourself, Dr. Chen. As you can see, I've picked up a little nick on my leg that I'd like you to take a look at."

"Of course, of course," he said. "Please step this way."

He led me into his dispensary and had me sit on his examination table. He sucked in his breath when he saw what was beneath the bandage.

"This is a bullet wound."

"Yes," I told him. "It came from a gun."

"Forgive me for asking, but of course you know that I am required to report this type of injury."

He didn't ask his question; he let it hang there open-ended. He wanted to know who had shot me and why I hadn't gone to a hospital or called an ambulance or anything else that I should have done. On the other hand he wasn't going to jump one way or another until he knew what the situation was. That's why I'd gone to him.

"Some person or persons unknown," I told him, "set a deadfall out in the rain forest. There was something out there they didn't want folks to know about. We're investigating. As for reporting it, you already have."

That wasn't exactly the procedure. He was supposed to report gunshot wounds to the state police in Honolulu. He set about cleaning the wound and stitching me up. He didn't want to hear that people were setting up booby traps in the hills again, in fact that was the last thing he wanted to hear.

He owns more than forty condominiums that he rents out on a weekly basis to tourists. He's highly leveraged, using each condo as security for the next loan, paying the mortgages out of current income. The Chinese fixation with owning land leads them into business strategies that more prudent investors would eschew. Anything that was bad for the tourist business—and another grass war would be hideous—was going to be even worse for Dr. Chen.

"This is bad," he said. "This is very bad."

"You can understand why we're trying to keep it quiet," I told him. "If the papers get wind of it, well, who knows where it might lead."

"Do not worry, Chief," he told me. "You may rely on me to keep this confidential. I would feel so bad if an unwise word on my part were to spoil your investigation. You may also rely on me to keep my maid silent as well. Please turn around and drop your shorts. I am afraid that this wound may become infected. Luckily you have bathed it in the ocean, but one cannot be too careful with such matters.''

The ocean is a long way from the rain forest. He gave me a shot and sent me on my way. I wasn't worried about the doctor. When I'd gotten out of the Marines he had been one of the men who had made the last chief hire me.

I went home and changed, then I rousted Harry Nagata—the local pharmacist—out of bed to fill the prescription Dr. Chen had given me: Tylenol 4's, but better than nothing.

I drove back to Hapuna and parked. It was still quiet and I couldn't think of a better place to search the bodies. They had California driver's licenses, L.A. in fact. I figured they probably got out that way at least once a year to take the kids to Disneyland. They had a Hertz rental car and if they were staying at one of the local hotels they had left their keys at the desk.

It was easy to spot their car: it was the only one in the parking lot with its windows open. Evidently they hadn't been planning to stay long. It also helped that Hertz had put the license plate number on the key chain. Their suitcases were still in the trunk. That made life considerably easier: there wouldn't be anyone calling to report missing guests. Even better were the Hawaiian Air ticket coupons—they're good on any flight anywhere in the islands.

All I had to do was get someone to take the car back to the airport and have a couple of Marty's men fly to Maui on the tickets and the two dead men effectively ceased to be my problem, officially. Of course the people who had sent them here would still know where they had been when they disappeared, but that was a separate issue. I didn't think they'd be calling in the FBI.

I called Marty from a pay phone. He wasn't just the AMNGWH anymore. He was also the Stine Development Corporation, Stine Enterprises, Stine Leisure Wear and a host of other things. His receptionist answered the phone, ''Martin Stine and Associates, may I help you?''

''This is Chief Yamasaki calling. May I speak to Mr. Stine, please?''

''I'm sorry, Mr. Yamasaki, but Mr. Stine is in conference right now and cannot take your call. May I have him return it later?''

Marty's receptionist is old-school Japanese, and she hates me.

''Well gee, Mrs. Onogata,'' I said. ''It's about that fifteen-year-old girl. If we can't get it all straightened out I'm afraid I'm going to have to come right over there and throw Marty's ass in the slammer and then lose the key.''

Marty came on the line about forty-five seconds later.

''Chief, you do have a way with the ladies. What's up?''

''Well, Marty,'' I said, ''it's such a beautiful day, I thought you might like to do some fishing.''

''Every day's a beautiful day in paradise, Chief.'' Marty knew something was wrong, but he wanted a clue. ''What's so special about today?''

''Oh, I don't know,'' I said. ''I just had more than enough bait for two and thought you might like to help me use it up.''

''And besides,'' Marty replied jovially, ''I've got a boat. How about four o'clock this afternoon?''

''That's fine, Marty, this bait'll keep.''

Like shit it would, but if Marty couldn't figure out why I had this sudden urge to go fishing he never would have made it to the top of the Stine Development Corporation. But anyone who was tapping his phone this week wouldn't have learned much from our conversation.

I drove out the coast road to Marty's house. Marty has one of the only private anchorages on this side of the island. He owns an entire cove fifteen miles outside of town. A developer offered him ten million dollars for it once and Marty laughed at the guy.

His house is set back in the hills, but his boathouse is down on the water of course, and it's bigger than most houses. You can drive trucks right into it. There's a winch to get speedboats into the water. Marty was waiting for me by the big double doors. He opened them for me and then shut them once I was in. His cabin cruiser was tied up at the dock. It was seventy feet long, all burnished brass and teak.

I had asked him once if didn't he think it was foolish to run his operation out of his home, and I'll never forget what he told me. "I don't shit in my own backyard." He'd built a huge fucking sign in the wilderness that screamed DRUG SMUGGLING HERE and then didn't conduct any business from it. I wonder how many hours the DEA has kept the place under surveillance over the years. Marty's a fucking genius, there's no doubt about it.

He looked like an unhappy genius today, though.

"You know, Marty," I told him as I looked admiringly at his boat, "they're taking these things away from convicted felons in Dade County." I paused to see if he had anything to say to that. He didn't. "Thought you couldn't make it till four."

"I hate to see fresh bait go bad," he replied. "Let's see it."

I opened the trunk and showed him the bodies. He didn't scream and faint, but I could tell he wasn't real happy.

"Friends of Smith?" he asked.

"Yeah."

"Wouldn't come sniffing around, I believe were your exact words."

"Not unless they knew something concrete," I told him. "And it looks like Smith made a full report just prior to you scrambling his cerebellum."

"How do you know?"

"They knew I don't enjoy being called Sheriff," I told him. "They were looking for someone named Stine. Have any idea who that might be?"

"No clue, let's get 'em in the boat."

I hadn't straightened out the bodies after dumping them in the trunk, and the bodies had frozen in the same awkward positions that I'd dumped them in. Marty had to get a sledgehammer to break their arms and legs so we could move them. It took the two of us to get them out of the trunk and into the boat. I threw my bloodstained shirt in on top of them.

"Get a plastic bag out of the galley," Marty told me. "I don't want to go swimming with that tucked in my belt."

He checked the vents on the scuppers and pressed the electric starter; the diesel's roar filled the boathouse. When the engines had warmed up enough he pressed another button and the boat door rolled up out of our way. He pushed the throttles forward a quarter and we were on our way. When we cleared the boathouse he pushed the throttles further and we surged ahead. Most people don't believe it when Marty tells them he can get his cabin cruiser up on a plane; he didn't even have the throttles past two thirds.

There really is a vicious undertow off Mana Kona; I hadn't been lying to Smith. It's posted NO DIVING and my men have orders to arrest anyone who even looks like he's thinking about diving there. They've never had to arrest anyone, though; except for their hobby, divers are a singularly sensible lot. I think it has a lot to do with diving. If being down at seventy feet and sucking on your regulator and getting nothing doesn't teach you how fragile life really is, nothing will.

The real danger of diving against a current is that you don't realize how much oxygen you're burning. Once again it's a case of the strongest swimmers getting themselves killed. They burn out their spare tanks and have to surface, where they have to dump their equipment. Usually they try to take a bearing so they can come back for it; mostly they never do. If they survive two or three days in the water they seldom feel like diving anymore.

That wasn't a problem for Marty. He's one of the strongest swimmers I've ever met. He's competed in every Ironman ever held on the island, and he wasn't a kid when that particular madness started.

He threw a spare tank over the side with a six-battery marine flashlight tied to it. Then he gave me a hand with the bodies. I'd weighted them down with anchor chain on the way over; Marty always keeps spares on board.

He went below to change and came back in his diving outfit. The water was warm, so he didn't bother with a wet suit. He was carrying a plastic bucket with a lid on it. I knew it would have quick-set cement in it.

"Might as well take care of Smith while I'm here," he said by way of explanation. I got a rod and reel and pretended to fish while I waited for him to come back.

To pass the time I tried to remember all the bodies that had gone down there. It was depressing because I knew I'd never get them all. There isn't much that passes for organized crime on the Big Island, but Oahu's pretty well sewn up. In the late seventies they had requested a piece of the action and Marty had had to say no. He might have cut them in for 20 percent, but they wanted 50. Marty might even have gone for that but I told him no.

Fifteen of them were down there now. And a shitload more than that had died in Honolulu before there was a change in management on Oahu. Before retiring to the life of gentleman farmer, Mad Dog had put a lot of freelancers down there as well. Throw in some assorted Mormons and those assholes the Evans brothers, and you've got a pretty fair-sized crowd.

I wasn't worried about someone stumbling across the bodies. The idea of banner headlines screaming about Hawaiian boneyards wasn't something we'd been willing to risk. That was why we used Mana Kona: because of the crabs. After a few weeks Marty would go back and gather up whatever was left and cement it up. Add a few limpets and it was just another rock on the bottom. It really was depressing that I couldn't remember how many of the rocks were ours.

Marty surfaced on the seaward side of the boat.

"Anybody watching?"

I scanned the coast with my binoculars. I didn't see anyone, but that didn't mean a whole lot; if they didn't want me to see them, I wouldn't.

"Coast be clear, Martin. Come on aboard."

He climbed up the ladder and rolled onto the floor. He

tied the line he was carrying to a davit and then went into the galley to change.

"Getting crowded down there," he called from below.

I was busy pulling in his spare tank and didn't reply. I knew there was plenty more room.

Marty came back up and picked up his spare tank. He took it back downstairs. I could hear him washing the salt water off of it. Marty's meticulous about his equipment—all good divers are. He came back above decks with his rod and reel and a bucket of beers. Conspiracies usually get blown because the conspirators get either lazy, stupid or greedy; we'd been at it for a long time and we were none of those things. When we got back to shore we'd have some fish, a pile of empties and that deep inner glow that only an afternoon blown off fishing can give you.

"You know, Chief," Marty began, "this kind of concerns me. I don't think these two were angry dads."

I sighed. "The Mormons probably have a hundred thousand missionaries out at any given time and they send them everywhere: New York slums, Catholic countries, Israel, you name it. It only makes sense that they have people out there looking out for them."

He pointed at the bandage on my leg. "People who shoot first and then ask questions?"

"Don't kid yourself, Marty," I told him. "You don't cross a thousand miles of wilderness and set up camp in the desert unless you're tough. Besides, they think Satan worshipers are good citizens in comparison to dope dealers." I paused. "And they like their kids."

"That's great, Carnac," he said. "They like their kids. What's your prediction this time?"

"One man with a twenty-power scope," I told him. "They've got to realize by this time that they shouldn't be fooling around with us."

"No chance they'll cut their losses and run?" he asked.

I didn't think so. Maybe if it were up to the guys who had to risk their necks they might let us slide. But somewhere there was an administrator who had an annual budget he had to justify. He had to convince the people giving him the money that they were employing a top-notch skilled organization. So far it was three-nothing, not including the four that the Evans brothers had gotten. That wasn't going to look good in the old annual report.

"No," I told him. "You can be sure that they know everything that Bellamy knew, which means they know about me and you." Marty gave a start when I mentioned Dave. I looked at him in disbelief. "Dave didn't know anything else important, did he?"

"Dave used to drive the truck."

Marty had tried to tell me how he got the local herb to the mainland once, but I told him I didn't want to know. I had to admit it was clever.

"We store the stuff in caves back in the hills," Marty told me. "That's the big secret behind the AMN-GWH, you know. Before I got those idiots organized they would harvest the best weed in the Western Hemisphere twice a year and dump it on the market all at once. It would depress the price for months. The sharp operators would buy the stuff up for pennies and make a killing three months later while the growers slit each other's throats.

"The way it works now is we trickle it onto the market at a steady rate and keep the price as high as practical. There's probably a three-year supply out in the hills. I've tried everything: I pay them not to grow; I give them free trips to Europe; I even try to reason with them. But they just don't feel right unless they're growing something. It must be the farming mystique.

"Anyway, once a month we load a container and put it on the ferry for Honolulu."

"A fucking shipping container?" I asked him. "That must be ten tons of the shit."

"Oh, it's more than that, more like twenty. We could sell twice that, but what's the point? It'd just depress the price and we'd lose market share to the Californians. There's a cachet to Kona AA that's worth millions, and we ain't gonna lose it for no short-term profits.

"Anyway, somebody's gotta load the container and drive

the truck. I've kept the operation small, and no one but me knows where more than two of the caches are, but there still must be thirty guys who know most of the story. Dave used to drive the truck to Honolulu."

"Did he know what happened to it once it got there?" I asked.

"He did." Then Marty did a strange thing. He laughed. "You know, Chief, we've been using the same route for five years and I've been dying to see a shipment get seized."

"You been out in the sun too long, Marty?"

He laughed some more. "Once a month Dave would go to Honolulu and drive his truck right on board the U.S.S. *Dirksen*. We've been shipping marijuana on a fucking Navy oiler for five years, and the best part is, we're not even paying anyone off. They think they're shipping Navy cargo."

Then I started laughing. The U.S.S. *Dirksen* is an oil tanker that supplies Pearl Harbor. It's plied the same route for twenty-five years: Los Angeles to Honolulu two weeks there and two weeks back. For twenty years it had sailed the Honolulu-to-L.A. leg empty, until Marty had had some orders cut that made use of it to ship Navy dependents' furnishings back to the mainland. I imagine there'll be some red faces at the Pentagon when the story breaks. Nothing could cheer me up more.

"Maybe you should warn your customers not to pick up the next load," I offered.

"No need," Marty was practically giggling, "Mayflower picks it up and delivers it to a warehouse in Burbank. I'll tell them to stay away from the warehouse, though."

He sobered up and took a long pull on his beer.

"Of course it's not due in L.A. till Thursday morning," he said. "If we want to be here to listen to Cap Weinberger's explanation we're going to have to do something about the Mormons."

"You think your customers may be of any help?"

"Sure," he said, "Mormons are crazy about motorcycles—every tabernacle has a club. Got any other bright ideas?"

"Well, I could chop you into little pieces and send you to them as a peace offering, except I don't have an address."

We sucked on our beers and killed a few fish and thought our own thoughts. No matter how I came at the problem, it always came down to me going to Salt Lake City. I have bad thoughts about the mainland. It seems like every time I go there somebody tries to maim me.

"Looks like I'm going to have to go to Salt Lake," I finally said.

"Glad you said it and not me" was Marty's reply.

I gave him the car keys and flight coupons I'd taken off the dead Mormons and told him what to do with them.

"And Marty, make sure you actually see them get on the plane. If they sell the tickets to the Presbyterian minister and his wife we're in deep shit."

He told me he wasn't born yesterday and that I could count on him.

"Terrific," I said. "I can count on you. There's one other thing: somebody's got to take care of Eiko while I'm gone."

He leered at me. "You want me to provide all of your services or only certain ones?"

Marty was never going to understand that relationship.

"Help yourself, Marty, but if I catch something from you, you better head for Sri Lanka."

The sun was low on the horizon when Marty started the engines and headed for home. People do come out in droves to catch the sunsets on the west coast of the Big Island. They're not something that I can describe, but almost all the old people on our side of the island have vision problems. We watch a lot of sunsets.

As we headed in, Marty turned to me. "You know, Chief, three of your bales are on the *Dirksen*."

"What's three bales among seven hundred?" I asked.

"Depends on what's in them."

"Marty," I said, "we've had this discussion before.

They're not likely to rip apart seven hundred bales of marijuana looking for something that they don't know is there. That's the whole scam, they've already made the big bust and everybody's happy."

I think Marty wanted to retire from the drug business, but he couldn't get out any more than I could. Once you board the tiger, you don't get off unless he asks.

"Maybe so," he said. We were quiet the rest of the way home.

CHAPTER SIX

□

HAWAII

The present

I have a one-bedroom bungalow outside of town. It's private there—you can kill people in your living room without disturbing the neighbors. It's not much of a place. Anywhere else in the world it'd be a dump. But where I live, it's just about as good as you can do on a chief of police's salary.

Eiko was waiting for me. She's twenty-seven and she's as beautiful as Japanese girls get, and that's very beautiful. She has long black hair that reaches her hips, and a dancer's legs. She was sitting in my favorite chair wearing just her panties and a T-shirt. I could see a streak of blood at the corner of her mouth where she had been chewing on her lip.

"You're late," she said accusingly.

"Sorry, I had business to attend to."

She ran to me and practically climbed up my body to reach my face. She kissed me, hard. I tasted the salt from her cut lip.

"Please don't be mad at me," she said. "I do the best I can, but when you're late I can't help myself."

"I'm not mad at you," I told her. "Wait for me in the bedroom, I'll be in in a minute."

I went to my office and got the kit out of my desk.

I took a riot gun out of my gun rack and did something that would get any of my men suspended for a month without pay: I loaded it with buckshot. I turned all the lights out and then walked around the house, checking the doors and windows.

Eiko was on the bed, waiting for me. She had pulled the shades and lit a candle; the red light played off her beautiful legs. She had one of them extended straight over her head and was slowly moving a cotton swab back and forth across the inside of her knee. My Marine Corps belt was fastened loosely about her thigh.

I sat on the bed next to her and took a sterile spoon out of the kit and thwacked the side of the Ziploc bag to break up the clumps. I measured an amount of powder onto the spoon. You have to be a fucking chemist these days because every batch is different, and the first person to use a new batch is a guinea pig for all the other users. I never let Eiko be first. The heroin melted quickly and I set it down to cool.

I took a disposable syringe out of the carton and checked that the bag was still sealed. Eiko moved the swab back and forth across her leg, but it was mechanical action now. Her eyes were fixed on my hands, on the syringe. I put the end of the needle into the molten liquid and drew it into the body. She had stopped moving her hands: she was mesmerized by the syringe.

I opened a disposable alcohol swab and rubbed it vigorously across her knee. It wasn't that I didn't think she had done a good job, it was just that it's always infections that kill heroin addicts. They're in a rush; they haven't got time to sterilize equipment. They share needles, and when needles aren't available, they open their veins with safety razors and sprinkle the powder in directly. They don't care; it doesn't seem that important to them. When I got her back from Honolulu she had weighed seventy pounds and been suffering from galloping hepatitis. She's much happier now, sings all day.

Marine Corps belts are designed to be used as tourniquets, never can tell when you might need a tourniquet. I cinched it tight around Eiko's thigh. She gave a moan like she'd been penetrated and threw herself back on the bed. I slapped the back of her knee to make the veins stand out and then rubbed the swab across her one last time. I found the vein and pushed the plunger home.

She let out a long low moan and arched her back, bringing her hips up off the bed. She lubricated heavily and her scent filled the room.

She reached down and grabbed the tails of her T-shirt and pulled it over her head. She was beautiful in the candlelight; her breasts were perfect, they rose and fell in time with her hyperventilation. She rubbed her hands across her inner thighs, not daring to bring them up to her clitoris. I recalled the medieval stories of the incubus.

I knew this phase would only last a minute, so I didn't disturb her. I took my clothes off and stood there, watching her in the candlelight. My leg hurt like a bastard and for a second I considered shooting myself up. But only for a second; I know where that path leads.

The climax passed and Eiko collapsed and lay there panting. She opened her eyes and looked for me.

I slipped off her panties and slipped into the bed beside her. I lay on my back and let her climb on top of me. I weigh about 170 pounds more than she does and I've always worried about crushing her.

I had an erection that you could drive nails with; watching Eiko writhe is the greatest turn-on you could ever imagine. She slipped herself onto my cock. Her vagina seemed incredibly tight, but it was me who was ripped apart. She's four feet ten inches tall, weighs all of ninety-five pounds and has a face like the Madonna. But she has voluntary muscular control over the sphincters in her vagina: the effect is indescribable. She had ruined normal sex for me. I'd have kept her even if she wasn't so useful for keeping her father in line.

She hadn't even cleared my glans when she started to orgasm. She gave a wild moan and thrust herself home. She put her head down and clenched her fists in the hair on my chest. She thrust herself against me again and again, moaning and whimpering. Her toes dug into the sheets and her fingers tightened in the hair on my chest. She looked for all the world like a football lineman surging out of a four-point stance. I watched the muscles clench and loosen in her back and her beautiful hair rippling like the sea at night.

I rested my hands lightly on her sides and let her move back and forth across them. I could feel the aliveness of her and I didn't want it to end.

When I finally came she gave a cry like a wild thing snared. I felt the muscles in her vagina contract. She reversed herself and wrapped her small mouth around my cock and sucked like she was demon-possessed, willing me not to lose my erection. When I didn't, she was on me again and rode me until she dropped exhausted. Oh, Judge Ohira, if you could only see your youngest now.

I still think that my four years at the University were the best years of my life. That's where I met Eiko's older sister. The University is nestled in a valley above Honolulu and further up the valley it rains every day, so there's a rainbow just about every afternoon. It's not quite the only school in town, but for the most part, it's where Hawaiians send their kids.

To play football for the Rainbow Warriors is just about the ultimate for a boy growing up in Hawaii. We don't have any major-league teams so a whole year's worth of adoration gets spent in the thirteen weeks of the fall football season. I could have gone to the mainland and played at Berkeley or USC. But when the offer came to play for the Warriors, I jumped at it.

They practically gave me the key to the village back home; it was the first good thing I'd ever done as far as most of the local establishment was concerned. Mom packed me a lunch and told me to study hard. That was the last time anyone mentioned studying to me for four years.

I lived in the athletic dorm and barely remember my freshman year. It's hard enough for normal freshmen to get anything done during their first year at college. For freshman football players it's damn near impossible. All the new and different things to do, the classes, the girls and the parties. If you're on the team you get invited to a lot of parties, parties that the girls who can't say no attend.

They didn't let frosh play for the varsity back then, and it's just as well because I probably would have flunked out. Besides, I had to learn a new position: 180-pound linebackers get creamed in big-time college ball. They put me on a weight-training program and taught me to play strong safety.

The upper classmen taught me the rest of the stuff that football players need to know: which alumni could be hit up for loans, which professors were to be avoided like the plague, which sororities attracted the sluts—all the stuff they don't put in the catalog.

By my junior year I was a Big Man on Campus. I was a fast, mean 205-pound strong safety and made all-conference that year. It's possible that I could have made All-American my senior year. But in our second game, against Montana, an offensive lineman had to tackle me to keep me away from his quarterback. It was a good play all around: we got fifteen yards and they got me out of the game. He hadn't meant to end my career.

I was still on crutches when I met Betty Ohira. She was from my hometown, but I'd never met her. She had boarded at the Punahou School in Honolulu. She was majoring in sociology and had ambitions of attending Stanford Law School. We fell madly in love.

The judge did not approve. As he saw things, I was a halfbreed no-account lout, who wasn't nearly good enough for his daughter. I flew home to talk to him. I had this crazy idea of asking for his permission to marry her, but it was like talking to a brick wall. He said a lot of nasty things about my father. He started to say something about my mother, but the look I gave him must have made him think twice. I told him we didn't need him and flew back to Honolulu.

When I arrived Betty was gone. She wasn't just not in Hawaii, she wasn't even in the country. The judge—he was actually just another lawyer back then—was a hard man. He had beat me home and told his eldest that she could either transfer to an all-girls academy in Japan, or she could forget that she had ever had a family.

She was in Japan for three months before she killed herself. One day she decided she wanted to go home and started walking. She didn't stop when she got to the shore.

I graduated anyway. The University was decent about the whole affair. They gave me some time off and extended my scholarship to five years so I could get my degree. After commencement I went home to find a job. I must have been pretty green, or maybe I'd just forgotten what home was like. The four summers I'd been at the University the alumni had always taken care of me. If there's a cushier job than lifeguard at a resort hotel, I don't know what it is.

I didn't think I was going to have much problem getting a job as a police officer on Hawaii. I was a local boy. I was a football hero. I had a degree in criminal justice. I was naïve as shit.

I must have forgotten that I was a half-breed, or, more delicately, of mixed descent: it just slipped my mind. The town fathers were happy to remind me, though. They told me in pretty certain terms that there was no place I was going to fit in the local establishment, especially as a police officer. They suggested bellhop at the Mauna Kea might be about my speed.

I did the only thing that a self-respecting football player could do under the circumstances: I went to the Whale and Lion, got plastered and broke the place up. It took four sheriff's deputies to arrest me. I was still conscious when they got me outside, but that didn't last very long. I suppose I'm lucky that it wasn't me doing the arresting.

Mr. Ohira came to visit me in my cell the next day. I had seen him at Betty's funeral but we hadn't talked. I really didn't feel up to talking to him. Besides having a roaring hangover I had taken a wicked beating. It made me wonder how long they had kept hitting me after I had lost consciousness. I wasn't used to the empty spot in my gum yet either. It bothered me more than the broken ribs.

"You are in serious trouble, James," he told me. "You

will be charged with more than eight counts of assault and battery, as well as a number of lesser charges such as malicious destruction of property, public drunkenness and corrupting the morals of a minor."

I vaguely recalled that the whole incident had started because they wouldn't let me buy Charlie Nianga's little brother a beer. I had seen Billy sucker-punch two of the guys who were holding me down, but I couldn't recall seeing him after the cops arrived. He must have been smarter than me and run. God, that hurt: outthought by a fifteen-year-old Tongan.

"Well, thank you for your concern, Mr. Ohira, but I can't afford a lawyer. And even if I could, I think I'd rather have an honest one."

"James," he said, ignoring my little attempt at humor, "if you are convicted of a felony in the state of Hawaii, you can forget about your ambitions to be a police officer. Your entire college experience will have been wasted."

"Doesn't matter," I told him. "I can still get a job servicing old rich white *wahines* at the fucking resort. That's about the best opportunity us mongrels have on this island."

"Perhaps on this island, but there are others. If you want to have any chance in life, you must not be convicted of these charges."

"What's the deal?" I asked. I was beginning to understand how life worked by that time. I knew there would be a deal.

"If you are willing to enter the armed services all charges against you will be dropped."

I thought it over for a while; I really didn't have anything better to do. Rake lawns for millionaires and service their wives while they were out killing marlin looked like my only other option.

"Why are you doing this?" I asked.

He looked at me a while and then said, "Because I do not wish to be constantly reminded that you exist. What is your answer?

I started whistling "You're in the Army Now," but the

Marine Corps recruitment station was closer to the jail. I've often wondered if that was a coincidence.

I told the recruiter that they could have me—and they were hot to get me (football, not B.S.)—if they'd ship me to Parris Island instead of San Diego. I was anxious to get as far from Hawaii as I possibly could. The recruiter looked at me gravely and said, "I think we can arrange that, son." I bet he was still laughing two weeks later when I got on the airplane.

My mother saw me off at the airport. I was to see her just one more time, and then only for fifteen minutes. She told me to keep my head down and work hard. I guess she figured that studying hadn't been my forte. Mrs. Ohira came as well. She gave me one of Betty's scarves. Poor Mrs. Ohira, she had such a rotten husband and such beautiful children.

That night I slept with Eiko curled into my armpit and dreamed about red-eyed demons who told me that I was damned in this life and damned in the next as well. I kept asking them why and they would just hold up bottles of Coke. That one would have been funny except it turned into the Vietnam dream. I hadn't had the Vietnam dream for years.

We were on a ten-day patrol in the Central Highlands. It wasn't an area of high VC activity, so we weren't as alert as we should have been. I was on point as we entered the village. I stopped on the outskirts and let the rest of the patrol fan out behind me. The first sergeant came up behind me, with the rookie he was trying to break in tailing behind him like an abandoned puppy.

Sergeant Wilson was from the ghetto in East St. Louis. People who knew him there said he had always been picking up strays and taking them home. In Vietnam he picked up white kids from the suburbs and tried to teach them how to stay alive. He didn't have much luck.

"What's goin' down, Yamasaki?"

"I don't like it," I told him. There were no people, but it was the middle of the day and there shouldn't have been any people. They should have all been indoors taking siestas. I still didn't like it. Wilson respected my opinion because I wasn't easy to spook. But I was spooked for sure in this place.

"Then we gonna take it nice and slow," Wilson told me.

That's when the kid appeared. In my dream it's always a little boy, but in the village it was a little girl, maybe eight years old. She was naked and screaming. She held up her little hand above her head where someone had cut off her fingers. Behind us I heard a *chuff,* as a Marine fired his grenade launcher at the hut she had run out of.

I swung my M-14 around, hating myself, but Wilson beat me to it; his M-14 cut the little girl's legs off at the knees. The rookie turned to Wilson, more surprise than anything else on his face. His lips formed a silent question, *Why?* But Wilson and I were already diving for cover. He turned back to the little girl and found out why—someone had epoxied a satchel charge onto her back.

There was no cover, but I didn't want to try outrunning the blast. I hit the ground and crossed my ankles, so the shrapnel wouldn't cut my dick off, and jammed my fingers into my ears. I put my fingers into my ears so I wouldn't be deafened. But at the time, I remember wishing that I already were. My fingers couldn't cut off the sound of the little girl's screaming. The satchel charge took care of that.

The rookie was blown twenty-five feet backward. He must have walked right up to the little girl. Incredibly he wasn't dead, but his eyes were gone and so were his ears. The last thing he ever saw and heard was the little girl. A doctor from the VA contacted us later to find out what had happened to the poor bastard. He had gone catatonic in the hospital. Vietnam had that effect on people.

While Wilson was taking care of his latest hurt kitten, I walked up to the hut the little girl had come out of. The guerrilla was still alive, barely. He was sort of crawling around looking for his eardrums. I picked up his rifle. The people who owned the hut hadn't been at fault; what were they supposed to have done? As I walked out I threw in a white phosphorous grenade anyway, what the fuck.

I got Eiko up at dawn and told her that Marty would be injecting her for the next couple of days. She said that she could do it herself, but I told her that that was all right, Marty would be happy to help her.

Letting Eiko inject her own heroin would be like letting a twelve-year-old guard the cookie jar, except you can't OD on chocolate chip cookies. She had injected herself just once since I'd gotten her back from Kuhio Street. I had locked her in a closet for two days. When I let her out, she was so strung out that she asked me to kill her. I didn't have to lock her supply away after that.

I haven't taken a vacation for six years. I worry that if I'm away for more than five minutes, my idiot lieutenant will decide that he has to do something impressive while I'm gone to get into my good graces.

Lieutenant Casey's a good man. He was the senior patrolman on the force when I first joined. I was the force's third patrolman, so I got stuck working Friday and Saturday nights to keep the local high schoolers in line. Casey gave me all sorts of good advice. "You gotta kick their heinies," he told me. "You gotta show 'em who's boss. You let the fuckin' natives get uppity. . . . You got a touch of the coconut brush yerself, dontcha, Yamasaki? Well, that's OK by me, I don't hold it against yah. Be careful around the slanty . . ." He sort of trailed off.

"Kikes," I said helpfully.

"Ah shit, Jim," he said. "You know what I mean. The assholes who run this town. They're out to get you foh sure."

I know what he meant, and I don't hold it against him. As a matter of fact I like him so much that one year when he was off on vacation, Marty and I buried three hundred thousand dollars and twenty-five pounds of cocaine in his backyard. Of course he's not likely to find out about it unless the state Bureau of Investigation digs it up for him. I'm planning on being truly shocked at his duplicity.

I called him at home and told him I'd be away for a few days and that I wanted him to mind the store. I made it pretty clear that if he implemented any of the ideas he'd gotten from Dick Tracy's "Crime Stoppers' Notebook" I'd fry his ass when I got back. He told me that I could count on him and I was glad he couldn't see me shuddering.

I gave Eiko her morning pick-me-up: a few milligrams of heroin in a glass of chocolate milk. She wouldn't be so high that she couldn't function, but she wouldn't get the shakes either. The tourists in the hotel where she's a desk clerk always compliment her on how cheerful she is. She just sings all day, a real joy to behold. She's always getting propositioned by rich tourists. But she just tells them that her boyfriend is the chief of police and that usually cools their jets. If it doesn't, meeting me always does.

Flights leave on the hour for Honolulu so I wasn't in a big hurry. I drove around town once to make sure everything was in order, just doing my job. I didn't detect any riots brewing so I headed out of town.

There was no one to see me off at the airport.

CHAPTER SEVEN

□

HAWAII

The present

Most residents of Hawaii—be careful who you go calling a native—consider tourists to be the lowest form of scum. It's not racism; they hate Japanese and *haole* tourists with equal fervor. As a matter of fact there's very little racial prejudice in Hawaii; who needs niggers when you've got tourists?

Hawaiians hate tourists because they're, well, tourists. They wear aloha shirts with the bright side out and insist on calling them Hawaiian shirts. They can't pronounce anything right. They have too much money. How could anyone not hate them?

Since the state's economy would collapse if it weren't for the tourists, you might think that people around here shouldn't hate them too much, but they do. The Visitors' Bureau has been trying to change folks' attitudes for years, but it's just so much pissing in the wind. Even after the United Airlines pilots' strike, which did more damage to the local economy than the *tsunami* back in '46, disc jockies still tell tourist jokes on the air, assholes.

Of course residents do appreciate some tourists: the ones who stick to the tourist attractions and spend every cent they've got while they're here. The unofficial state motto is "Not one thin dime gets back on the plane." Don't get me wrong, though; Hawaii's a great place to visit. . . . Come on out, bring lots of money.

Considering the local attitude problem, the folks who work for the local airline are definitely out of place. One of the nicest memories most tourists bring back from Hawaii is a flight on Hawaiian Air. It's by far the nicest airline in the world. It's owned by an old missionary family that cleverly convinced the last king to give them huge tracts of land in what would one day be downtown Honolulu.

Somehow or another they've managed to hire just about every nice person in the islands to work for their airline. From the pilots to the people who answer the phone, you'll never meet friendlier folks. This is truly amazing when you consider that the typical Hawaiian refers to tourists as maggots. "I'd rather be seen talking to a native" is a pretty typical comment.

I usually ask for an aisle seat in the back, so I can get off without being trampled by a thundering herd of old people in loud shirts. This trip I asked for a window. I wanted to see the islands one last time in case I wasn't coming back. The pilot gave a running description for the benefit of the passengers, Maui, Lanai, Molokai, Gilligan's.

On the approach to Honolulu International we flew directly over Hawaii Kai, Koko Head, Diamond Head and Pearl Harbor. It was dead low tide and I could see the hulk of the *Arizona* resting on the bottom at Battleship Row. More than a thousand men are entombed in it. It wasn't an auspicious omen.

I had seen the *Arizona* on my way to Parris Island. The Marine Corps had paid for a one-way ticket to Los Angeles and told me that if I really had my heart set on Parris Island it was three thousand miles thataway. They gave me a week to make the trip. I didn't really mind; I'd always wanted to see the U.S.A.

Parris Island really isn't that bad. Well, it isn't as bad as sailors will try to make you think that it is. Parris Island builds character. There's nothing quite like having a six-foot-eight Negro with stripes telling you that you're a pea-brained urinal licker to build character in a young man.

Despite all that, I learned to love the Corps at Parris Island. The Marines didn't give a shit what color my parents had been, or that they hadn't quite been a matching pair. All they cared about was that I could shoot straight and that I wouldn't let my buddies down in a fire fight.

The best friends I ever had I met at Parris. I was still thinking about them when the captain turned on the FASTEN SEATBELTS sign, getting ready to land in L.A. The Marine Corps was the best thing that had ever happened to me. When I left the island I didn't care if I never saw Hawaii again. The Corps was going to be my career.

One of my friends died at Khesanh, fighting to protect William Westmoreland's honor. Another came back, but he died of lung cancer three years later. A third came back too, but his legs stayed in Vietnam.

I wrangled a leave and went to see him at the big Army hospital in Saigon. It wasn't Ted. It was some stranger lying on a hospital bed hating the world, hating anyone with legs, hating me. Vietnam had that effect on people. When I got back to the States I wrote him four letters, but he never replied. He didn't forget about me, though: I was the beneficiary of his GI life insurance policy. I thought about trying to find out how he'd died, but I never did. I decided I didn't want to know.

As for the rest, we've never gotten together, too many ghosts between us.

I had flown United to Los Angeles. L.A., the city of night, an endless stretch of highway with degenerates at every intersection and stars behind every wheel. Jim Morrison loved L.A. I've never been there. The airport looks just like everybody else's. I went to the Delta counter and bought a ticket for Salt Lake. They had loads of seats and flights left every hour.

I used my American Express card, wouldn't think of leaving home without it. I figured that the people I wanted to see would be looking for visitors from the west, and I wanted to make sure they didn't miss me. If I couldn't locate them, that meant going back to Hawaii and waiting for the guy with the twenty-power scope to show up. The idea didn't thrill me.

I had no idea where I was going to find them. It didn't seem like a real good bet that they'd be listed under "Goons" in the church directory. I was worried that if they didn't find me I would have to resort to drastic measures, maybe running an ad in the personals column of the local paper. "SJPHM drug runner from fiftieth state wishes to contact Mormon CIA, object: reconciliation. Sincere replies only, please."

I wasn't real worried about putting myself in the lions' den, so to speak. I was hoping that the Mormons wouldn't be any more anxious to shit in their backyard than Marty was in his. That was the other reason I wanted the world to know I was going to Utah. I figured the Mormons would be reluctant to have the FBI searching the tabernacle looking for me.

I had a plan, of course. I wasn't just going to Salt Lake because that was where the Mormons were—that would have been pretty stupid. I figured that our only chance for survival was to convince the Mormons that it was in their best interests to leave us alone. There was no way we were going to win a shooting war. Besides outnumbering us several million to one, they reproduced faster. Utah has the same demographics as your typical third-world nation.

Convincing the Mormons that it was in their best interests to leave us alone was going to be tricky. I'd have been willing to try bribery if I'd thought for a second that it would work: protecting Marty's profit margin isn't high on my list of priorities. Somehow, though, I couldn't see the Mormons being beguiled by the promise of easy drug money. But have them I did. I had them by something better than their balls; I had them by their religion.

I personally belong to the Holy Order of God the Ruthless Practical Joker—the main tenet of which is that God is there to maximize human suffering as part of an extremely complicated practical joke. As for other religions, we Holy Jokers are ready for the worst. It wouldn't surprise us to get to Judgment Day and find that all the world's religions, the ones that we've been killing each other over for the last umpty-ump years, were completely true. Father Coughlin and the Ayatollah sharing a party line with the big man upstairs.

All religions are pretty much alike as far as I can tell. I would hate to have to rate them in order of lunacy. But if I did, the Mormons would be right up there with the Christian Scientists at the top of my list. Now I'll admit that the Mormon religion does a fine job of all the things that religions are supposed to do, much better than Catholicism, for instance. The Mormons are close knit. Widows, orphans and the infirm are all provided for. Societal values are reinforced, etc., etc. The religion explains all the great mysteries and provides a framework that every Mormon can feel that he or she is a part of; it gives life meaning. But God, the Book of Mormon reads like science fiction.

Mormonism was founded by Joseph Smith, one of the great con artists of the nineteenth century. He claimed to have found a set of gilded leaves (they were pointed out to him by Jesus) upon which was written the history and moral philosophy of a race—either a lost tribe of Israel or folks from Atlantis, I forget—that had lived in North America around the time of Christ.

Why this philosophy is supposed to be relevant to modern Americans is a total mystery. After all, those folks wiped themselves out in what must have been a really nasty war. It not only left no survivors on either side, it wiped out all traces of their civilization. Well, all right, maybe there is some relevance there, but not much. Why we should adopt their philosophy and head down the same path is just one of those questions that politeness forbids you to ask.

Another good one is why the church isn't sponsoring archaeological digs all over North America looking for other buried nuggets of wisdom. I mean really, could everything that God wants us to know have fitted onto a few lousy golden leaves?

Actually, I'm being much too harsh on Joe. Any man who could invent the concept of "Spiritual Marriage"—an excuse to have sex with other men's wives—couldn't have been all bad. And if, when the last trump blows, I find him sitting there on the right hand of God, it won't surprise me a bit. I can take a good joke as well as the next guy.

The Mormons began settling in Utah after they had been, in quick succession, kicked out of New York, Missouri and Illinois. They were the nineteenth-century equivalent of the Palestinians: everyone felt sorry for them, but nobody wanted them settling in their state. The Mormons were beaten, robbed and threatened with extermination everywhere they went.

The real problem was that they were an industrious people who stuck together and voted as a bloc per their leader's instructions; earlier settlers were worried that they were going to be displaced. The people who lived in that village in Oregon where the Bhagwan took over can probably relate to the feeling.

After Joe was lynched in Illinois, thereby providing an object lesson for those who would follow in his footsteps—L. Ron Hubbard and the Bhagwan, for instance—Brigham Young decided that the Mormons' only chance for survival as a people was to move somewhere that no one else would want. He decided on the Rocky Mountains.

Prior to the arrival of the Mormons the area was known as the Great American Desert. Immigrants passed through it as quickly as possible on their way to California. The great dead lake in the middle discouraged settlement. Young figured that no one would bother them there, and no one did, not for a few years anyway.

The Mormons labored for ten years in the valley of the Great Salt Lake, building their civilization in the wilderness. The first two years were tough, but the Mormons shared and no one starved. Though most folks did go hungry while they got the hang of dry-land farming. They built settlements and dug canals and sent missionaries all over the world to call the Mormons to Zion.

And the Mormons came. They made the trek in large groups along trails that had been blazed by the first

Mormons—their leaders had decided early on that it would be a good idea to avoid the trails used by more orthodox pioneers. Brigham Young sent back men who had already made the trip to act as guides for the people who followed. The Mormons planted crops along the trails and tended them so that the next year's caravan would be certain to have food, something no other group of settlers had thought to do. The call of the church was so strong that Mormons in northern California left working gold mines behind them and went to Utah to be farmers, and this was in 1849.

Naturally this situation was too good to last. Too many people hated the Mormons and they weren't just going to sit back and let them set up shop in the West and flout American values. The United States invaded Utah in 1857. It came as a complete surprise to the Mormons; they hadn't seceded from the Union or anything. They were perplexed as to why Washington felt it was necessary to send five thousand soldiers out to Utah to restore order. One thing was certain, though: the Mormons had been kicked around once too often and they weren't just going to sit back and take it anymore.

The Mormon-American War is one of the oddest events in the sad history of the United States Army, and I'm proud to report that the Marine Corps had nothing to do with it. It's possible that somewhere there may have been a more badly botched campaign, but I doubt it. The invasion was conceived in Congress as an answer to the "Mormon Problem," and like all military campaigns run by the politicians, it was a disaster.

The poor dogfaces had to march across a thousand miles of wilderness to get to Utah. They could have made it before winter, but, in the grand tradition of the U.S. Army, their leaders were indecisive and couldn't make up their minds what they wanted to do. They pissed away the summer and fall worrying about what Congress would think and ended up short of Utah, stuck in the mountains, when winter hit. Winter in the Rockies is cruel; a lot of dogfaces didn't see the spring.

Brigham Young turned out to be a political genius, one

of the reasons it's Brigham Young, and not Joseph Smith, University. Young knew it was futile to fight the United States Army. The politicians in Washington weren't about to lose a war to the Mormons. On the other hand, he also knew that fielding an army of that size—at the time it was the largest peacetime army in American history—and keeping it supplied two thousand miles from Washington was expensive. He figured that Congress wasn't going to be willing to support an unpopular war forever, and that eventually it would be willing to come to some sort of mutually agreeable arrangement.

Just to make it easier for Congress to see the error of its ways, the Mormons adopted guerrilla tactics. They burned supply trains and captured pack animals. They scorched the earth in front of the invading army. Fodder is scarce in Utah during the best of times, and the Army's pack animals began to die at a horrendous rate. The expense began to mount.

In the meantime, the same newspapers that had been screaming for the government to whip those polygamous Mormons into line were now, predictably, howling about corruption and the cost of the war, assholes. The papers dubbed it "The Contractors' War." President Buchanan was backed into a corner. His dream of a short sweet successful campaign, with a minimum number of casualties and a clear-cut victory—in other words, a popular war—was evaporating like spit on a griddle. He did the only thing a politician could do. He declared himself the winner and sued for peace.

He sent special envoys to the Mormons carrying a complete pardon for Young, and instructions to end the war at all costs. Naturally the colonel leading the invading army wasn't too pleased to hear the news. He hadn't marched a thousand miles to slink away without covering himself, and his men of course, in glory. He wanted to invade Utah anyway. As part of the compromise he was promoted to general and got to build a fort well away from Salt Lake City. He was killed in 1862, fighting for the South.

The war officially came to an end in 1858, without

either side firing a shot in anger. The compromise that the politicians worked out with the Mormons left the federal government nominally in charge. The real power in Utah stayed with Brigham Young.

I doubt if you've ever heard of the Mormon-American War, but it should sound real familiar. Think about what the U.S. Army was doing between 1961 and 1972. I wish I could report that the Marines didn't have anything to do with that one either.

But anyway, the Mormons' history is why I had them. They'd been kicked around for 140 years and the one thing it had taught them was that their religion came first. That was my leverage. I had once belonged to an organization where the members were supposed to be, and gladly were, willing to sacrifice their lives and sacred honor for the good of the whole. The Mormons weren't any different—they'd make good Marines. I suspected that seven men dying for nothing wasn't too high a price to pay to protect the good name of the church. I didn't think it would be a problem convincing them of that. The only problem was finding them.

I needn't have worried.

There was a little old Mormon lady standing outside the terminal collecting donations for the Missionary Protective Society. I flipped her a fin and asked for a receipt. The telephone number was printed right on it. Things really were beginning to look up. If the MPS was what I thought it was, and if it collected its budget by soliciting donations on street corners, maybe the boss didn't have to justify himself to some committee after all. Maybe he really would just write us off as an uncollectible debt.

I called the number. The lady who answered the phone said, "MPS, how may I help you?"

"I'm trying to get in touch with a Mr. Smith," I told her. "I think his first name is Joshua. I understand he works for you people."

"I'm sorry, sir," she replied. "There's no Mr. Smith working for the Society. Perhaps I can help you?"

"That's odd," I told her. "I just met Mr. Smith a few

weeks ago in Hawaii, and I'm sure he told me he worked for the missionaries. Is there some other organization in town that he might have worked for? He asked me to deliver a package for him.''

There was a pause on the other end of the line. She came back a second later and suggested that I probably wanted to talk to Mr. Anderson, who was running the office while the chairman was away. I told her that would be fine. She didn't scream and drop the phone when I gave her my name. She did give me an appointment for six o'clock and tell me they would be expecting me.

I had an hour to kill, so I rented a car and tooled around the city. Salt Lake is a pretty town; they keep it immaculately clean. The city is laid out in a grid with the tabernacle in the center. You can always tell where you are in Salt Lake City because the street names are all in reference to the tabernacle. North Second Street, for instance, is two blocks north of the temple and runs east-west.

It was a beautiful day. The burghers looked tanned and prosperous. There were no boarded-up storefronts that I saw. And I noticed that everyone, and I mean everyone, took excellent care of their homes. I didn't see any peeling paint or even much crabgrass. It seemed like there were an awful lot of car washes. I wanted to drive back to the airport as fast as I could and get back on the plane.

The Missionary Protective Society's headquarters was in a residential district and looked like every other single-family home on the block, except for the sign. Standing there in the street, I remembered the cold feeling I'd felt when I'd found out who it was that the Evans brothers had murdered. All four wallets had contained little ID cards with TCJCLDS imprinted on them, The Church of Jesus Christ of Latter-Day Saints.

''Marty,'' I'd said, ''we are in deep shit.''

''What's the problem?'' he asked.

''Jimbo there murdered four Mormons. Why'd he have to go and murder fucking Mormons? Why couldn't he have killed some scumbag frat boys that nobody would've missed?''

"So? What's the problem?" Marty asked. "People will just have to look a little farther to get that stupid magazine."

"Marty," I asked, "you aren't by any chance confusing the Mormons with the Jehovah's Witnesses?" From the blank stare he gave me, I gathered that he was.

It must be a continuing source of embarrassment to the Mormons to be mistaken for Jehovah's Witnesses. I almost got mad at Marty for not knowing the difference. But it occurred to me that besides being educated by the Little Sisters of the Poor—whose idea of a comparative-religions course is explaining the difference between the Franciscans and the Jesuits—Marty was also from the east coast. He had no clue.

"Marty, suppose these guys had turned out to be card-carrying Jesuits with autographed pictures of the pope in Rome tucked safely in their wallets. Do you think that maybe somebody might be coming along to investigate their mysterious disappearances?"

"Sure, but these guys aren't priests. What are the Mormons likely to do?"

"Oh, cut off your balls and make you eat them."

"Shit, what would've happened if they had been Jehovah's Witnesses?"

"The human race's aggregate IQ would have shot upward. Let's get the stiffs loaded."

"Do you think the Mormons'll buy the story?" Marty asked as he bent down to get Jimbo's feet.

"I sure hope so." That's what I had said back then. It didn't cheer me up any to be standing outside the Missionary Protective Society thinking exactly the same thing about my new story.

I walked up to the front door and rang the bell. A fortyish woman in a tasteful black cocktail dress opened the door after just a short wait. I wondered how often she attended cocktail parties. She said that she had stayed to wait for me, but that she had to get moving. She looked me over very carefully, and then brought me back to see Mr. Anderson. If she was a housewife doing volunteer work for the MPS, then I'm the reincarnation of Kamehameha II.

Anderson met me at the door. He was older than the woman, but not by much. He wore frameless glasses and a tropical-weight wool suit; he looked like a lawyer. He had that air of other-worldly casualness that college professors like to affect. But he still reminded me of a shark. His eyes seemed to be meeting mine, but I had the impression that they were really focused on my hands. I wondered if the chairman was really on vacation.

His office was tastefully furnished, no reproductions of nineteenth-century portraits of Mormon politicians to be seen. There were prints of the Utah countryside on the walls and a bust of Brigham Young on Anderson's desk. The furniture was solid, but didn't look extremely expensive. There was nothing that would look out of place in the headquarters of a charitable organization.

"So," he said, "Chief Yamasaki, I've been looking forward to meeting you."

"I'm glad I've finally met someone from Utah who's got my job description down right," I replied. I had told them my name was Jim Yamasaki; I hadn't mentioned that I was a chief of police. "Since you know who I am, you probably know why I'm here."

"Perhaps," he said, "but just so there's no misunderstandings, why don't you tell me exactly what you want."

"It's very simple. I want you people to stop using my town in your fucking drug-smuggling operation."

If my little bombshell had rocked him to his very innermost core he managed to hide it well. Considering that the typical Mormon considers caffeine to be a dangerous drug, abused only by hardened addicts, it wouldn't have been easy to convince any sensible person that the Mormons were mixed up in drug smuggling. Luckily there are damned few sensible people in this country.

Anderson took his glasses off and held them up to the light. He must have seen a speck, because he took out his handkerchief and polished them for about two seconds. He put them back on his nose and gave me his full attention.

"Those four boys who disappeared last summer were up to their necks in marijuana smuggling, but they tried to cheat a grower and they ended up dead. It was a real nice cover, going on a mission to save the souls of people in Hawaii and all the while ruining lives all over the world with dope." I didn't think I had to mention how that was going to look in the papers, and the implications it would have for other Mormon missionaries.

He didn't believe me for a second, but that was all right. He knew I was lying; he even knew that I must have known that he knew I was lying. It didn't matter. What mattered was that there were millions of people all over the world who would be all too ready to believe every word.

"These accusations are completely absurd," he replied. Then he opened a desk drawer and turned off the tape recorder with a flourish. That was supposed to impress me so much that I'd admit to snatching the Lindbergh baby. "Perhaps you will tell me why you have come here and what you want."

"We depend on the tourist trade for our living in Hawaii," I told him. "Otherwise I'd have the FBI breathing down your neck so fast it would make your head spin. But as it stands we don't want adverse publicity any more than you do. As for what I want: I want you to stop sending professional hit men to Hawaii. I want the drug dealing stopped and I never want to see another Mormon in my jurisdiction." Actually all I wanted was no more hit men; we both knew that.

"In return we won't go to the papers with the absolute proof that we've accumulated about your organization and its involvement with the Mafia."

"What sort of evidence," he asked, "have you managed to fabricate?"

"Fabricate, shit," I replied. I was still talking for the record. It wouldn't have surprised me at all to find out he was videotaping our conversation. Come to think of it, it would have surprised me if he wasn't. "Your precious missionaries are in a boat lying on the bottom of the ocean less than a mile offshore somewhere in the islands, you don't need to know exactly where. The boat's on the Coast Guard's 'Board and Search' roster, and they're not the only bodies in it. How's it going to look when they raise the boat and find your boys' bodies along with the bodies of a pair of notorious drug runners and several tons of marijuana?''

He seemed to think it over for a minute. When he finally did say something it was so completely off-topic that it disoriented me, probably what he had in mind in the first place.

''Hirohito,'' he said. ''Did that name get you in trouble in grade school?''

Hirohito is my middle name. James Hirohito Yamasaki, and yes, it got me into heaps of trouble when I was a kid. Not so much with the *haoles* as with the Japanese. Naming me after the Divine One was very disrespectful. My father had done it to piss off the local Japanese community, who didn't care for his choice in wives.

''It was my father's name,'' I lied. ''I'm proud of it.''

''How interesting,'' he said. Then he opened a file folder that had been lying on his desk and began reading. ''James Hirohito Yamasaki, 2693566; born, 12 March 1941; entered Marine Corps, 8 July 1963; height, six feet one inch; weight, two hundred seven pounds''—he looked over his glasses at me—''although you seem to have added a few pounds over the years. Color eyes, brown; blood type, AB negative; religious preference, none.

''Basic training: Parris Island, South Carolina, 15 July 1963 through 10 November 1963. Advanced infantry training: Camp Pendleton, San Clemente, California, 19 November 1963 through 13 January 1964. Refused transfer Officer Candidate School, 6 January 1964. Strange, you don't appear to be unambitious.''

''Getting shot in the back wasn't one of my life goals,'' I lied to him. He didn't need to know the real reason—it was Ohira—and besides, it seemed like the less he thought of me, the more careless he was likely to get.

''Requested transfer Vietnam, 7 January 1964. Served

in advisory role to the South Vietnamese Army, 12 February 1964 through 19 September 1964. Awarded Vietnamese Cross of Gallantry, Bronze Star, Purple Heart with cluster. Promoted lance corporal, 22 August 1964. Transferred Third Marine Division, 21 September 1964, served through 9 July 1965. Awarded cluster for Purple Heart, Presidential Unit Citation, Navy Cross." He paused and looked up at me when he got to the Navy Cross. "The citation is for conspicuous courage under heavy enemy fire."

"How was I supposed to know there was a colonel in the helicopter?"

"You were rescuing a fallen comrade, a Vietnamese Marine."

"If he had been American they would have given me the fucking Congressional Medal of Honor." He looked at me disapprovingly; I halfway expected him to tell me that medals don't fuck.

"Would he have done the same for you?"

"Yes, but he died on the way to the MASH unit." I could tell Anderson didn't believe it, asshole.

"Refused transfer stateside, 18 March 1965, after receiving second cluster for Purple Heart. Eleven July 1965, requests transfer to combined action unit. Promoted sergeant, 31 July 1965. Combined action unit, Quang Nam province, 15 July 1965 through 19 December 1965. Reported missing in action and presumed killed, 21 December 1965, while on CIA-sponsored mission in Laos.

"Twelve April 1966, arrives U.S. mission, Bangkok, Thailand. Reports that remainder of unit was pinned down in an ambush and subsequently wiped out . . ."

I cut him off there. "You know, the rest of that file is classified. You could get yourself in real trouble for having seen the cover." My report really had been classified, "most secret" or some such bullshit. The brass had been very anxious to make sure nobody ever found out what had happened in Laos. They didn't want their names associated with a disaster.

". . . wiped out by friendly air strike. Requests hardship

leave stateside, 18 April 1966. Terminal leave, 28 April 1966. Honorable discharge, 23 August 1966."

"How do you happen to have access to classified information?" I asked him.

"Some things have a higher calling than governments," he replied.

"In that case, it's a damn good thing the Russians have to be atheists or we wouldn't have a country anymore."

He ignored my comment, beneath his dignity no doubt. "Your report states that you managed to escape while everyone else was killed because you had been sent to the rendezvous point to attempt to make contact with the choppers. I find it hard to believe that the Green Berets would send a Marine on a mission like that."

That had always been the weakest part of the story. "I was the most familiar with conditions in Laos. It was logical."

He leaned back in his chair and made a steeple out of his fingers and rested his chin on the point of it. He watched me for a while, to see if I was going to volunteer anything. "Tell me," he said, "what really happened in Laos."

CHAPTER EIGHT

□

KINGDOM OF LAOS

December, 1965

All my life people have taken pains to make sure that I understand that I'm not Japanese. *Haoles* don't even bother pointing out that I'm not white; it's self-evident. I can't even claim to be a half-breed. I'm a *poi* dog: a little of this, a little of that. I've gotten used to it over the years, not belonging. So to have Monsieur Fourier suddenly accuse me of being Japanese, and at such an inopportune time, seemed like the fucking height of injustice.

I had known from my first day in Vietnam that the Japanese weren't very popular among the locals. All of Southeast Asia had been included in the Greater East Asian Co-prosperity Sphere, and the Japanese occupation forces hadn't been handicapped by the moral qualms that had troubled the French and Americans. The occupation had been long and brutal. But the local hatred for all things Japanese had never affected me. I'm an American. The Vietnamese saw only the uniform.

The villagers in Quang Nam hadn't cared; the Japanese had never come to Quang Nam. There wasn't anything there that they'd wanted. Laos, with its rubber plantations, had been a different story. The Laotians remembered the Japanese occupation very well.

The mob was on me in a second, flailing and kicking. They were too disorganized to do me any real damage. But after a few minutes a leader appeared and organized them.

Eventually the ones the leader had selected to deliver the local greeting ceremony—the three biggest ones—got tired of kicking me. When they were through they tied my arms behind my back and hung me by my ankles from a branch about twenty feet above my head. I was spinning around in slow circles, but that didn't stop me from noticing what they were doing on the ground beneath my head. I started swearing at them in Polynesian.

Fourier laughed. "Yes, James, it seems that not all Asians are equal after all. There is not much nostalgia in this country for the last war. How do you call it, the Big One?"

"De Gaulle fucks little girls," I told him.

He laughed. "See if you can keep up your spirits when the fire gets warm. I have seen them do this before. It will only be a small fire, yes? But they will add sulfur to it oh so slowly. You are not in such fine condition now, but I think you may last two or three days in any event, yes? Of course you will be begging to be killed after the first day, at least while your voice lasts."

"Pétain fucks sheep."

He had to think about that one. I could see him working it over in his head. When he figured it out he laughed all the louder. He poked me in the ribs with his cane and said, "You are a very funny fellow. Of course the marshal fucks sheep." He paused and considered me.

"Do you know why they add the sulfur? It is for the smoke, it will get in your eyes and make the sulfuric acid. Your eyes will literally melt out of your head. But of course, that will not kill you. If you are strong, you will drown, yes? You see, the acid will form in your lungs as well. Soon you will be choking and gasping and begging to be killed. You will drown oh so slowly while on dry land. See if you can make the jokes then."

He paused dramatically, waiting for me to start begging for mercy. I disappointed him. When I didn't have anything to say, he continued.

"Now if you will forgive me, I have other more pressing matters to attend to. Perhaps I will come back tomorrow to see if you are still so funny, yes?"

He left me there slowly swinging back and forth, wishing for a breeze. I wondered what Marshal Dillon would have done. Probably ask Festus what took him so long. I looked around for Festus, although I would have settled for Washington. All I saw were interested Laotians. They were making bets and it didn't take a real genius to figure out what they were betting on.

I tried to think pleasant thoughts. I was determined not to put on a show for the Laotians. If they wanted an evening's entertainment, they could go out and get a TV like normal folks.

In one of the Tarzan novels, I forget which, Tarzan and another white man had been in much the same position I was in now, except without the sulfur. The other guy, not Tarzan, started blubbering. Tarzan told him to keep a stiff upper lip and show the Ubangis how a white man dies. What an asshole.

The ancient Laotian woman who was tending the fire threw on another twig and added a pinch of sulfur. A segment of the crowd started howling; evidently they were betting on sooner rather than later and wanted more than just a pinch. The old woman shook a stick at them and screamed right back.

"*Merci,*" I said.

She spat in my face. The later-rather-than-sooner crowd gave a whoop and started laughing. It dawned on me that the old woman was probably an artist. She wasn't going to be happy if I didn't last at least three days. I saw more money changing hands in the crowd.

There wasn't a lot of smoke, but the rotten egg smell was making me gag. My left eye was swollen shut, and my right one wasn't much better, but I could feel the sulfur irritating them anyway. They were watering badly and the crowd was beginning to blur. The worst part, though, was the pounding headache from being hung upside down.

I determined to die like a brown man. The idea was so

funny I started laughing; it wasn't exactly an old-fashioned belly laugh, but under the circumstances it was the best I could do. The old woman looked at me with concern—delirium this early wasn't a good sign.

"When was the last time you got laid, you old bag?" I asked her.

She smiled at me contentedly, sat back on her heels and threw another twig on the fire. I thought about home.

There is a beach on Hawaii. The sands are white, not gold or black like most on the island. It is more than three quarters of a mile long and extends a hundred yards inland. Along the edge, far above the high high-tide line, is a stand of coconut palms. They are old, and more than thirty feet tall, but they produce the sweetest coconut milk.

There was a Polynesian girl. She was slender and tall and her hair was as black as the ocean at night. We met under the coconut palms one night, when the moon filled the sky and bounced reflections that shimmered and blurred in her hair. She asked me to climb the palm and bring her a coconut. The coconut was sweet, but she was by far the sweeter. Before the moon had sunk into the Pacific I had lost myself in her sweetness.

But the beach was gone, along with the coconut palms, along with the maiden. They cut down the trees to make room for a refinery, and they raped the beach to make a breakwater for the tankers. All so tourists could fill up their rental cars and Hawaiian Air could fill up its planes and Hawaiian Electric could power air conditioners. But memories can't be taken from you. I opened my eye.

The crowd had dispersed. I wasn't cooperating by being entertaining. The old woman looked at me disgustedly. She threw one last branch on the fire and stalked off. The rain had started, and I guessed that she didn't want to stay out in it and aggravate her rheumatism. Especially if I wasn't going to be cooperative. I tightened my stomach muscles and curled upward so that the rain could wash out my eyes. When I could see again, and the fire had fizzled out, I relaxed and dropped back to my original position.

My momentum carried me past vertical and I swung like a pendulum. It started me thinking.

I hung there for a couple of hours and thought pleasant thoughts about a few of the women I'd known and unpleasant thoughts about all of the Army assholes I'd ever met. I amused myself by making up a list of all the scores that I wanted to settle. The list had gotten a lot longer in the past two days.

When the village was at its quietest, and the rains had become torrential, I started swinging. I tightened my stomach and got most of the way through a half-pike. On the downswing I threw my head back and arched my back. I was using my ankles as a pivot and keeping the rope taut at all times. After six repetitions I was swinging wildly through more than 240 degrees of arc. On the last upswing I bent my knees and pulled my feet behind my back.

My body bent like a bow and the rope came up into my crotch like a hammer, grinding my testicles into my groin. I threw my face at the rope and caught it with my teeth on the way by. I held on for dear life as my momentum tried to rip my teeth out by their roots. I leaned into the rope with my body and after a few seconds the gyrations stopped. Carefully balancing myself, with most of my weight squarely on my crotch, I started chewing.

The rope was rough manila: it cut the shit out of my lips. After a few minutes I had managed to break one of my incisors and the rough edge made a fairly good saw. I figured I'd be through the rope in about an hour. Just as the first strand parted, Fourier spoke up from behind me.

"And what, James," he asked, "do you intend to do when you get to the wire core?"

He walked around in front of me where I could see him. He was wearing a poncho and was dressed for traveling. He had a dozen men with him; they all looked like they were ready to hit the road. I rested my head against the rope. My breath came in ragged bursts. The downpour mixed with the blood flowing from my ruined mouth to make a steady red stream running down my chest. For the first time, I noticed that my broken incisor hurt like a bastard. It was a pretty low moment in my life.

Fourier took a step forward and his arm slashed upward, right at my face. The self-preservation reflex is strong. I saw the machete in his hand and jerked backward. As I pivoted on my ankles it occurred to me that I should have let him slit my throat. It would have been a lot easier on me.

His machete touched the rope and didn't even slow down on the way through. I was in free fall for a second before landing heavily on my bound arms. It hurt. Fourier caught the wildly swinging rope and held up the end where I could see it.

"You see," he said, "the joke is on you. There is no wire core."

He laughed and signaled for his men to help me. They cut my arms and legs free and picked me up. I couldn't have walked ten feet if there had been a loaded .50-caliber machine gun right in front of me. We made our way to the other end of the village where it looked like the entire populace had been assembled. They were dressed for traveling: everyone had big bundles on their backs and many had hand carts loaded with household goods. I noticed that none of the old people who had been at the barbecue were in the crowd. I looked over at Fourier.

"We are going on a little hike into the hills, James. I think I would enjoy your company."

"Well, of course," I said. "I'm happy to come along, but couldn't it wait till the morning?"

"I am afraid not, James. I am expecting your Air Force to be paying a call on poor Tiehereaux in the very near future. I do not wish to be here when they arrive."

He ordered two of the villagers to dump their possessions and load me onto their cart. They complied without a word. With a wave of his hand Fourier set the crowd in motion. He walked along beside me.

"I don't mean to be rude, Monsieur Fourier," I said, "but I don't think your village is very likely to be bombed."

"Please, James," he said, "you must call me Pascal.

Why do you think that we will not be bombed? Perhaps you feel that your government will not drop the bombs on neutral nations? If so, I could show you the craters."

"As far as they know," I told him, "there are thirty-two Americans on the ground in this village. They wouldn't bomb their own troops."

"Ah, James, you are so naïve. You are no different than Captain Ho, who also does not expect to be rudely awakened by American jets. He is asleep in his bunker back at Tiehereaux with all those lovely automatic weapons that you so kindly brought to us."

He told me to get some rest and marched off to the front of the column where he spoke in rapid French, evidently ordering greater speed. We walked for four hours. The path was smooth and well worn; we made good progress in spite of the rain. In the hour before dawn we stopped to rest.

A Laotian girl came to clean my cuts and scrapes and to rinse my eyes with clear water. She was lovely and my entire attention focused on her, until the flare went off.

I craned my neck and looked back along the path, down into the valley. A parachute flare was floating serenely toward Tiehereaux. Fourier got up from where he was resting and walked over to sit down beside me.

"Listen," he said. "It is so far away. So high."

And then I could hear it. It wasn't a close ground support aircraft. I knew without being told that it was a B-52.

"Let us hope that your Air Force's reputation for pinpoint accuracy is well deserved."

The first bombs fell and exploded in the village. We saw the flash and right behind it came the thunder, a rising crescendo that was like a physical blow, more than mere noise. The flashes went on and on, and the rolling thunder of the explosions was like a thousand deranged drummers announcing Armageddon. After an eternity the flashes changed color and the noise lessened. Fourier looked to me for an explanation.

"White phosphorus," I said dully. "Much worse than

napalm; it burns underwater. If it gets on your skin you have to cut it off with a knife."

"A shame," he said. "Such lovely rifles."

The girl next to me was sobbing quietly. I recalled that no old people had been allowed to accompany us. Well, except Fourier. He put his index finger under her chin and lifted her face so he could see her eyes. Crooning to her in French he smoothed her hair. I turned back to the fire. Fourier looked at me. "Why such a long face, James? Your grandmother was not in the village."

"They didn't know. How could they have known?"

"That you were all dead?" he asked. "But of course they could not have known. And as it happens, one of you is still alive. However, it was expedient. They did not wish to allow the North Vietnamese to parade thirty bodies, or even worse, thirty prisoners, through the streets of Vientiane. Do not place the faith in generals, James."

"What about me?" I asked. "They didn't get me."

"And what about you, James? Perhaps you are a deserter. Perhaps you were captured in Vietnam and brought here. You are not important. You are not even in the Army."

Fourier looked disgusted when he saw that I was refusing to be philosophical about the fucking Air Force dropping white phosphorus on its own troops. "I too was once a young man . . . with a young man's way of thought. When I was sixteen, I lied about my age and enlisted in the French Army so I could go and fight the Boches. Can you believe this? I lied about my age to go murder other young men for the greater glory of France." He shook his head as if he couldn't believe it himself. "I had three older brothers who had already enlisted and I did not want to miss the great adventure.

"We served together in the Twenty-first Division of the Grande Armée. By 1916 two of my brothers were dead and it was no longer an adventure. At Verdun we fought the Boches for ten months. More than a million men were killed. For the first three months we did not even see any enemy soldiers. Ninety days of continuous artillery barrages.

"The Germans used four-hundred-twenty-millimeter cannon. Imagine, James"—he spread his hands about two feet apart—"four hundred and twenty millimeters. Entire platoons were wiped out by a single shell.

"It was hell, James. It was worse than hell. We did not dare to bury the dead. More often than not, to attempt it was to create two new bodies that also needed the burial.

"I cannot describe the stench. Thousands of bodies, men and horses, rotting in the mud. The barrage continuing day and night disinterring those bodies that were buried and spreading them across the fields in smaller and smaller pieces.

"What food there was had to be ported to the front by men from each, how do you say . . . from each unit. The horses could not get within artillery range, you see, they could not take cover from the barrage. Some nights every man who went for food was killed by the shells. I saw men watching each other, wishing that the inevitable would occur so that at least some of them could go to hell with a full belly."

He wasn't looking at me as he talked His eyes stared into the past and I knew he was seeing a familiar nightmare. He looked haunted.

"There was no water. I saw men lapping like dogs from green puddles, ignoring the blackened faces of the dead that looked up at them. Dysentery was the norm. There were no latrines, the stench from our bodies blended with the stench of the dead hanging like the miasma of hell over the battlefield.

"The battlefield was hell, but the hospitals were worse. You have heard of 'triage,' James? It was invented at Verdun. The doctors divided the wounded into three parts. The men who could be salvaged and sent back to the front received immediate attention. The men who could be salvaged but not sent back to the front would receive five minutes of a doctor's attention." He made a cutting motion with his hand. "Without chloroform. The last third were labeled untransportable. They were left lying in the open in the hopes that a German shell would finish them quickly. To be labeled untransportable was worse than a sentence of death.

"I made a pact with my brothers, Jacques, Henri and Pierre. We would not allow one of us to be taken to the hospital if there was no hope. The *abbé* told us it was a mortal sin. Pierre told him that we must have already committed the mortal sin, because we were already in hell. A shell killed Jacques, but Henri, he was split open from here to here"—he indicated his groin and his sternum—"by a German bayonet. Pierre found him trying to put his intestines back inside himself. Henri begged to be taken to a hospital. Pierre said, 'Of course, Henri, it is only a scratch,' and then he shot my brother. It was very kind, James, it was really very kind.

"And the generals, fifteen miles behind the lines dining on fresh quail and emptying the cellars at Taittinger. Planning the next offensive that would send waves of young men against machine guns. They did not care for us. They did not care about the French at all. All they cared about was France. They cared so much that half the houses in the villages of France have stood empty for fifty years.

"We were paid five sous a day, that was not even enough to buy a loaf of bread. When we could get leave, we had no place to go. And if by some miracle we could get transportation to our homes, we found our families starving—for what money could we send them?

"They supplied us with cheap red wine in the rest camps and encouraged us to drink ourselves into oblivion. But the odd thing was, our morale, it was very high. We stopped the Boches at Verdun, and our generals assured us that in 1917 we would have them out of France altogether.

"General Nivelle" he spat "planned the grand offensive. He promised the politicians that he would roll the Germans before him. And he told us that we would meet no resistance. We marched forward from Verdun, confident that the war would be over by Christmas, and we were annihilated. Some divisions, including my own, took more than fifty percent casualties.

"We were finished as an army. When the generals

ordered us back to the front, we did not go. The mutiny spread like wildfire through the ranks. There was not a single division that was willing to go over the top to face the German machine guns. Some units raised the Red Flag that had lately become so popular in Moscow. At least one general that I saw was hanged by his own troops.

"My regiment threw down its arms and decided to march to Paris and let the government know that we were willing to learn German, if that was what it took to end the war.

"Do you see, James," he asked, "the fatal flaw in our plan?"

"You shouldn't have thrown down your rifles."

He laughed. "I like you. Yes indeed, we should not have thrown down our rifles. A division of special forces, they had never been to the front to face the barrage, or the German machine guns or the phosgene gas or any of the other terrors we faced day after day. They caught us without our rifles.

"They surrounded us and forced us to line up in formation before our own machine guns. And then a captain reviewed us. He stopped before every tenth man and shot the man between the eyes. Sometimes it was not the tenth man, sometimes it was the ninth, sometimes the eleventh. We did not know. Imagine if you will. He would stop in front of you; if you were the seventieth man he would reload there—while you watched—and then he would kill you. Or perhaps the man next to you. You did not know.

"We were lucky compared to some units; it was only every tenth man. Another battalion in our division was told that they needed rest, they did not know what they were doing. They were marched to a peaceful valley, and then *hachés*, by their own artillery. The mutiny did not last very long."

"Did you return to the front after that?" I asked.

"Many did, but as a schoolboy I had read about our colonies in Asia, and I had always dreamed of traveling to the exotic Orient."

I grinned at him. "You mean you deserted."

He looked at me disapprovingly. "Why must you look on the negative side? I prefer to look on it as redirecting my talents in the best interests of France. I was certain that our colonies were going to ruin due to neglect."

"How did Pierre feel about it?"

"Ah, Pierre, lucky Pierre. He was the luckiest man alive. No one would gamble with him, but everyone wanted to be near him in combat. We were certain that we would not be killed by a shell if we were near Pierre. Many, it is true, were killed by bullets while standing near to him, but it was of the shells that we were most afraid.

"Lucky Pierre," he said with a sigh. "Odds of one in ten were nothing for him." He didn't say anything for a moment, and then he gave me a sad smile. "Do not place the faith in generals, James.

"Get some sleep," he said as he stood up. "We will be walking tomorrow, and I am afraid your taxi will be staying here."

I knew I should sleep; I had this feeling that if I were to slow Fourier down he would kill me without a second's thought—despite how much he liked me. But I couldn't. The dawn had come up early in Tiehereaux and I had to watch.

The rain forest was as saturated as it was ever going to get; the fire couldn't spread to it. The village, actually the phosphorus, burned quite nicely, though. I watched for an hour, until it burned itself out. Then I slept.

It turned out that we didn't go anywhere that day. Fourier and his men helped the villagers build makeshift shelters in the forest, camouflaged against aircraft. It was late in the day when they were finished and Fourier decided that we might as well stay for the night.

He sent men back to the village to look for salvable items. He warned them to be on the lookout for helicopters, and under no circumstances were they to fight if any arrived. The men came back in the early afternoon. They brought back the twisted barrel from an M-16. Fourier looked at it sadly and then flung it into the jungle.

Fourier and the headman came to visit me after lunch.

"Duc," Fourier began, "does not think that you will be able to travel by tomorrow morning, James. Is this true?"

It certainly seemed like a reasonable assumption, but I didn't see Fourier leaving me behind. I couldn't see him carrying me either, which left only one other possibility. "Shit," I said, "I'll race you all the way to Vientiane."

Fourier laughed. "We are not going to Vientiane, though, and I am too old to race." He turned to the headman and spoke to him at length in French. When he seemed satisfied with the headman's answers he turned back to me. "James, Duc is not a Western-trained surgeon; however, he is going to do some things for you. You would be most wise to let him."

"Bring on the voodoo dolls," I told him.

The headman built a small fire next to me. Damn clever with small fires, these Laotians. When he had it burning merrily along, he took a straight razor out of his pocket and held it in the fire. After a moment, he wiped it on a clean cloth and said something to Fourier.

"You must be very still, James."

He tilted my head back and lanced the swelling below my left eye. I felt a gush of warm blood and pus run down my face. I didn't even wince. I suppose it hurt, but I was so overloaded on pain that a little more didn't seem to affect me any. After a few seconds the swelling was gone and I could open the eye.

He opened an olive-green packet—it was from an Army med kit—and sprinkled the contents into the cut. Then he sewed me up with a needle and thread from a government-issue sewing kit. I watched his hand come and go beneath my eye; I was mildly interested. He said something in French when he was finished. Fourier replied and they chatted for a few minutes. Fourier asked me to take off my shirt. I complied, trying to hide how much effort it took.

My chest and rib area looked like raw meat. It didn't surprise me: my urine had been bright red that afternoon. Fourier whistled when he saw his men's handiwork. The headman poked and prodded and actually managed to hurt me once. He wrapped a bandage around my chest and gave me something to drink—my estimation was 160 proof.

"Try to sleep," Pascal told me. "It will be a busy day tomorrow."

They gave me a shelter all to myself and didn't bother to set a guard; it was pretty clear that I wasn't going anywhere. I slept fitfully and dreamed. The pain woke me whenever I rolled in my sleep. Late in the night I awoke and realized that I wasn't alone. The girl who had cried for her grandmother was beside me. She undressed me, and shocked the hell out of me by getting me erect. Once she had me excited she did some very odd, but pleasant, things on top of me.

When we were finished, she stayed and massaged my legs. It felt wonderful and I fell back asleep quickly. This time I didn't awaken until dawn.

The girl woke me at first light and made me eat something and helped me get dressed. I needed the help. Fourier came along shortly.

"To up and be at them, James," he called out.

I crawled outside and was delighted to see that all of Fourier's men were heavily loaded. It meant we were going to go slow and take plenty of breaks. My legs felt fine and I decided I probably didn't have a serious concussion. As long as we weren't going to go more than fifteen or twenty miles I figured I could keep up. I was well motivated; I knew what stopping would mean.

We set out along the trail heading north. Fourier sent one man ahead, but didn't bother with a trailer. He was dressed in his white suit and boater and didn't seem to use his cane at all. He looked like he was in a good mood.

"Did you sleep well, James?" he asked.

"Well enough," I replied casually. Then I ruined my attempt at displaying *savoir-faire* by leering back at the village.

"Yes? Duc must have been very impressed to send you his daughter. There were probably other girls in the village who were fertile."

"What?"

He looked over at me, surprised. "What did you think, eh? That you had swept the girl off her feet with your American charm? Perhaps you would like to borrow my mirror, yes? Duc wanted your son and ordered the girl to sleep with you."

I thought about it for a while. I wasn't sure how I felt about it. I decided it wasn't worth thinking about because I sure as shit was never going back. If she did have my son, he would be half Laotian, one-quarter Japanese, one-eighth Polynesian and only one-eighth white. An odd thought struck me. He might be born in Laos, but he would be fulfilling the American dream, only one-eighth *haole*. Every generation a little bit better than the one before it.

CHAPTER NINE

□

KINGDOM OF LAOS

December, 1965

By ten o'clock I knew that I was going to die. It wasn't the pain, the waves of agony that shot out of my broken ribs with each new step. It wasn't the heat or the flies that swarmed around me, seeking the crusted blood. It wasn't the concussion that had put a halo around everything in direct sunlight and made even the throbbing of my bruised kidneys seem distant. It was the fever that was going to be fatal. Not that I thought it was going to kill me. I figured the Frenchman would take care of that.

We walked along together, Fourier whistling a happy tune from some long-forgotten opera with my wheezings serving as his rhythm section. Duc had set my broken nose back at the camp, but it was going to be a long time before I used it for anything but storing dried blood.

I counted my paces and told myself that I would take a hundred more, and then another hundred. I never would have made it through the first morning if all of Fourier's men hadn't been overloaded. He didn't want to burn them out. We stopped and rested for ten minutes every hour. After each stop it seemed to take more and more effort to get moving.

"James," he said after our third stop, "you do not look well."

"I'm fine," I told him.

"In fact," he said, "you are not. However, we are

already late and my employer worries when I am late. I am afraid we cannot stop and we have no doctor. Will you keep up?''

''No sweat,'' I told him. As it happened, I wasn't sweating and it worried me.

''Perhaps these will help,'' he said as he handed me a vial. They were Penicillin VK, worth their weight in gold on the black market. I swallowed four dry and hoped that they hadn't lost their potency.

''What exactly is our cargo?'' I asked him. He had a dozen men and each of them carried a large bundle besides his rifle and personal gear. The bundles looked like they were more bulky than heavy. I noticed that the point man never carried his: it was always taken by someone from the main party.

Fourier laughed. ''It is the most valuable and dangerous of all cargoes,'' he told me. ''If we are caught with it . . .'' He paused, and then drew his hand across his throat.

I was confused. ''You're taking heroin into Thailand?''

''You are indeed silly, who would smuggle heroin into Thailand? We are smuggling currency. More than one million American dollars, in fact. If the Thai police catch us it is unlikely that they will report it to their superiors . . . or leave any of us alive to tell the tale. To know that we are here is to be tempted beyond the strengh of most men. We are not safe from the Pathet Lao, or even the North Vietnamese.''

''You don't appear to be overly worried.''

''My employer has a long arm. The bandits who swarm this country would think twice before stealing from him. Perhaps they would get away with it. But if they did not, he would murder their entire families out to the fifth cousins. The things he would do to those directly responsible . . .'' He shuddered. ''It is not to be spoken of. Perhaps he could not reach into North Vietnam, but it is not certain.''

That started me thinking about the North Vietnamese troops back at Tiehereaux. I wondered if Fourier had really mentioned his concern about a visit from the American Air

Force to the Vietnamese captain. The more I thought about it, the less likely it seemed. He must have left the old people behind—there hadn't been that many—so the North Vietnamese wouldn't think the village was deserted. That started me thinking about Lucas's question: how had the North Vietnamese known we were coming?

I mulled that over for a while and then started thinking about Fourier. It would've been one thing if he'd evacuated the village immediately after the massacre. But to wait more than forty-eight hours and then evacuate the village a couple of hours before the B-52's arrived to conveniently rid the area of a troublesome company of Vietnamese Regulars? It was asking too much. He must have been warned.

I knew it was pointless to ask. I couldn't see the Frenchman admitting to being less than a genius. And besides, it seemed like the kind of question that would probably lead to me getting my throat slit. I didn't have to ask, anyway. I moved Horus to the very top of my "deal with later" list and started thinking about where I might find some sulfur back in Quang Nam.

I looked at the bundles and did some quick math. Each man had the equivalent of the lifetime income of three generations of Vietnamese peasants on his back. The temptation would have to be enormous. "Your employer must really trust you and your men."

"Perhaps," he replied, "but I do not think he understands this Western concept of trust. Each of these men has a family that has stayed behind. If we do not return, they will all be murdered. If one of us disappears with his pack, it is one child from each family. Two men and it is the wives. Three men and we had better not return. Watch carefully tonight: they will chain themselves together and give me the key. They do not trust even each other."

"Why does your boss trust you?"

"I have worked for his family for thirty years. I have never been disloyal—even in the worst of times when the Japanese Army hunted us like dogs in the hills. Too, I am an old man and have little reason to betray him now."

"That doesn't explain it."

We marched along in silence. Finally he sighed and said, "No, I suppose that it does not. Perhaps he does trust me.

"When I separated from the French Army I made my way back to Paris with stolen leave papers. The special police were everywhere and I did not fool myself that I could escape them forever. I had come from the front and the stench of death was all around me. It surprised me that people could pass me on the street and not be revolted.

"If the police were to pick me up and determine that my papers were stolen"—he shrugged—"well . . . the best that I could hope for was that I would be sent to the penal colonies in South America. That was the best I could hope for. I knew, in fact, that I would be summarily executed.

"I determined that I would not hide. I was not afraid of death. I was only afraid of dying at the front in some stinking shell hole with my insides spread out for the crows to peck at. I needed money, of course; Paris was not cheap. But that was no problem. I had killed enough innocent young German boys that killing a French industrialist presented me with no difficulty. I stole a taxi and waited outside a fine restaurant by the Seine. The papers were full of it the next day. A patriotic industrialist slain by German spies. He was in the chemicals, James; I have never for a moment regretted it.

"With my money difficulties momentarily a thing of the past, I set out to make up for my lost youth. I was nineteen but could pass easily for thirty. I told people that I was medically unfit for service and hinted that my father had arranged it with the Ministry. All were only too willing to believe it; I think that they must have heard this story all the time.

"I cut a swath through the seamier side of Paris. I do not know how long I could have kept it up, three years at the front and I had lost much stamina. Also, after only a few weeks I was already short of funds, although credit was easy and I was not planning to stay long enough to worry about when the bills came due.

"And then one night, in a notorious brothel on the Rue Hermite, who should I run into but the captain who had murdered Pierre and one hundred and fifty of my comrades. He had been promoted to major since I had seen him last and the war appeared to be treating him kindly.

"I asked him how one so young could have risen so fast, and he told me that it was because his troops loved him so well. 'They are dying to please me,' he said."

"Did you kill him?" I asked.

"James," he replied, "I am shocked that you would think that I would usurp the Deity's privilege and judge this man. Me, a good Catholic."

"So you didn't kill him?"

"Of course not."

I kept walking. What the fuck, if he wanted to tell me fairy stories that was OK by me. He looked over at me and smiled when he saw the look of disbelief on my face.

"Well, perhaps I did cut out his eyes. And maybe his ears as well. And perhaps a few of his tendons, the ones in his neck and wrists and elbows and knees and ankles. And, after I had done that, I started to worry that since he would be spending the rest of his life in bed, perhaps he would be tempted by self-pollution . . . so I removed that temptation as well. But kill him? Never. I hope he lives to be a hundred.

"Anyway, I suddenly found myself in the possession of a major's uniform, as well as orders that would take me to Marseilles. Enough people had seen me leaving the brothel with the pig that I did not think it would be so clever to stay in Paris. Besides, the climate is so much nicer in the South, don't you think?

"I took the night train to Marseilles. It was a long trip and I had time to think. I decided that I would never be safe in France. My name was on a roster somewhere, and I knew that eventually someone would decide to do something about it. Ten years in French Guiana did not appeal to me—and neither did being stood up against a wall and shot.

"In Marseilles I discarded the uniform and began looking for some way to get across the Mediterranean to Morocco. It would not be easy, I knew. Many would have the same idea. Once I saw the police dragging a deserter back to their headquarters. They were beating him with their clubs and spitting on him and calling him a coward. If I had had a gun I would have killed them. What did they know of cowardice?

"The underworld in Marseilles teemed with men such as myself. Desperate men with no papers or passports anxious to leave France as fast as possible. I fell in with a group who were acting as enforcers for a local crime family. One day we heard that a man was looking for some men to go to Africa with him. The word on the street was that he had money and a boat and that he had the Coast Guard in his pocket.

"We went to talk with him. He said that he was an agent for a Berber chieftain who was looking for some Europeans to go on an expedition to cross the Sahara to East Africa. Five of us discussed it. We saw it as a chance to get to Indochina and we jumped. Perhaps we were fools, but we knew that to stay was to court death each day.

"We crossed the sea to Benghazi aboard an ancient freighter. If there is a less pleasant city on the face of the earth than Benghazi, I do not know of it. There we met Sharif Ibn Faoud Rahzuli. He was a pirate of the worst stripe, and a more despicable crew of unhanged murderers you have never seen.

"He had somehow come into the possession of two Vickers machine guns. He wanted us to operate them for him. We should have pressed him more closely about what he was planning to use them against, but we were not in such a good position to bargain. A word to the Italian authorities and we would have been on our way back to France in chains within the hour. We assumed that he was smuggling some form of contraband, gold probably, to India. He promised us passage to Cambodia when we arrived in French Somaliland."

"Was it gold?" I asked.

"I am not proud of this, James. No, it was not gold.

"We crossed the Libyan Desert in caravan. I will not forget this. The hardest leg was thirteen days between oases. The temperature was well over fifty degrees each day—which would be more than one hundred and twenty of your silly degrees Fahrenheit—and well below zero every night. We had no water on the last day and the camels had had none for two weeks—even the Berbers were beginning to look worried.

"When we finally came to the oasis, Rahzuli ordered a celebration. We slaughtered the weakest of the camels and feasted. The Berbers smoked their hookahs and we took small sips of the last of our wine. That night, while the camp slept, I crept to the camels and searched our baggage. We were loaded down with chain, slave chain.

"I told my friends the next day. But what could we do? We did not know the desert. If we left the Berbers we were sure to perish. We voted to stay with Rahzuli and leave at the first sign of civilization. But it was not to be. We headed east from the oasis, deep into the Sahara. We crossed the White Nile far to the south of Khartoum. Our destination was a small village in southern Sudan. I do not believe it was a random choice. Rahzuli had been consulting maps and talking with his guide for days before we arrived.

"It was a small village, far from the main caravan routes. Rahzuli did not think anyone would miss it. They did not need our machine guns. A wooden plow is not much good against swords and rifles. When they were finished, Rahzuli had all of the villagers that he thought could make the trip chained together by the neck. The ones that he did not think could make the trip, the old and the young, they were murdered as casually as you would swat a fly.

"Rahzuli told us we would earn our pay protecting his cargo from pirates. People who would steal the profits of an honest laborer. We were fools to believe him. We crossed Abyssinia through Eritrea, traveling for days without seeing a soul. It seemed like every day the slave chain was shorter. Rahzuli had been optimistic in his predictions as to who would survive the trip.

"I cannot say when we determined not to desert. It became easier day by day to stay with him as the Indian Ocean came nearer. The cries and whimpers of the Africans became just another noise from the land. Rahzuli had told us that we would be given passage on the ship that would be taking the slaves to India. But we had come to see his true self on the trip across Abyssinia. We did not believe him for a moment.

"We entered the Côte Française des Somalis, French Somaliland as you would say, after six weeks of travel. We Frenchmen were worried about being back in French territory. The war still raged in Europe. We wrapped our scarfs around our heads and tried to look like Arabs. The caravan traveled only by night. Naturally Rahzuli did not want any of the local French officials to see his cargo, and as you can imagine, we too were not so anxious to be seen.

"Our plan was to turn the machine guns on Rahzuli and his men when we got to Djibouti. With the help of the Africans we planned to hijack the ship. One of my compatriots had been a merchant sailor before the war. He thought that with a little luck, he could sail the vessel all the way to Cambodia. Our plans were well laid, perfectly conceived.

"Djibouti is an open sore on the shore of Africa where the Gulf of Aden meets the Red Sea. A city of cutthroats and beggers. Whirling dervishes danced in the marketplace in front of starving children sitting behind empty begging bowls. We entered the city at noon, when the sun was at its zenith. There were no white men on the streets. No one remarked over our unusual cargo.

"A fat Indian sea captain met us at the docks; he rubbed his hands gleefully when he saw the blacks. 'Excellent,' he cried, 'and did you bring my machine guns as well?' 'Yes,' I shouted. 'And if you so much as move a muscle, you will see them in action.'

"We had set up the Vickers guns and had the entire mob in our sights. The Indian practically squealed with delight. 'Oh, Rahzuli,' he said, 'and you have brought me white men. I could kiss you.' "

Fourier smiled ruefully. "And with that Rahzuli reached into his robes and pulled out the firing pins from our machine guns. 'I think you will find your guns somewhat ineffective without these, gentlemen,' he said. Then he gave a great laugh and went on board the ship to do business. His men relieved us of our weapons and added us to the chain. There was plenty of room.

"And that, my friend, is how I came to the Orient: as a white slave in the hold of a stinking pig of a ship commanded by a mad, homosexual fat man. It was not a pleasant trip."

"Kind of out of the frying pan and into the fire," I said.

He looked at me sourly. "I said it was unpleasant; it did not leave me yearning to return to the once-green fields of Verdun. As I said, the three years at the front had taken their toll on me. I was no longer the fresh-faced young man that I had once been. Most of the captain's attentions were paid to a young Gascon, and he, at least ate better than the rest of us.

"The captain unloaded the blacks somewhere on the west coast of India. I have no idea who wanted them or why, only that the price was more than enough to make the risk worth his while. During our stay in the port he locked us in a bilge tank and invited us to make noise. There was a twenty-centimeter inlet to the tank. He told us that it opened directly to the sea and that it could fill the tank in less than a minute.

"I think he may have been planning to sell us in India as well. But by that time he had fallen madly in love with the Gascon. It was disgusting, but at least it made him forget the rest of us. After a month of his unwelcome hospitality we made port somewhere in Cambodia and the local factor for the French Indochina Rubber Company paid us a visit.

"He made it clear that he did not care one way or the other how we happened to find ourselves in our present predicament. He was willing to 'buy out' our contracts, as he put it, as long as we were willing to sign on with the rubber company. In return for five years' service, at a fair wage, we would be protected from people prying into our histories. It was much like the Legion, only without the foreigners.

"As it turned out—for what choice did we have—our protection would be five hundred miles of rain forest. We did not get many visitors in southern Laos, and those that did come, generally they were not quick to delve into someone else's past."

At that point in his story we came to a clearing where the point man was waiting for us. The sun was directly overhead and Fourier called for a break. "We will eat nothing in this heat, James, and we will not start again until two-thirty. Try to drink some water and rest. I will continue my story later."

I collapsed under a tree, wondering how I would feel at two-thirty. In spite of the heat I was asleep almost instantly. The last thing I noticed was how Fourier's men rested. They sat with their backs against trees with their rifles cradled in their arm. None of them was out of sight of any of the others. They rested with their eyes open, watching each other.

Fourier woke me at two-fifteen. He looked into my eyes to see if I knew where I was. To see if I could continue. I looked up at him through bleary eyes and offered to race him to Peking. He laughed. "But we are not going to Peking, James, and I am too old to race. We start in fifteen minutes."

I stood up with a groan, and turned my back on him to piss. I closed my eyes tightly and prayed that the world would stop spinning by the time I was finished. My kidneys throbbed and it seemed like it took a long time to empty my bladder. I decided not to look. I didn't think it was going to do me much good to know what color my urine was.

The spinning did stop, allowing me to take stock of my aches and pains. There were so many of them that I thought about going public. I figured I must have the pain market cornered. I took two more of Fourier's pills. Not the way you're supposed to take penicillin; but I figured I would worry about next week, next week.

I started to stretch but stopped immediately. Instead I hobbled over to Fourier and asked for some water. He gave me his canteen and watched as I chugalugged.

"You are very strong. That is very good. Most men would have given up by now." He turned to his men and said something in French and we started out. The afternoon wasn't nearly as bad as the morning had been. I still wasn't very optimistic.

"So did you stay with the rubber company for the whole five years?" I asked.

"More than twenty," he replied. "They were very wise. They needed men willing to lose themselves in the jungle. Men who were not afraid, men of action. They needed our cooperation, our willing cooperation. At first I planned to leave them as quickly as practicable. But I talked to the other backcountry foreman and soon I had changed my mind. We were not slaves of the company; we were valuable employees. We brought them the raw rubber. In return the company treated us like kings. At least when we met our quotas.

"I soon found out that after my five years I would be free to leave. The company would not suddenly start asking what I had been doing in 1918 and dropping hints about Devil's Island. That made all the difference to me. I was not a slave or a hunted fugitive. I belonged, the company would look after me and treat me fairly. And if I chose to leave them, well, it was my decision. The other growers said I would be mad to quit. We were like princes in our jungle castles. We had large company houses and servants to keep them clean. The company sent fine food and wine upriver to us. The natives treated us like gods, for it was we who had control of the Western goods.

"And then too, I found a very profitable side line."

"Oh?" I said, expecting to hear a sordid tale of drug smuggling.

"It is probably worse than you think, James. World demand for heroin was not quite so high in the twenties as it is today. However, the yearning of people to be free," he said sarcastically, "knows no era. I spent the 1920's running guns into French Indochina and even into China itself. This is why it is possible that we have an agreement with the North Vietnamese—we have been doing business with them since before you were born.

"The weapons came from the Soviet Union, mainly. They came by freighter to Burma and then overland through Thailand. My present employer's father was a warlord in the mountains of Thailand. For a price he saw to it that the weapons made their way into Laos—where I saw to it that they made their way to their final destinations.

"The company loved me. While all the other foremen had labor and sabotage problems, I exceeded my quota by at least fifty percent every year. I could have done much better, but I did not want to look too good. I thought it might raise suspicions. I had no labor problems, you see, because the workers in my district knew that if they were to strike, someone would come for them in the night.

"I became invaluable to the company. By 1925, I was in charge of the company's operations in Laos. Tiehereaux, that very pleasant little village that your Air Force has just paid a visit to, was my home for many years.

"I convinced the company that it would be well to make a deal with the guerrillas. Of course we all knew that giving them real money, with which they were certain to buy arms, was suicidal. But I think that in fact all of my bosses were only interested in the current year.

"As early as 1927 we could see the Japanese on the horizon and I feel that we all knew that our time in Asia was limited. At least the businessmen felt that way; I think the soldiers thought they were running the Roman Empire: they talked about their grandchildren serving in Indochina.

"It was a good life in the jungle. I took money from both sides and lived like a king. The Communists loved me, the capitalists loved me, the people in Tiehereaux loved me. I made a great deal of money, James, millions in fact. My only regret is that I invested it all through a bank in Singapore, the Gibraltar of Asia. How long did they keep the Japanese out of this Gibraltar? A week, was it?

"The French Indochina Rubber Company did not last much longer, I'm afraid. I did not even find out that my escape had been cut off until I got word that the Japanese were actually on their way to Tiehereaux. I considered the possibilities. I did not think that there would be much of a future in working for the Japanese. It became necessary to run, either to the Communists or to the bandits. I picked the bandits and have never regretted this choice.

"Mr. Han, who was the warlord who had controlled the smuggling route through Thailand, took me in as an adviser. He needed all the help he could get. The Japanese were not interested in working with him either, and had set out to exterminate his army. In the West you heard of the Bataan Death March and perhaps of the Changi prison. But these were mere nothings. The war that took place in Southeast Asia made the war in Europe look like a picnic. Entire villages were wiped out to the last child for even the smallest offenses against the Japanese occupiers.

"Not meeting the rubber quota for two months in a row was cause enough to have entire districts depopulated. The Japanese would make harvesters watch as they tortured their children. On the other hand, the Japanese were very careful not to be captured alive. One guerrilla group managed to kidnap a Japanese official's wife. They skinned her alive and sent him the skin. They had written on it that she was still alive; they asked if he wanted her back.

"The Japanese went on a killing spree after that. No one was safe. They went through the markets in every town in the district and emptied their machine guns into the crowds. Thousands died. Their war with the guerrillas turned to new heights of savagery. They would go to the towns and tell the elders that the next sign of guerrilla activity in the area would be the death knell of their village. They were not bluffing. The elders came to the guerrillas and begged them not to cause trouble. The guerrillas laughed in their faces. 'Why should we discourage the Japanese,' they asked, 'when they are doing such a wonderful job recruiting for us?'

"Mr. Han was not by nature a political man. I think he would have gladly done business with the Japanese, if they had been interested. They would have none of him, though. They did not deal with brigands, is how they put it. They forced him to side with the anti-Japanese guerrillas as a matter of survival. He did not like it, there was no money in it.

"In the first years of the war things went very badly for us. We had no food or medicine and ammunition was in very short supply. It was hard to keep our spirits up under the circumstances, but somehow we did. I told them that things were not nearly so bad as they could be.

"In 1943, the British opened a supply route for us through Burma. It was mainly to supply the Chinese, but we took our share. After the supply route was open things were not nearly so bad.

"And then we began to hurt the Japanese, sometimes very badly. But we could not defeat them. In the end it was the American submarines that turned the trick. There was not much point in harvesting rubber only to have it rot on the docks. In 1944 the Japanese left. They returned to Japan to defend its sacred soil from the Americans. After they left, it was over very quickly.

"Those who had collaborated with the Japanese were hunted down and exterminated. That business with the sulfur, I saw it a dozen times without going out of my way. The new Thai government issued pardons all around and Mr. Han became a legitimate businessman—well, at least for two or three months.

"I expected that once the Japanese were taken care of, everything would return to normal. But it was not to be. The embargo on rubber had forced the Allies to look elsewhere. Our markets had been captured by the South

Americans and by the synthetics. The French Indochina Rubber Company did not even have enough capital to attempt to compete. I was suddenly a middle-aged middle manager with no prospects. Luckily there were still many people yearning to throw off the colonial yoke and be free.

"With the rubber industry no more, the people in Tiehereaux were again very poor. They were more than willing to act as porters to take arms across Thailand and Laos to the Viet Minh. The late forties were very good years. The superpowers were at each other's throats and there was plenty of money to be made by enterprising fellows such as myself. The Communists paid me to supply arms and your CIA paid me to tell them about it. Once again I was making money, only this time I invested it all in New York.

"The problem is that this revolution business is always either boom or bust. First you fools in the West let the Communists take over China. Suddenly there was no need to smuggle arms across Laos. My people starved. Then the French cut off the supply routes through North Vietnam—good times. Then the French lost the war—bad times. Then the Russians fell out with the Chinese—good times. And now the Americans are dropping bombs on us—bad times.

"By the mid-fifties it became clear that we could not depend on this war business for our living. We cast around looking for some alternative, and it was right there beneath our noses. We began growing poppies in the hills. The fields are very beautiful, James, they remind me of the fields of Flanders. Business has never been better. We are taking in money faster than ever before."

"Ever have any qualms about fifteen-year-old junkies selling their bodies on the streets to pay for their habits?" I asked him.

"James, the world has done very little for me besides kill the people that I loved. If your people want to kill themselves slowly by eating the fruit of the lotus, it is no business of mine."

We marched until shortly before dusk. Sunset in the

tropics is as sudden as sunrise. So we didn't march on into the coolness of the night. We stopped and made camp, and as Fourier had predicted, his men chained themselves to a tree and gave him the key. I surprised myself by being hungry. I don't know why it came as a surprise; the only thing I'd eaten in the past three days had been a bowl of clear soup that morning.

Fourier gave me some cold rice with soy sauce and told me not to push my luck.

I slept like a baby. When I awoke I felt clearheaded for the first time since I'd been clubbed running from the village. I was mad with hunger, but we had only meager rations and Fourier told me that I could have no more than any of his men.

We started out no more than a half hour past first light. I wasn't worried about dying anymore, at least not about dying because I couldn't keep up. I was still plenty worried about dying. Fourier had a new tune to whistle and seemed to be delighted to be out and about. That may have been because he didn't have a pack to carry.

"And so, James, although we no longer ship much in the way of arms—because you Americans are too timid to sink a few Russian boats in the harbor at Haiphong—business has never been better. You should see the happy Thai peasants going out to tend to their fields. There can be no more pleasant task in all of horticulture than the growing of flowers.

"What's more, we do not see anything but good times ahead of us. Your generals have refused to learn anything from the mistakes of the French generals, and soon you will be bogged down in a war that you cannot possibly win, not without using atomic weapons anyway. Think of it, tens of thousands of potential customers. It will be a sad day when you Americans decide to pack up and go home."

"What makes you think," I asked, "we're going to go home?"

"Because, James, you are human beings. And even the stupidest human being learns that there is no profit in putting one's hand in the fire. I am convinced that the

Vietnamese would leave if there was any place for them to go. It is a very depressing country; they have been killing each other for a thousand years.

"The killing will not stop after you Americans leave. Eventually the North Vietnamese will win, of course; it is inevitable. They will pick some day to celebrate the great victory over the Americans. It will be a national holiday long after the Communists have been swept aside by some new order. Much like the Mexicans celebrate the Fifth of May: El Cinco de Mayo, the day they beat the French—the ungrateful fools.

"But even that will not stop the killing. The Vietnamese will win, but you Americans will have your revenge." He laughed. "You will leave enough weapons behind you for the Vietnamese to be killing themselves for a hundred years. The damage you will do while you are here is nothing compared to what the Vietnamese will do after you are gone."

I gained strength each day in spite of the food. On the fourth night Fourier invited me to sleep with his men, and how could I refuse? It took us two and a half weeks to cross Laos. Fourier insisted on sticking to backcountry trails and wanted to cross into Thailand as far north as possible. The trip was pleasant, although not something I would have chosen to do for fun.

Fourier was a fascinating companion. He regaled me with tales of his childhood in France and of the history of Indochina. As I grew stronger he drew me out about my own childhood. He was interested in my unusual ethnicity but not out of morbid curiosity; he was genuinely interested. I told him about my father and growing up on the Big Island. He was fascinated by Hawaii. He spent an entire day asking me questions about the state, about the government, about the people. He was especially interested in the power blocs that ran the state and local governments.

I told him about how I happened to become a Marine and he was far from sympathetic.

"And what did you expect, James? You say your police

department has three officers and you expected them to hire a fourth who was not certain to be loyal to the men who gave him the job? Perhaps you walked in off the street one day and said, 'Excuse me, I have come for the job that you owe to me.'

"If you had really wanted the job you should have gone to the men who were in charge and said, I am a loyal fellow and I wish that you would allow me to prove my loyalty in some manner. Perhaps you could have broken a few arms for them or convinced some undesirables to move to some other island. Once you had convinced them that you were a loyal vassal, that would be the time to ask for the job that they owed you. Remember this, James, because it will be no different when you get back."

I liked that, when I got back. That started me wondering why I was still breathing. I didn't think it had anything to do with my sparkling wit, and it certainly couldn't have been my looks. I was beginning to look a lot better than I had. But I still had a face suitable for frightening children.

"Pascal," I ventured, "what exactly do you have in mind for me?"

He thought for a few moments. "I am not sure. You are a strong man. The will to live seems to burn inside you. I think that perhaps my employer will have some use for you. And James, if he offers you a job, you would be most wise to accept it, most wise."

One morning Fourier announced that we were in Thailand. I hadn't seen a sign or anything, and the jungle looked exactly the same, but I had to believe him. We slowed down considerably and there was no talking in the column. I found myself carrying one of the bundles and two men were on point at all times. On the third day we came to a road where we stopped and made camp.

"Not long now, James," Fourier told me.

The next morning an ancient Fiat truck came wheezing by. One of Fourier's men waved it down and checked in the rear to make sure it was empty. When he gave the all clear we came out of hiding and got aboard. We rode in silence for three hours; Fourier's men were even more alert than they had been in the jungle.

"If there is to be a betrayal," Fourier said, "this is where it is most likely to take place."

At the end of the road we were met by an armed party of thirty mounted men. Everyone looked relieved to be home and the welcoming committee seemed happy to see us. There were smiles all around as the men greeted each other. After they had reacquainted themselves, we mounted small horses that they had brought for us and began the climb into the hills. We arrived at the warlord's camp shortly before dusk.

They had been very clever how they camouflaged it—they hadn't. Or really they had. From the air it would look like a small farming village complete with fields, twenty or so huts and a Buddhist shrine. From the air you wouldn't be able to see the gun emplacements or the barracks. The larger houses were all built under tall trees.

Fourier took me to his own home. The household was lined up to greet him as if he were a returning conqueror. His wife, or maybe she was a concubine, was at least thirty years his junior and she was very beautiful. At last I knew why his boss trusted him. There were a number of Eurasian children in the house, ranging in age from two to sixteen. There was probably a baby somewhere.

"Pierre," Fourier called out, "show our guest to the spare bedroom." He had said it in English to the sixteen-year-old. It was evidently a cultured home he ran here. As I followed Pierre out of the room, Fourier called out after me, "Do not try to run. You will not get very far and it will only serve to embarrass me."

After I finished bathing I found that Pierre had laid out one of his father's suits for me. At first I laughed, but then I looked down and stopped. Instead I wondered what was going to keep the pants up. I couldn't have weighed more than 150 pounds. The suit fit fine.

Walking back to the parlor I found Madame Fourier setting out a plate of cold food for me. I decided that a good Catholic like Pascal wouldn't go in for concubines, so it had to be Madame Fourier. She told me that Pascal had left, but wouldn't tell me where he had gone. I guessed he was making his report to his employer. I hoped they could think of some use for my talents, and, if not, that people around here weren't dying for some entertainment of the upside-down variety.

He came back around ten and told me to come with him.

"Mr. Han wants to get a look at you," he told me. "It is very important, James, that you control your sense of humor because, believe me, Mr. Han does not have one. There will be a translator who will translate what you say into dialect. But please do not think that Mr. Han will not understand what you say. He only admits to speaking one language. But he was educated in Europe and it is certain that he speaks French and I would be willing to bet that he speaks some English as well."

"Why would he hide something like that?"

Fourier looked at me in exasperation. "Because knowledge is power. Listen to what I say: your life is hanging on a whim. Do not ask any stupid questions of Mr. Han. His answer is likely to be to have your head taken off."

The warlord's compound was modest. There was nothing palatial about it except the guards. They all carried AK-47's and looked like they were aching to use them. Fourier handed them his cane without being asked and then submitted himself to a very thorough body search. I was wondering what they were going to do to me, but my search was no different from Fourier's. It was evidently SOP for everyone.

The guards ushered us into a windowless study. The room was lined with books and there was a row of chairs lined up before a massive wooden desk. The warlord sat behind the desk.

He was naked above the waist; the light from the candles gleamed off his massive shoulders. He had a weight lifter's body and an executioner's hands. He looked to be in his late thirties, but it was hard to be sure because he had shaved his head. That was all incidental. I was drawn to his eyes. There was only a hint of an epicanthic fold in the corners, much less than I have. His nose would have been right at home in Gstaad or Paris.

He looked back at me, and in faultless, unaccented English said, "Welcome to Thailand, Sergeant Yamasaki."

CHAPTER TEN

□

KINGDOM OF THAILAND

January, 1966

Pascal gave a visible start when he heard his boss speaking in English. Everything he had told me screamed in my head, *This man is a killer, this man is a killer*. The room felt suddenly cooler as the sweat dried on my body. I tried to think but the only thought that would come was, what difference did it make what I knew, if I was never going to tell anyone.

"It's nice to be here," I told him, not knowing what else to say. Thailand beat the shit out of Laos and that was a fact. But I doubt he needed to hear the news from me. I decided to heed the advice an assistant coach had once given me and not say anything, leave him in doubt.

"We have much in common, you and I," Han continued. "We are both half-cast, a little of both, belonging to neither. We have no natural allies. To survive we must be strong. Pascal tells me that you are very strong."

I looked down at the scrawny body that was all that was left of four years in the weight room. "I was a lot stronger four weeks ago."

"No," he said. His eyes burned. "You have never been stronger. You have been through the fire and returned. You have been tempered and tested. Few could have survived what you have gone through and remained anything but husks. Pascal did well to bring you to me. I can use men such as you. But will you serve?"

Pascal had relaxed when his boss patted him on the head, but he got all tight again when he heard my answer. "Who can say?" I replied. "It would depend on what was asked."

"You know the alternative?"

"Yes."

He watched me; his eyes were shadows. Finally he indicated that we should be seated. "Yes, of course, it would depend on what was asked. Would you betray your country?"

"I know my duty," I said.

"Yes, you know your duty, but you did not answer the question. No matter, I shall not ask it again. To whom do you owe your loyalty, then? Is it to your homeland?"

"To my men and my service," I replied. It was hokey, but I meant it. I had ceased to give a shit about the good old U.S. of A. when I'd seen the first white-phosphorus charge go off. Loyalty is earned.

"That is the correct answer, of course. But do you mean it? Perhaps you do. We shall see. Tell me about your village, the one in Vietnam. We shall come to the one in America soon enough."

I told him about the village and the men who guarded it. He asked for names, Marines and militia. I think if I'd hesitated for a moment while I was reeling off the Vietnamese names he would have killed me out of hand. He quizzed me on Vietnamese grammar and the domestic habits of the Vietnamese peasants. Then he started on the Viet Cong. He wanted to know what I knew. But I think what he was really going after was whether I respected them as soldiers. I did. Killing people you respect is much more satisfying than killing slugs, more of a feeling of accomplishment.

When he was finished with Quang Nam, he moved on to Parris Island. He seemed to be fascinated by basic training. He didn't ask me to analyze it based on what I'd learned in Psychology 101, he just asked for facts and opinions. How did I feel about the drill instructors now?

Would I attempt to even the score if I ever ran into one? Where were my friends now?

From there we moved on to my college days. I started to explain the rules of football, but he cut me off, not important. He asked about my teammates and what the difference between good and bad coaching was. How we handled defeat.

Then he moved on to my childhood. From the questions he asked it was clear that he saw my father as the loser that he had been, married to a half-caste, drinking himself into the grave leaving a wife and baby behind him.

I don't remember my father; Mom never talked about him.

It was well after midnight when he finished with me. "Yes," he said, "I think you are capable of loyalty: to your comrades, to the precious Marine Corps, to me. But I am afraid that I must earn it, must I not? I cannot buy you, because what you want is not for sale. I cannot threaten you, because there is nothing left that you fear. I should destroy you, because you are dangerous. But you are strong, and strong men are so rare."

He glanced at Pascal.

"Pascal is not strong. He goes, but he always comes back. How many women could you buy with your money, Pascal? How many children could you father? You know I would not come looking for you, unless you betrayed me, unless you made it a matter of principle. It would not be worth the effort. I would not even harm your family, because what would be the need? You would have already destroyed them. I would probably give them to someone else, perhaps to Enrique, yes?"

If there was a hint of sadness in his voice, I couldn't hear it. "You come and you go and eventually the Communists will betray you. Then I will have to find someone else."

Pascal just shrugged his shoulders. Han turned back to me.

"I am strong," Han continued, "for the same reason that you are strong, Sergeant Yamasaki. Hatred burns within me and all the blood on this poor tired planet will not quench the fire.'' He leaned over his desk, but his expression never changed. ''I would kill and kill and kill until I was shot down like a mad dog, and I would be content. But I am a prisoner to duty, duty to my people, duty to my soldiers. That is why you are strong, Sergeant Yamasaki, hatred, tempered with duty. Hate without duty is a tiger that will turn and devour. With both you become strong. And strong men are so rare.

''Leave me now. I must think what it will take to win your loyalty. Perhaps I will think of something, perhaps not. No matter.''

Pascal got up at once, and I couldn't think of any good reason to stick around either. The guards followed us out and made sure we found the door. Pascal got his cane back and we walked into the night.

''So,'' he said, ''that was very strange. I have never heard him offer to take on anyone as a partner. That is what he has offered you, you know, he has offered you the partnership.''

''Great,'' I said, ''I can get the first Southeast Asian heroin distributorship in Hawaii. In on the ground floor. Just what I fucking need.''

''Perhaps you should not talk like this, yes? Everything that occurs in this place is reported and I do not think he would enjoy hearing this.''

''Speaking of his royal tutti-fruitiness, what put a hair up his ass? Why's he all pissed at the world?''

Pascal walked on in silence for a moment before he spoke. ''Of course I know the answer. I have known him since he was a small child. But it is not for me to tell you, he would not like it to have people telling stories about him.''

''Not a pretty story?''

''He would not want me to tell you what he eats for breakfast, let alone his life story.''

As we entered his house I asked him to at least tell me if Han drank his blood hot or cold. Pascal laughed and suggested that even though I was a very funny fellow, Mr.

Han was not auditioning a jester this month, so perhaps I should save my best jokes for vaudeville.

His wife had stayed up waiting for us. She looked relieved when Pascal came through the door. He excused himself and told me that if I needed anything during the night I should wake Pierre, who would be happy to get it for me. I went to my room and undressed in the darkness. I stood by the window looking out into the jungle. You can see motion at night. The guard was very still—it took me twenty minutes to spot him. It would have surprised me if he was alone.

I'd slept between pressed sheets for three whole days during the previous two years; the sensation was odd, but not unpleasant. I awoke late the next morning much refreshed. The smell of roasting coffee had me out of bed in a flash. I washed up using the pitcher and bowl that had mysteriously appeared in my room overnight, and then wandered out onto the veranda.

Pascal looked like a new man: he was freshly shaven and wearing a crisp new linen suit. He had on a wide straw hat with a green band and wore an apricot ascot at his throat.

"Ah, good morning, my friend. Did you sleep well?"

"Very well, thank you," I replied. "And yourself?"

"Well, it has been such a long time that I have not seen my wife, as you can imagine we had much to catch up upon." His wife blushed furiously; she was very pretty. "There was all the news of the children, and Mrs. Tang has new curtains, and the weather has been so hot. You cannot imagine what a relief it was for me to get all this news." He gave a great laugh and rested his hand on his wife's knee. The randy old goat. It didn't surprise me that he kept coming back. I would have too.

They invited me to sit with them and break the fast. Mrs. Fourier called for a maid, who came and poured coffee into a fine porcelain cup for me. Breakfast was bread and fruit; there wasn't any butter or any other kind of dairy product. Cows look a little out of place in the rain forest. I had missed coffee.

We talked about breakfast in different parts of the world. Pascal thought the idea of bacon and eggs in the morning was revolting and I told him that people who ate amphibians in glass houses shouldn't throw stones. Mrs. Fourier took it all in without saying a word. When we'd finished eating she excused herself and went to see what the children were doing.

"You're thinking bigger than just Hawaii, aren't you?" I asked.

"Of course," he said. "Hawaii is not much of a market compared to Los Angeles. It is not even much of a market compared to Da Nang. And we shall need new markets if we are to survive the end of the war. And," he said, jabbing a crust of bread in my direction for emphasis, "there is no bigger market than the United States.

"If we cannot penetrate this market, we will get very hungry. It will be a long time before we will be running guns into Vietnam again. The North Vietnamese are so organized, it may be three or four years until the next rebel organization springs up to fight for justice and liberty for the poor suffering peasants. And even then you Americans will have left so many weapons behind you that there may be little demand. There is no doubt that we must steal the American heroin market from the Turks."

"That won't be easy," I told him. "The New York Mafia controls heroin in the States. If they don't want to buy from you, I don't think you'll be able to sell to anyone else. At least not if you want to retire and enjoy your golden years."

"Ah, James," he sighed, "you have been watching too many movies. When the Sicilians first came to your country, they were the most despised segment of the immigrant population. They were spat upon by even the Neapolitans. But this gave them strength. When you have nothing to lose, you are very dangerous. People who do have things to lose would be well advised to keep away.

"This is how the Sicilians obtained their fearsome reputation. It is easy to kill people who have things that you will never have. It is easy to rob and steal and kill when you think of how happy their children are and how sad are your own.

"But over the years the Sicilians obtained the things that they could never have, the fine cars and the large estates and the beautiful women. They began to send their children to the schools where their mothers had scrubbed halls and where their fathers had shoveled coal. Soon enough, as they rode in their fine cars with their, how do you say, their button men beside them, looking out of their windows, what do you think they saw, James? They saw young black men who hated them so badly that it made their stomachs churn, yes? They have things to lose, Michael. They are not so dangerous anymore."

"So you're just going to move right in and take over?"

"Of course not, James. What do we know about America? We are going to send you, and then you will buy heroin from us for the next thirty years. We will all get very rich. I will be able to send my children to the Sorbonne, or perhaps to Harvard. You can use your share to establish a home for the orphans of Marines killed in Vietnam. Everyone will feel much better about themselves."

"And just why am I going to go along with this wonderfully utopian vision of yours?"

"Well, you will be killed if you do not, but you do not seem to be much impressed with this line of reasoning. But no matter. I will think of something, or you will think of something, or perhaps Pierre will have an idea. If not, we will find someone else. Perhaps this Washington, yes?"

I could just see Washingon strung up by his ankles trying simultaneously to blow out the fire and explain that "muthafuhka" was a term of endearment. "I don't think Washingon and Mr. Han would hit it off."

"Perhaps not. Mr. Han has invited you to supper, by the way, which would be about nine o'clock."

People in the tropics eat the main meal of the day after the sun has set and never eat anything substantial until after the hottest part of the day.

"Would you like a tour of the village?" Pascal asked.

"Aren't you afraid I might see something that I shouldn't?"

"But James, we are all friends here. And besides, you have seen much too much already."

Pascal didn't dwell on defensive measures, although he did admit that there were bandits in the hills and one couldn't be too careful. He showed me the communal laundry facility and the medical clinic. He pointed out the advanced, for Southeast Asia, hygienic standards of the village and was quite proud of the infant mortality rate—less than 2 percent per year. He took me up into the hills and showed me the poppies and the happy farmers.

Women from the village were slicing the poppy bulbs and collecting the raw opium that oozed from the wounds. They really did look happy.

"We can manufacture morphine here," Pascal told me, "which is not only much easier to transport, but it is also much more valuable. Some day we hope to be able to actually produce heroin here. And then we can cut the middlemen out altogether. Value added, James, that is the secret of a productive community."

"What stops the middlemen from going to other suppliers and cutting Mr. Han out of the picture?"

"Well, James, they are reasonable men and reasonable men do not seek to get themselves killed." He looked at me reprovingly. "Mr. Han has more than one thousand fighters in his army. This is why we have turned to the heroin, it is a very expensive operation. If the chemists in Bangkok were to join with the other growers and attempt to cut Mr. Han out—he would simply murder all his competitors. Then he would have the government arrest the chemists so that he could replace them with more reasonable men."

"Why would the government be so accommodating?"

"You should be the last person to ask this question, James. Have you not spent the last two years trying to kill Communist guerrillas? We could be running a slave ring here and the government would ask only if we needed more chains. Many of our weapons came from your CIA."

"How do the North Vietnamese feel about it?"

He sighed. "James, please to try and think like an adult. As long as we are useful to them we could be torturing Karl Marx and they would not care. The trick is to decide when we are about to become a liability, and cease doing business shortly before."

"Is that what Mr. Han meant when he said that the Communists would eventually betray you?"

"Yes, but I think I am safe for a while. Things are actually going quite badly for them. They cannot believe that you Americans have come in such numbers and are so willing to die for such a futile cause so far from home. I am afraid that things will get much worse for them before they get better. I just hope that things do not suddenly get better while I am in Laos. It would be most unfortunate.

"But enough of this!" he shouted. "We must have lunch and there could be no finer place for it than here, with such a fine view of the poppies."

We sat beneath a mango tree on Pascal's poncho. I unpacked the lunch that his wife had made for us. There was wine and bread and a can of pâté, along with fruit and some cold Chinese dumplings, a feast. We spent a very pleasant afternoon eating and watching the field hands. We told stories about our first loves—his stories were considerably better than mine—and generally had a good time. We returned to the village around dusk.

I went to my room to take a nap, Pascal had told me that he would wake me for supper. I slept well, having no dreams. He woke me at eight and told me not to worry overly about appearance—Mr. Han would not care. I asked what Pascal was planning to wear and that was when I found out that he hadn't been invited. He didn't seem very put out.

"James," he said as I was leaving, "if not for your own sake, then for mine, control your sense of humor."

"No Heinz Fifty-seven jokes?" I asked.

He looked at me blankly and shook his head. "No jokes at all, and especially no Heinz Fifty-seven jokes. Whatever they are."

Mr. Han had sent an escort, and there were other shadowy figures in the background as well. Pascal was responsible for me being here. It wasn't very likely that he was going to risk having me become an embarrassment. I decided to be on my very best behavior.

Whatever Han had learned in Europe, appreciation of fine food wasn't included. Supper was plain, heavy on starches and vegetables. "It is what my men eat," he explained simply.

The waiters were obviously soldiers. They didn't have their rifles with them, but I could tell. They worshiped him. Their eyes were fixed on him all through supper. I could see them trying to anticipate his every desire. They were clumsy, but he didn't berate them.

"They compete for the privilege of being in my household," he told me. "Once a year I rotate my bodyguards and a new contingent moves in. It is well for soldiers to know their leaders. Why else would they be willing to fight and die for them? My personal life is no mystery to any man who carries a rifle for me. He knows that I do not live like a prince, he knows that my life is duty. And knowing this makes it easy for him to devote his life to duty. It is a very good practice."

"It's not how we do things in the Marine Corps," I told him.

"Perhaps your situation is different. But somehow I do not think that it is so different that you could learn nothing from me."

He told me about the leaders who had been most beloved by their troops and why. I was embarrassed to find out that Pétain was on his list. He described the wonders that such men could work with dispirited, broken soldiers. He had a pretty killing argument. He asked me how many soldiers I'd met who'd be willing to die for William Westmoreland. I couldn't think of any. I didn't doubt that any of Han's men would have gladly taken a bullet meant for him.

His men cleared away the dishes when we were through. I noted how carefully they picked up my silverware, making sure I hadn't hidden a soup spoon up my sleeve. When they were finished clearing, Han waved them out of the room. I was certain they would be waiting right outside the door in case I tried something. I decided not to try anything.

"You may call me Claire if you wish," he said. "It was my mother's husband's name. Another of my father's little jokes. My father was a curious man in his youth. He wondered what sort of children he would produce with a Caucasian. He wondered if they would be different than his Chinese children. Since he was in a position to satisfy his curiosity, he did. He kidnapped a pair of French missionaries, a husband and wife. The man, he murdered. The woman . . ." He stopped and held out his palms.

"I understand that my mother prayed for deliverance for the entire nine months that she bore me. She was delivered from him the day I was born. He had grown tired of her constant crying and strangled her that day.

"It is possible that you, if anyone, could understand what it was like for me as a child. I was not my father's son. He did not recognize me as his child. I was a mere curiosity. People had no reason to fear reprisals for mistreating me and I was an easy target. At the time I wondered how I survived. But now I realize that no one would have wished to harm me too badly. That could have drawn my father's attention. Drawing my father's attention was often fatal.

"My father let me stay in his house until I was eleven. On my eleventh birthday he threw me out in the street and invited me to fend for myself or starve. I survived by cleaning huts for the soldiers in my father's army. They fed me and in return I did odd jobs and ran errands. Soon I was their mascot. As a joke they trained me to shoot and use a knife, only it was no joke for me.

"I was sixteen in 1943 and already one of the best killers in my father's army. I led patrols against the Japanese and always came back with trophies from the hunt. That was where I first met Pascal. He taught me how the enemy thought, and how to use this against him. When the war was over, my father sent me to Europe as a reward for my loyal service. The next year he sent one of my half brothers to kill me. He had decided that he did not need any bastard sons plotting against him.

"I returned in secret to Thailand and recruited a dozen of my former soldiers to back me. Then, in the space of six months, I murdered each of my half brothers. One after the other."

"That must have made your father's last few months very sad ones," I said.

His voice didn't change inflection. "My father is not dead, he has retired to an honorable position fitting for one of his advanced years and long service."

I couldn't suppress the involuntary shudder. I had no trouble not asking what the local pension plan was like. I decided it was time to change the subject.

"Was your army always this large?" I asked.

"No, but men wish to serve and there is always work to be done. There are the Chinese bandits and the Communist guerrillas. And of course we find it prudent to discourage the Pathet Lao from coming here. And then there are our other duties, guarding caravans and keeping competitors in line. It is a busy and fulfilling life."

"What do you do with the money?"

"As you can see, I spend it all on lavish parties."

I figured there was a lot of money coming into the village. Besides the heroin, I was sure he was taking money from all comers. I wanted to know what he was doing with it. It was possible that he was planning to retire to Switzerland and live like one of the local bankers, but I couldn't see it. He would die in Asia. I knew it. His men knew it. He knew it.

When he saw that I was waiting for an answer he sighed. "It is expensive to drag an entire people into the twentieth century. I send young men, and a few young women, to America or Europe for educations; many do not come back. I educate the people here, so they will know why their babies die so young. I hire men to come from Germany to explain modern farming. And of course, I must protect them all from outsiders. It is very expensive.

There is no money in Swiss bank accounts, if that is what you wish to know. Money means nothing to me, except for what can be done with it. I plan to do great things, Sergeant Yamasaki.

"And what would you do with all this money? Perhaps buy a great estate in California, where no one would care who your parents were. Would you buy women? Would you gamble it all away? What would you do?"

This time he was quiet, waiting for me to respond. I thought for a while. What would I do with the wealth of Croesus? "Buy back an island," I finally responded. He looked disappointed.

"And what would you do with this island?"

"Tear down the refineries."

He drummed his fingers on the table—it was the closest thing to emotion I'd seen coming from him. He thought about closed refineries and finally decided that there probably wouldn't be much in them for me.

"I would like you to help me with my army," he said. "They are very brave, often too brave. They have no real training, however. I think it would help if you taught them some of the things that you learned at this Parris Island." He pointed his finger at me. "Mind you, they do not need to know how to today to officers."

"Are you so much better than the men you're fighting?"

"Pascal has shown you the village. Are you so blind that you cannot see?"

I thought for a while; he was right. The village was worth fighting for.

"When do I start?"

"I think perhaps that you should observe my men in action first. There is a gang of bandits terrorizing a district north of here. I am sending a patrol out tomorrow to find them. Would you be willing to go along? It would be a chance to do what you do best."

I didn't have to ask what he thought I did best; I knew. He was offering me a chance to kill people. My mother always says that the way to a man's heart is through his stomach. Han had different ideas, better ones. "When do we leave?" I asked.

"Before dawn tomorrow. The commander will speak English."

I got up to go, thinking that I should try to get some sleep. Han held up his hand. He stood and went over to a closet, where he took out my AR. "You will probably find some need for this," he said as he tossed it to me.

I took out the clip and checked the action: everything worked fine. Han really was suicidal. I had no doubts. I slung the rifle over my shoulder.

"Thanks. I should get some sleep."

"Dawn, shortly before dawn" was all he said.

I threw him a snappy salute and turned on my heel. His guards didn't say anything when they saw the rifle. I gathered from the looks, though, that I needn't bring it back. I walked home alone.

Pascal was waiting for me. There was an empty bottle of Haut-Brion, 1945, sitting on the end table next to him. His eyes were moderately glazed but he didn't have any trouble focusing them on my rifle.

"Poor Ng," he said. "He loved that rifle. His wife claimed it was ruining their marriage. He wouldn't sleep without it and she wouldn't sleep with it."

"Just call me James Yamasaki, home wrecker," I said. I held the bottle up to a lantern to see if there was anything left in it. Just dregs. *What the fuck,* I thought to myself as I upended it. "Thanks for saving me some."

"Ah, James, I have had that bottle since 1954. We liberated it from the governor's mansion in Hue and I have carried it with me to this day. I was saving it for a special occasion. But I decided to wait no longer."

"How was it?"

He looked sad and I thought I detected a tear forming at the corner of his eye. I braced myself for drunken nostalgic ramblings about the green fields of France.

"Ah, James," he said sadly, "red wine and the tropics, they just do not mix." He got up and headed for the back of the house. "Pierre will wake you at three-thirty. I will see you when you return."

"How did you know I was going somewhere?" I asked.

"Because I am a very clever fellow," he replied. "And I do not believe in ghosts. Get some sleep." He disappeared into his bedroom. I went looking for a toothbrush.

Back when I'd been with a regular Marine outfit I'd always hated long-range patrols. Living on C rats and shitting braced against a tree worrying about getting my dick shot off while my pants were down around my ankles. Sleeping in a rain poncho under a leaky tree and then wearing wet clothes for days. Jungle rot slowly accumulating on various parts of my body. I'd had no idea how good I'd had it.

Han's men didn't have automatic weapons or ground support aircraft. They didn't have medevac helicopters and nobody was likely to come along and drop supplies to us if we ran low. If we got our collective ass in a sling, there wouldn't be a battalion response team to get us out of it.

We had assembled in the village square, twelve men, including me. I shuddered when I saw the size of the leader's med kit. He might have had a bottle of aspirin in it. I didn't think we had nearly enough food for two weeks. No one looked worried, though.

Tam, the leader, did speak English, after a fashion. He told me to stick close to him, but not get in his way. It reminded me of the time headquarters had sent a fucking captain to the village, to act as an observer. The asshole had decided he wanted to come along on a night patrol. I'd been more afraid that the jerk would get us all killed than about having to report him killed in action. But either way it had been a losing proposition. I could sympathize with Tam's predicament.

We rode ponies for the first two days and ate about half the food. I asked and found out that meant that we were going to be traveling light, not that we were going to be resupplied somewhere. *Fucking great,* I thought to myself, *just when I was beginning to feel like a human being again.*

I had pretty much recovered on the long walk from Tiehereaux. I didn't have any trouble keeping up with Han's men. Tam wasn't interested in anything I had to tell him about how the Marines worked these things, so I was pretty much on my own. I started to miss Pascal.

We avoided the main trails and headed steadily northwest, toward China. We didn't pass through any of the villages and the few farmers we passed were careful to mind their own business. Tam was pretty sure that we got where we were going unreported.

Han's men might not have had air support, but they didn't have the Viet Cong to contend with either. After we arrived in the district with the bandit problem, Tam dressed up as a farmer and went into a strange village and asked for the news. Everyone knew about the bandits and the unfortunate village that had them as guests. They had been there for a week and had worn out their welcome in the first half hour.

I couldn't believe my eyes when we got to the village the bandits were occupying. There were no guards and the bandits strutted like schoolyard bullies through the marketplace. We corralled a farmer and pumped him for information. He was only too eager to help; he tried to plan an ambush for us.

Gangs of armed men terrorizing lightly populated districts in Southeast Asia aren't that uncommon. But usually they stay in the jungle, where they're almost impossible to track down. Typically they're made up of soldiers who got tired of the Army, or who had to get out in other than the usual fashion. These ones were unusually overconfident. I sure hoped that they really didn't have any reason for it.

There were nineteen bandits in this gang, armed mainly with Chinese carbines. The leader, though, packed what had to be a Thompson submachine gun, based on the farmer's description. They had moved in one day and expropriated a number of huts and a few wives and didn't look like they were in a real hurry to be moving along.

We invited the farmer to eat with us. He wanted to go home, but we were insistent. We didn't have much food left, but we figured we would either restock in the village or die there. There was no need to conserve in either case. We waited till long past midnight.

The bandits posted one guard, who sat by a fire and looked lonely. Tam handed me his knife and waited to see what I would do with it. I stripped down to my shorts and gave him my rifle. The guard never knew what hit him.

The patrol came out of the bush, making even less noise than I had. Tam smiled at me and we traded weapons again. He set me out in front of the hut that had the most bandits in it, because of my rifle. And then left with the farmer who was fingering the huts with bandits in them. I saw Tam enter one of the huts with his knife in his hand. He only stayed for a minute.

Tam had told me to wait for a signal, but hadn't told me what it would be. I recognized it when it came, a woman's scream followed by rifle shots. The bandits came pouring out of my hut. They were half naked and confused. Some of them were actually loading their carbines on the way out the door.

There was a momentary traffic jam as three of them tried to get out at once. I added to their troubles by emptying a magazine into the crowd. Little blood volcanoes erupted across their bodies. They looked black in the moonlight. I popped the first magazine and in the same motion inserted the second. Then I slid into the hut and selectively emptied the second magazine. There was nobody shooting back.

I stepped back out of the hut and listened to see if there was still any action going on; but the village was dead quiet. After a bit Tam came by with his knife and checked out the hut. He wasn't taking the chance that I might have missed one or two. I think he was hoping that I had.

The villagers weren't exactly dancing in the streets celebrating the liberation. They stayed in their huts and waited until dawn to find out who ruled the village now. When the dawn came they appeared one by one and looked around to see who the bodies belonged to. When they saw it was to their erstwhile guests they looked somewhat happy, but not overjoyed. They were waiting to see if it was out of the cooking pot and into the fire.

Tam stood on a crate in the marketplace and addressed them. The only word I caught was "Han," and it was followed by a roar of approval from the crowd. They still didn't do any dancing, but at least they stopped looking like they were about to have their taxes doubled.

One of Tam's men had been killed while attempting coitus interruptus. It was a real lesson to be learned by everyone: don't watch when you've got work to do. The villagers gave him a great funeral and us a great feast.

We rested in the village for two days and then headed back. I wished we could have stayed longer—the local ladies had been very grateful. Despite losing a man, we started back with two extras. Every young man in the village had volunteered to go fight with Han's army. Tam arranged for an athletic competition and then talked to all the winners. He selected the three best. I think he probably wanted only one, to replace the man he had lost, but we had a lot of extra rifles to carry.

It took us a week to get home. Tam led the victory procession. He carried his new machine gun like a trophy and we marched through every village along the route home to display our prizes.

Pascal was glad to see me.

CHAPTER ELEVEN

□

KINGDOM OF THAILAND

April, 1966

We circled each other warily, watching. He was small and very quick, very dangerous. He was just a blur behind a wickedly curving knife when he made his move. He aimed for my face, a stupid place to aim a knife. I sidestepped and grabbed his arm with my right hand, which surprised him because that was the hand that my knife was supposed to be in.

He had never seen the switch. He'd been too busy watching my eyes. My left hand curled forward in a jabbing motion and suddenly he could see the knife: the blade had been hidden beneath my forearm. His eyes opened very wide as I buried the thick leather sheath in the folds of his neck.

I leaned forward until I was about a quarter inch from his face and gave him my favorite drill instructor's favorite line, "You're dead."

Pierre translated for the crowd, eliciting a laugh from everyone but my victim, who was looking pretty glum. I held up my hand and yelled for silence. "Shut up, you stupid motherfuckers" was one of about fifteen Thai phrases that I had memorized; it made the training go a lot more smoothly. I put on my stern expression to show them that it wasn't a game.

They quieted down and paid attention as I explained, through Pierre, the proper way of killing a man with a knife. I showed them how to switch hands and how to hold a knife so that your opponent couldn't be sure where it was. The more things your enemy had to think about, I told them, the closer he was to being dead. I told them to watch the other man's knife, not his eyes; he wasn't going to kill you with his eyes.

I'd been teaching "squad" leaders everything I knew about killing for nearly two months. They weren't really officers because Han's army had only one officer, and he got pissed whenever anyone saluted him. But they were as quick as anything you were likely to meet at OCS, and a hell of a lot better motivated. They had a lot to learn about everything except unarmed combat. I'd found out they didn't need any help in that department on the first day when one of them nearly kicked my head clean off. I had to use my best dirty tricks to beat him. If I'd lost it would have meant losing a lot of face. In my position, losing face could have been fatal.

I taught them the things they needed to know to fight against airplanes and tanks and how to fight old-fashioned wars more efficiently. In short, the things I had learned at Parris Island and Camp Pendleton. I learned a lot from them too. I was going to have some nasty surprises for the Cong if I ever got back to Quang Nam. When I got back.

I had them practice against each other for a few hours with sheathed knives and then called it a day. I was having supper with their boss and wanted to be sharp. Han wanted a progress report.

Pierre and I walked back to Pascal's, where I had become a fixture. Pierre had adopted me and become my indispensable guide and translator. He was a good kid. We took our boots off on the veranda and left them at the door. Pierre's father greeted us with a bottle of red wine.

"It is from Australia," he said. "And surprisingly, it does not taste too much like the kangaroo piss. Only the smallest amount seems to have snuck into the vat."

I gathered that meant it was good shit. I took my glass and swilled it down; it all tasted the same to me. I excused myself and went to wash up in the bathhouse. Pierre came along shortly with my suit and hung it from a nail set in the wall. Pascal had insisted on having a suit made for me after his became too small. It was a white suit. He had insisted on that too, but I liked it anyway.

Pierre sat on a stool and looked up at me like an eager puppy. He watched every move I made. Lately I'd begun to see my mannerisms reflected in him. Luckily I have very good posture. Sergeant Beller back at Parris Island had seen to it. Pierre had made me tell him over and over again how I had come by my scars. Hero worship made me nervous; no one had ever done it to me before. I finally sent him back to the house to clean my boots—anything to get him away from me for five minutes.

When I got back to the house Pierre and his father were engaged in an animated conversation in French. As I entered they switched to English. A very polite family. Pierre was relating the day's events. He had just gotten to the "You're dead" bit.

"The training is going quite well," Pascal said. "Mr. Han is well pleased."

"How can you tell?" I asked.

Pascal laughed and said, "Because he has not sent someone in the night to slit your throat."

Pierre gave a start. Pascal ruffled his hair and told him not to worry, no one was going to slit his friend's throat. We passed the evening away playing pinochle with Pierre's little sister as a fourth. They played cutthroat pinochle in Pascal's house. The bidding was even more complicated than in bridge. The time passed quickly.

Pascal finally took out his watch and told me it was time that I got going. I said good night to Pierre and Mei Ling and headed for Han's compound. It was my fourth invitation to dinner and several of the guards were in my class as well. They greeted me cheerfully, but the body search was just as thorough as it had been on my first visit. I would have felt obliged to kick some asses if it hadn't been.

I didn't really look forward to dinner with Han. It was usually pretty awful. I had asked Pascal about it and he told me that Han ate worse than his troops. Whenever they tried to cook him something fancy he got angry, and no one wanted to see him angry. Personally I think he went a little overboard on the fearless-leader routine. Dinner was typical.

After his men had cleared away the dishes and retired he asked for a report. I told him his men were pumping me dry.

"I think," he said, "that you have been here long enough. If you stay much longer, you will have trouble explaining your absence."

"I haven't decided about your proposition," I told him.

"That does not matter, you will or you will not. What matters is that you will not betray us."

"How can you be sure?"

"Of course," he said, "I cannot be. But the safety of my people requires that I make decisions, that I take chances. I do not think you will betray us, and if you do I do not believe that you can do us much harm. Perhaps you can be of great service. A truck will take you to Bangkok in the morning."

I knew when I'd been dismissed. He didn't want me to stick around and get maudlin. He wanted me to leave and make up my fucking mind. As I walked back to Pascal's I began to wonder what kind of story I was going to tell. I'd been gone close to four months, and it's not that long a walk. I decided to keep it simple; it's the complicated lies that get you in trouble. I'd seen enough jungle that I figured I could tell a pretty convincing lie. Laid up for weeks with jungle ague, etc., etc.

Pascal was waiting for me. He always waited.

"James," he said, "we must talk."

"I haven't decided," I told him.

"That does not matter, you will do it. I know this because Mr. Han would never let you go if you were not. I wish to talk to you about Pierre."

"What about Pierre?"

"I am sending him to America soon. I want you to look after him."

"America's a big country."

"He is going to board at the Punahou School in Honolulu. That is not so far."

I started to ask him how he had arranged that, but stopped. It occurred to me that Pascal was rich and that there were probably people all over the world anxious to do him favors.

"How does Mr. Han feel about it?"

"You mean about losing one of his hostages? That was just talk. He knows that I will not leave him. I will die in Southeast Asia. I have known this since they let me out of that pig of a freighter and I saw the shore for the first time. It is my fate, James, I do not complain.

"I have sent money to Hawaii. A doctor named Kwan Chang, who is incidentally your contact should you decide to join with us, is the trustee. His office is at the intersection of University and Wainiha. He will sign over the trusteeship to you. And James"—he paused for emphasis—"he is not to know that my son is in Hawaii. Pierre will travel under the name of Pierre Arnaud. Can you remember all this?"

"Dr. Chang, University and Wainiha, Arnaud. I've got all that, Pascal. But, you know, I'm still in the Marine Corps. I can get leave and go home to arrange everything, but I don't think I'll be home very long. My mother will have to take care of Pierre."

Pascal gave me an odd look—I thought it might have been pity. "Yes, of course, James, you are still a Marine. Do the best you can." He said good night and that he would wake me at six. My escorting party would leave at seven-thirty.

Breakfast wasn't very cheerful. I hate good-byes. Pierre was close to tears: evidently his father hadn't told him he would be seeing me again in the near future.

"I am afraid," Pascal told me, "that your suit will have to stay here."

I looked down at it and decided that he was right. It didn't jibe very well with my three months in the jungle. I had been wearing the suit in the evenings and black pajamas with combat boots during the day; life's little ironies never fail to amuse me.

"Did you throw out my uniform?" I asked.

"No, I thought perhaps that one day you might need it. In fact, it has been fermenting for several months now, and is certain to add an air of credence to whatever fanciful story you are planning to tell your superiors." He gave the same nasty chuckle I remembered hearing in Tiehereaux.

Fermenting was the right word, and an air of something it was definitely going to give. I wouldn't have wanted to put it on in the house, even if Madame Fourier would have let me. It literally made my skin crawl and even Pierre moved upwind. Pierre was brushing back tears—it was like he'd lost his only friend in the world.

I wanted to give him something, something to remember me by. But I had nothing left. I checked out my uniform, hoping that the Laotians had left me something. Not a chance. I noticed that my Marine belt was still intact, after a fashion. I took the canvas out of it and gave the buckle to Pierre.

"Marines don't cry," I told him.

He threw himself into my arms and cried a little bit, not much; he was busy holding his breath. I laughed and tousled his hair. I mounted up. At least the pony didn't seem to mind my aroma.

"*Au revoir,* y'all," I called out. I looked back once—they were all waving.

I wasn't certain that my escort wasn't planning to shoot me in the back as soon as we were out of sight of the village. But, since there wasn't shit I could do about it, I decided not to waste time worrying over it. I listened for the click of a safety being released, though, and I vowed I'd have an escort to Valhalla.

I was only slightly surprised when the truck came and they let me get on it. I didn't stop worrying, though: I remembered Han's story about his stepbrother. It had occurred to me that he might not want his people to know what kind of reward they could expect for loyal service. I figured I would be safe when I got to the embassy in Bangkok.

The trip across Thailand took more than forty hours over the worst roads you can possibly imagine. At the river crossings there were no bridges. If there wasn't a ferry, the driver would just plow into the river and hope we didn't stall before we reached the other side. The only good part of the whole trip was that I couldn't smell myself after the first couple of hours.

I knew we'd arrived when the driver stopped and indicated that I was to get out. He didn't like the way I smelled either. He wasn't the same driver who had started the trip—they had switched about a third of the way to Bangkok. I wasn't sure if that was for security or just standard operating procedure. One man couldn't possibly have driven the whole way, I knew that. I hadn't slept a wink the entire trip.

I got out of the truck and stretched. It looked like he had let me off in the northernmost suburb of the city. It was a residential district and evidently not where the rich people resided.

I'd taken leave in Bangkok after my first tour was up, so I knew the city. The stories I'd heard about Thailand had sounded like wild lies, but I had wanted to check them out anyway, in case there was even a shred of truth in them. It turned out all the stories had been watered down, probably because even the people who had been there didn't believe what they'd seen.

In Thailand, prostitute is just another phase in a girl's life, somewhere between puberty and temple harlot. Something like one in six of all Thai women have been prostitutes at some point in their lives; there's no social stigma attached to it. They've created an art form, and believe me, they're damn good at it. My platoon sergeant had told me that I'd come before I was hard. I'd thought that was impossible till it happened. Being back in Bangkok made me suddenly realize that I'd lost my wallet, what a fucking pity.

I knew where the American embassy was, but I figured

that traipsing through Bangkok dressed in rags with an automatic weapon over my shoulder was probably not a great idea. The AR was a serious problem. It was worth probably two or three thousand dollars on the black market, about ten times the Thai per capita income. Carrying it around dressed like I was made me a prime target, but abandoning it never occurred to me.

Daybreak was due any minute and that would bring people out of their homes and onto the streets. I could already hear them stirring. There was a Buddhist temple nearby and it looked like the best bet for a place to hide.

The temple was built entirely out of intricately carved brown sandstone. The interior was dimly lit and deserted. It made me wonder where the monks slept. There was only one large room, which stretched back between two rows of massive columns to a large gilded statue of the Buddha. The floor was tiled and worn smooth by five hundred years of meditators' sandals. There was room behind the Enlightened One, so I stretched out and went to sleep. I didn't wake up till after dusk.

The monks stared right through me as I walked out, getting psyched up for some strange Eastern rite no doubt, probably fucking. Three rifle cartridges bought me a bowl of noodles at a sidewalk stall. I had eaten the last of my food on the truck and I was ravenous. I couldn't figure out if one of us was getting a lousy deal. On the one hand I wasn't in a position to bargain, and on the other the noodle lady probably didn't want to haggle with a wild man carrying a rifle. I held up three bullets and she seemed to be happy. Maybe she was.

It was a long walk to the embassy, but I didn't feel like trading bullets with a cabby. For the last half mile I saw the building in the distance, with mixed emotions.

Legation duty is one of the assignments that Marines pull. It's supposed to be an honor and they don't let just anyone do it. As I was walking I wondered who the lucky assholes were who had pulled Thailand. To pull legation duty in Bangkok while your buddies were getting their asses shot off in Vietnam had to be one of the all-time great deals.

Most places the guards wear their pretty dress blues and try to give a good impression. In Bangkok, they wore fatigues and flak jackets and tried to look like killers; maybe it wasn't such a plum assignment after all. When they saw me in the floodlights they dropped their rifles to the horizontal and pointed them at my belly. I kept walking. I stopped when I was about six inches from the end of the closest rifle.

"Point those somewhere else, vermin," I growled, "or you'll be seeing your neighborhood proctologist to get them out." It occurred to me that I was a natural for DI. I decided to apply for it after the war was over. I impressed the sentries so much that they pointed their rifles about a quarter of an inch to my sides. "Don't just stand there like fucking GI Joes," I told them, "go get somebody who doesn't have to be told when he can take a shit."

They were good soldiers; they didn't look at each other to see what they were going to do. They both kept their eyes locked on me. They didn't ask me any stupid questions either and I was careful not to scratch any of my itches. The older of the two told his partner to call upstairs. He shouldered his rifle and disappeared into the guardhouse. After a while, he came back and pointed his rifle at my feet.

"Consul's coming," he said. He didn't say anything else.

The consul turned out to be an elegantly dressed man in his early sixties. He was dressed formally, evidently getting ready to go out. He looked at me in disbelief.

"You called me down here for this?"

"He's an American, sir," the older of the two guards said. "Or at least he talks like one. He might be a Marine."

The consul turned to me and raised one eyebrow.

"Yamasaki, James H., sergeant, United States Marines Corps, 2693566. On loan to the Vietnamese Defense Forces, Quang Nam province, Republic of Vietnam. I've come from Laos, sir. I have important intelligence information."

"What is the Marine Corps motto, Sergeant?"

"Show us your tits," I replied, doing my best to keep a straight face. Semper Fidelis is the officers' motto, and then only when they're on duty. The two sentries shouldered their rifles. I'd convinced them.

"Well," he said, with a sideways glance at the two Marines, "perhaps you better come with me. Leave your gun here." He turned to the older guard, who had winced in unison with me at hearing my rifle called a gun. "Jenkins, come along. I'll have a relief sent down to replace you."

I leaned my rifle in the doorway out of sight of passers-by and gave the younger Marine a look that boded ill for his health if something happened to it. We entered the embassy, official territory of the good old U.S. of A. I reflected, with the consul leading me in the middle and Jenkins bringing up the rear.

"Are you hungry, Sergeant?" the consul asked.

"Yes, sir," I replied. "But what I really need is a shower."

"And some new clothes," he added. I had to admire him. I might have smelled like the freshest of roses for all you could tell from his expression. "Jenkins, take Sergeant Yamasaki to the Marine quarters and get him cleaned up and fed. I'll send down some clothes. About a size forty-two, Sergeant?"

My last suit—I'd bought it for graduation—had been a forty-six long. I looked down and said, "Yes, sir."

The consul was good to his word. It wasn't exactly the most fashionable suit I'd ever worn, but it was serviceable. By the time I finished cleaning up, Jenkins and I were best buds. We had a lot in common. He put his rifle away and brought me down to the Marine mess and rustled up some food. He was curious. But when I told him he didn't want to know, he believed me and didn't ask again. He may have believed I was who I said I was, but he never let me out of his sight for a second.

I was finishing up my third piece of apple pie when the consul walked in. He sat down across from me and rested his hands on the table. He still had on evening clothes, but he had loosened his tie.

"Forgive me for asking, Sergeant," he said, "but do you have a four-inch-long scar along your right side about six inches below your armpit?"

I was about to answer when Jenkins piped in that I did. He had watched me take my shower in case I had been planning to sabotage the embassy's plumbing.

"Hmmmm. Your sudden appearance in Bangkok seems to be causing large amounts of distress to the east." He drummed his fingers on the table for a bit and seemed to be lost in thought. "Well, we shan't be bothering you with any questions tonight, Sergeant. A number of people will be flying in tomorrow morning to talk with you. Is there anything we can do for you tonight?"

"Well, sir, I haven't collected a paycheck for about four months now and I'm kind of anxious to see the sights, so if you could . . ." I stopped when he started shaking his head. I had just been jerking him around, it comes natural to me.

"I don't think that would be wise, Sergeant. I think it would be much better if you stayed here and rested."

"Well then," I said, "it sure would be nice if I could phone home, my mom probably thinks I'm dead."

He didn't pause for a second. "I'm afraid that's not possible, all transpacific telephone service is out. If you give me your mother's address and a short message, I'll see that it's telexed at once. Your mother will have it first thing in the morning, which will be coming along very soon in Hawaii."

As I wrote out the message I wondered how he knew I was from Hawaii. I didn't think it was a lucky guess.

They gave me a room to myself, but I wasn't tired; I'd slept all day. I didn't have to stand by the window and stare to spot the guard. He was smoking a cigarette and watching my window like it was the shower in a girls' dormitory. I walked out into the hall and said hello to the guards. There were two of them and they were at opposite ends of the corridor, making it tough to get them both at once. Neither of them wanted to play rummy.

I went back into my room and lay down. I went over my story in my head, trying to pick it apart. I may have been overlooking something, but no story is pat, not even the true ones. When I got bored with fantasy, I went back into the hall and asked the guards to have someone bring me a uniform in the morning. Then I went to sleep. I still wasn't tired, but one of the things you learn in boot camp is how to sleep in your spare moments. You never can tell when you might need some reserve stored away.

The Marine who got me up the next morning brought me a uniform. It didn't fit real well but it had the right number of stripes on the sleeve. I washed up in the adjoining bathroom—they had given me an almost VIP suite—and ate the breakfast a steward had brought me. My debriefing started at seven-thirty.

There were five of them. It didn't surprise me to see my old friend Horus. I said hello and tried to picture him hanging by his ankles from a banyan tree. It wasn't very hard. One of the other gentlemen introduced himself as the ambassador. I couldn't quite figure out what he wanted. Maybe he was worried that I hadn't had my passport stamped at the border. The other two civilians introduced themselves, but didn't specify their agencies. That was all right; I'm a good guesser. The last member of the team was a recording technician. He got in the first word. He clicked on his reel-to-reel and spoke into the microphone.

"Zero seven thirty hours, 13 April 1966. This tape contains classified information and is to be physically destroyed upon completion of the transcript and no later than zero seven thirty hours, 15 April 1966. Subject is debriefing of Yamasaki, James H., sergeant, United States Marine Corps, 2693566." He clicked off the recorder. "Gentlemen, please identify yourself before speaking for the first time. If there are any problems with the equipment I'll be waiting outside." With that he turned the machine back on the left the room.

"Horus, Clifford J., colonel, United States Army, 4930557. OK, Yamasaki, take it from the top."

I didn't think I had to introduce myself, me being the star attraction and everything.

"The choppers set us down ten clicks from the village. The air recon photographs had indicated a trail and it led right where we were going. Captain Lucas put me and one of his men on point and had ten men in a trailing party. He kept the main force with him. We got to the village with no problems and with no indications that we had been spotted.

"We entered the village at ten hundred hours; it was deserted. We were doing recon on the village when we heard heavy fire coming from the direction of the rear guard. Lucas ordered us to spread out and take cover. He had the mortars set up and tried to contact the rear guard via walkie-talkie. There was no answer and the firing died out after a few minutes. I estimate that it was five minutes before the first of the rear guard caught up with us. Three men came out of the jungle running as fast as they could.

"Lucas ordered covering fire from the mortars, but it didn't come in time. Two of the men were down before the first round landed in the jungle. Our cover fire became effective and Lucas led a party out to make pickup on the fallen soldiers. He was killed at that time by enemy fire. His first sergeant took command at that point and we retreated into the center of the village with our wounded."

"Why didn't you request air support?" Horus asked.

"Our radio operator was killed in action with the rear guard. We couldn't pick up any channel with the radio we had with us—it was either defective or there was no one out there listening.

"The fire was coming from NVA regulars. . . ." One of the mysterious civilians cut me off there.

"Simpson, Barton A., State Department," he said. The ambassador gave Simpson a sour look when he heard "State Department." "How can you be sure that they were North Vietnamese regulars?"

"When they began to infiltrate the village I saw their

uniforms. And besides, they were too effective to be anything but NVA regulars.

"We were pinned down in the village the rest of that day and all of the next. We were all scared shitless. They had captured someone alive and were torturing him in the jungle close enough for us to hear; but the first sergeant didn't want to waste a mortar round trying to get them. The guy they were torturing lasted till noon the second day, or at least his voice did.

"Sergeant Hansen told us we had to hold out and wait for the cavalry. We all expected relief by the second day and figured we could hold out that long. We dug in, expecting artillery, but the North Vietnamese seemed reluctant to shell the village.

"On the second night the first sergeant asked me to try and get to the rendezvous and signal for a chopper."

"What were you going to signal with?" Horus asked.

"He had a twelve-by-twelve international-orange ground cloth that I was going to lay down on the field. I also had the walkie-talkie."

"Did he send you by yourself?"

"Yes, sir. He thought one man would have a better chance of getting through undetected.

"I had no problems getting through the North Vietnamese lines. They were evidently expecting we would be reinforced as well, because they had pulled back well into the jungle. I had no trouble reaching the rendezvous and was there when the B-52's came. That was pretty shitty what you did."

I was looking right at Horus as I said it. He didn't seem to be offended. He took an eight-by-ten photograph out of a file folder and stared at it for a while. If any of the rest of them had been rocked to their innermost cores by the news that they had killed twenty of their own troops for policy reasons, they were taking it well. Horus put his photograph away.

"Why didn't you attempt to make contact after that?" he asked.

"I thought you might have more bombs left," I answered bitterly.

"That's enough, Sergeant," he barked. "We are, of course, truly sorry that those men were killed. But at the time we were certain that it was in the best interests of the United States that that den of heroin smugglers be sanitized. It is tragic that there were Americans left on the ground, but I will not stand for any implication that we might have knowingly bombed our own troops. Besides, the decision did not originate with this section."

"Sorry, sir."

"Did you see any evidence of heroin activity in the village?" Simpson asked.

"No, sir."

"Carson, Alan E., State Department. Did you see any Europeans or evidence that a European may have been in the village recently?"

"No, sir."

"Please describe, in your own words, everything that you can remember about the village. Anything at all that looked out of place. Any evidence of money or materials of foreign origin. Take your time."

It went on like that all day. I described the village as best I could remember, filling in gaps that I thought I should know based on Quang Nam and Thailand. I knew it wouldn't be smart to give too many details. My version of history had me in Tiehereaux for only two days and that had been four months ago.

The two men from the "State Department" asked most of the questions. They would ask questions about the village, and then questions about my walk to Bangkok. It went on and on, with them trying to poke holes in my story. They would ask the same question three times at hour-long intervals, trying to see if the story changed any. But it was a simple lie. Parts of it were even true.

Toward the middle of the afternoon I pretended to get angry, as if I thought they didn't believe me. They soothed me by explaining that it was a scientifically proven method of debriefing. It was the most efficient way to recall all of the valuable intelligence I had stored in me. What jerks.

The recorder took two-hour tapes and the technician had to change them five times. Toward midnight I think they ran out of steam. Hearing the same story over and over again began to get on their nerves. I knew I was getting pretty bored by the whole ordeal. The ambassador had checked out after dinner—he'd never said a word while the recorder was running. Simpson seemed to be calling the shots; he called it a wrap at one A.M. The technician came in and packed everything up, gave the tapes to Simpson and cleared out. Horus stayed behind.

"Tell me, Yamasaki," he said, "what did you think of Sergeant Hansen?"

"He had a good head on his shoulders," I replied. "Why do you ask?"

"Just curious. I'd known him for years. I never would've thought he'd send a Marine out for a loaf of bread, let alone to make contact with an Army helicopter. But I guess you never really know, do you, Sergeant?"

That was Horus's cute way of telling me that he knew I had been selling them a crock of shit. That was OK. I didn't care one way or the other what Horus thought, as long as he was willing to go along with my version of history. I kept my mouth shut. When he saw that I didn't have anything to say, he reached into his shirt pocket and handed me a note. It was the message I'd sent my mother.

"I'm afraid your message didn't get through. Your mother killed herself last month." If he was sorry, he didn't say so. He watched me like I was a rat in a cage, waiting to see how I would react to a new stimulus. I crumpled up the note and threw it away.

"Am I dismissed, sir?"

He walked right by me, not saying a word.

I didn't blame the Army for my mother. I knew what had killed her. Betrayed by her father, who'd married out of his race and expected the rest of the world not to notice. Betrayed by her loser of a husband, who'd thought he had married beneath himself and never let her forget it. Betrayed by her son, who'd gone off to fight in a war she didn't understand and then didn't even have the courtesy to send back a body for her to grieve over. She had been betrayed by everything she'd ever loved and she hadn't been about to let it happen again.

When I got back to Vietnam I found out that I wasn't going to be a Marine much longer. I didn't blame the Army for that either. Something crazy had happened to me in Laos. The Marines couldn't be sure of me anymore. The colonel made it clear that it was in the best interests of the Corps that I didn't re-up. At least he wasn't hypocritical about it: he never said a word about my best interests. I couldn't blame the Army for that.

I couldn't even blame the Army for what had happened in Quang Nam. While I had been lying in Lucas's tent listening to the B-52's pounding the North, a battalion, an entire fucking battalion, of NVA sappers had taken out the fort. They were in and out in a half hour, long before the action team got there. They found Washingon draped over the machine gun in the mess hall. There had been way too many bodies for the Vietnamese to carry them all off. My replacement had died nobly and in the best tradition of the Corps. I couldn't blame the Army for Quang Nam; if I'd been there it would have been just the same.

So way did I become Mr. Han's partner?

What else was left? I'd lost everything: my family, my friends, my Corps. Even the chance to die honorably There was nothing left, nothing but Han; and of course, there was an island.

CHAPTER TWELVE

□

SALT LAKE CITY

The present

I blinked twice and Anderson came back into focus, his smug Mormon face waiting for me to come clean and be forgiven. What an asshole. I hoped that if I'd phased out for a few seconds he had written it off to my impassive Oriental demeanor. I resisted the urge to look at my watch. Maybe I'm getting too old for this business, except that can't be it. I've been old ever since Mom called to tell me about Betty. Maybe I'm just tired.

"Nothing happened except thirty dogfaces got themselves killed and almost took me with them," I told him. "I laid low for a week until I figured the Pathet Lao had stopped looking for me. Then I headed south, for Cambodia. When I got there I thought it would be safer to try for Thailand than Vietnam."

"You were missing for almost four months. Surely it couldn't have taken that long to walk to Bangkok?"

"Unless you've been there you wouldn't understand: it could take a day to go five miles. I was alone . . . and in enemy territory. I couldn't use the roads and I had to travel at night by moonlight. I played it right by the book, and I got out alive. What are you going to do about Hawaii?"

He leaned forward and put his hands on his desk. "Of course I have absolutely no idea what you have been talking about. I am shocked to learn that those four young men were murdered. I do not know for certain, but I find it scarcely credible that they were mixed up in any way with illegal activities. It is barely possible that they were duped in some manner by hardened criminals who would find it easy to take advantage of their innocent natures. But I do not believe for one minute that they would knowingly become involved in smuggling drugs.

"Further, I am shocked that a police officer would abet the obstruction of justice by hiding the true facts of this case. You are in very serious trouble, my friend, if even one tenth of what you have told me is true."

He was bluffing. I knew he was bluffing. He knew that I knew that he was bluffing. He was speaking for the record, in case I'd brought my own recorder. I hadn't been that smart. "Well la-dee-da," I said, "you better race me down to the federal building to report it before your conscience blows a gasket."

"Unfortunately, all I would have to report is hearsay. Are you planning to spread these malicious lies in the media?"

I had him; we had a deal. I rose from my chair and glanced at my watch; happily there weren't any unaccounted-for gaps. "You mean like drop a note to Dan Rather? I doubt it, Mr. Anderson, the case is still under investigation. We never closed the file on your boys. It's still on the books as a possible multiple homicide." We really hadn't closed the file: our secretary had been laid off in 1983, and our files are at least that far out of date.

"Tell me, Chief," he said as I headed for the door, "how much does a decorated war hero cost?"

I turned in the doorway and looked back at him. "A lot," I told him. "More than you can afford."

I let myself out, Anderson didn't show me to the door. I got into my car and momentarily wondered if it would explode when I turned the key. I sat there for a minute and decided that the pieces really would land in their backyard: nobody would be that stupid. I fired the car up and headed back to the airport, having no desire to stay and hear the choir sing. I would tell people back at the station that I just hadn't felt right being on vacation. I worry too much. It was sure to add to my reputation for being a dedicated public servant.

I dropped my car off at the lot. I was in such an expansive mood that I even let Hertz sell me a quarter tank of gas, at twice the going rate, for the fifty miles I'd driven their car. I took the shuttle up to the terminal and booked a seat on the nine P.M. flight to Los Angeles. Since I had an hour to kill I went looking for a bar. I spent an amusing half hour familiarizing myself with the local liquor laws and ended up sipping an orange juice and reading the local paper. Lots of doings down to the tabernacle.

The plane was fifteen minutes late boarding. That didn't surprise me, it was just the way I remembered air travel. It wasn't until we got out to the taxiway and stopped that I started getting premonitions. After another fifteen minutes the captain came on the intercom and announced that they were having minor technical problems with one of the engines. "Nothing major, folks, so why don't y'all settle back and have a drink on us while the mechanics check it out."

I was suddenly thirsty in a major way. Maybe it was engine trouble; somehow I doubted it. We were still sitting on the taxiway when the ten o'clock flight left. It was right on time.

The rest of it was entirely too predictable: a truck came to tow us back to the terminal at ten-thirty. I'd have been willing to abandon my luggage, but the eleven o'clcck flight was booked for probably the first time in its history. Just as well, I was sure that if I'd managed to get on board it would have had even worse problems than the nine o'clock flight.

I thought about renting a car and driving to Denver, but it's a long way and you have to drive through a lot of empty desert to get there. Lots of places to have a fatal accident. The airline was real apologetic about marooning us in Salt Lake. "Sorry, no other flights till the morning. No, no planes available to take you tonight. Of course we'll foot the bill at the airport Hilton. Seven A.M. sharp."

I wasn't paying that much attention. It had been obvious

since the captain had come on the intercom that I'd be staying in Salt Lake that night. It was why the Mormons were going through all the trouble to keep me there that was bothering me. They could have just followed me back to the airport and murdered me there. Maybe it had something to do with the chairman being out of town.

I tried to call Marty, but nobody was home. I called the station house to ask them to have someone swing by my house. I told them that I would be back the next day. They sounded disappointed. They had probably been planning to have a big poker game down at the station while I was gone.

I took the airline up on the free room, but not without some internal debate. If I stayed in the airport they'd know I was expecting something and they'd just make their plan more elaborate. On the other hand, there was a good chance that if I took the room they'd expect to get me in my sleep. Maybe they'd be overconfident—the last two sure had been. It wasn't a real good chance, but then again they weren't exactly the KGB either.

The shuttle to the Hilton was full of angry passengers. Some were more philosophical than others, although it's hard to see why anyone would want to spend an extra night in Salt Lake City. The town doesn't exactly rock till it drops.

At the hotel there was a crowd milling around the front desk. They were even angrier than the folks on the shuttle. Two harried clerks were busy assigning rooms and explaining that they had to get credit card numbers anyway, even if the airline was footing the bill.

They gave me a room on the fifth floor; that was the lowest they had. Eastern European secret police like to throw people out of windows. I'd always thought it was a particularly nasty way to go. I was surprised when the room turned out to be in the middle of the floor instead of on one end or next to the elevator. It made me wonder who was next door.

I broke a soda bottle inside one of the hotel towels. It wasn't much of a weapon, but I figured it would do for the first person through the door. And after him, anything could happen. But no one came. I spent the night behind the door sitting on the floor with my back to the wall. I almost wrote the whole incident off to paranoia, except the front desk forgot my wake-up call.

I snuck out the back door without checking out and walked to the terminal. I paid cash at the United window and had no problems, but I doubt my departure went unnoticed. I tend to stick out in a crowd; it's my tan. I arrived in Los Angeles at eight. It was still early in Hawaii, but I tried to call Marty anyway; no one home. I was starting to get worried. I got to Honolulu at noon local time and called the station and asked for Benton and Kitamura to meet me at the airport. Sam's tall and it would be easy to mistake Kenny for me from a distance. They would have guns.

I asked for an aisle seat in the back on the interisland shuttle, and was home before one.

One of the nice things about the Kailua-Kona airport is that there aren't any good resting places for snipers. Funny how you never notice things like that. Sam and Kenny were waiting for me. Good thing for them. Kenny went to get my cruiser while I grilled Sam about what had happened during my absence. It was pretty clear he thought I was an asshole, gone one day and expecting the world to end because of it.

He was surprised when I wouldn't let him carry my bags. Ordinarily he would have, but today I wanted to keep his gun hand free. I was edgy and had an itch between my shoulder blades right up until I got my riot gun out of the trunk of my cruiser. Even then I wasn't what you could call happy. I threw my luggage onto the backseat and told Sam and Kenny that I'd be at home and that anyone who needed to talk with me should call before coming out.

Marty's motorcycle was parked in my driveway and he was inside waiting. He would have waited forever. His mouth was stretched back in a horrible parody of his typical grin. His face was black, so black that you couldn't see the permanent tan he'd acquired over the years. Whoever had murdered him had left the garrote looped around his neck. My first thought was that Marty looked silly wearing a tie.

It's really very simple. Go to any bicycle store and buy a brake cable and two handlebar grips; throw away the receipt. Cut about eighteen inches of cable and thread it through the grips. Fasten the little metal ball around the free end and you have a professional-model garrote, all for about $3.95. It depends on where you shop. Wear gloves and don't forget to leave the garrote behind you when you're finished; you wouldn't want to have it on you if you're stopped for a faulty taillight.

I opened the riot gun's choke wide and checked the house. There was no one home. I went back to the living room and sat down. It didn't make any sense. Marty would have told them everything they wanted to know—he was no fool, and besides, he'd seen Dave's hands. They knew there was no boat, no bodies, no nothing. So why was I still breathing? And then I felt really trapped. Was the FBI outside, waiting for me to sneak Marty's body out and dump it somewhere? "Whatcha got there in the rug, Chief? Mind if we take a peek?" That would be the smart thing to do; it's what I would have done. The scandal would have gone on and on. Marty would have told them where all of the pot was stashed; clueing NBC to several hundred tons of marijuana stashed in my jurisdiction wouldn't do much for my credibility. If the Mormons ever came up, it would just be to mention that I'd probably murdered four of them who had accidentally stumbled on my organization. It would be very neat, and they could always finish the job later. Leave me dangling in the breeze.

The only other explanation I could think of was that they had left for some reason. Maybe the cruiser I'd had float by had scared them. I wasn't betting on it, though. So I sat there, totally at a loss. Action or inaction, fight or flight? I could feel the acids building up in my stomach. I didn't know what to do.

I went to my office to get the Rolaids I keep in my desk. I opened the center drawer and my eyes were drawn to the empty space. It took me a second to realize what it was and a few seconds longer to get the full implication. The heroin was gone. They had snatched Eiko. I couldn't stop the huge grin from spreading across my face: they thought they had a hostage, assholes.

I would have laughed out loud, but I remembered the tape recorder in Anderson's office. Since they weren't planning on killing me right off, it was a good bet they would probably be interested in what I was doing. I pounded on my desk a few times for effect and sobbed, "Eiko, Eiko!"

I would really miss Eiko. Maybe I even cared for her a little. But business is business and Eiko was a very small cog. She wasn't important in the overall scheme. The organization comes first.

I started looking for microphones. I didn't find any, but that just meant that they were using good ones.

I got my gun-cleaning kit and left the Rolaids in the drawer. I walked back into the living room and took the AK-47 down off the wall and looked it over. I'd had to get a flyboy to mail the stock from Thailand. Cost me a month's pay. Whenever people see it they always ask if it isn't illegal, even for me. I always tell them that maybe it was illegal to bring it into the country, but having it here is OK. Then I show them the concrete in the barrel and how the chamber is welded shut.

I dug the solder out with my thumb nail and let it fall to the carpet. The plaster of Paris in the barrel came out just as easy. I looked through the barrel and saw Marty and winked at him; he had always enjoyed a good joke. Then I set about field-stripping and cleaning. In an hour it was as good as the day it had come out of the factory in Czechoslovakia.

There was still the problem of Marty's body. It was for shit-sure that I wasn't going to go swimming with it. But even that wasn't a real problem; the reason we'd taken to burial at sea in the first place was that we were expecting large numbers of bodies and we didn't want happy campers stumbling on them. I was still expecting large numbers of bodies, but I figured they were about to become somebody else's problem.

I covered Marty's body with a sheet, in case the Avon lady came by, and then went to take a nap. I woke up at ten feeling like a new man. I'd have been at peace with the world if Marty hadn't been stinking up the house.

There are loads of roads that cut through the rain forest on Hawaii. The jungle comes right up to the side of the road and the smell of rotting vegetation is overwhelming; I figured Marty wouldn't add to it appreciably. I waited till after two, and then gave him his last ride.

While I'd been at Parris Island, one of the DI's had gotten loaded in Beaufort and killed a baby deer on the way back to the base. He'd roused the whole barracks and insisted on having a proper funeral for his "little buddy." Ted, the platoon clown, gave the eulogy. Marty got less of a funeral oration than Bambi had, but then, nearly everybody does. The only appropriate thing that came to mind was *Sayonara,* although *See you soon* kept running through my head.

I had a bottle of Taylor port at home, vintage 1928. Pascal had sent it to me for my fortieth birthday. I didn't even want to think how much something like that would cost, though I doubt he paid for it. I'd been saving it for a special occasion, but it didn't look like I should wait much longer. I opened it and it was as good as advertised.

I waited for dawn.

I didn't think it would take them very long to contact me, and it didn't. I was still drinking my morning coffee when the dispatcher yelled out that I had a call.

"Chief Yamasaki here," I said.

"Good morning, Chief," came the reply. "My name is Smith, Jedediah Smith. My cousin Joshua came through here last September and he told me to be sure to look you up"

"And how is old Joshua?" I asked.

"Solid as a rock, Chief. Would it be possible for us to

meet somewhere for lunch? I'm sure we have mutual interests that we could discuss to both our profit.''

We settled on Hapuna Beach. There would be hundreds of people there at noon. We both felt safer that way.

I pulled into the parking lot and drove around till I found a rangy blonde wearing denim. God, they all looked alike. He was wearing mirrored sunglasses and evidently shopped for boots at the same place as the last two.

''Mr. Smith?'' I asked.

''Afternoon, Sheriff,'' he replied. He paused waiting for me to go into my fag politician routine, but it was getting stale. I asked him if kidnapping wasn't against the Jehovah's Witnesses' creed and enjoyed the dirty look he gave me. He held up a box in front of me and seemed to be satisfied when it didn't make any obnoxious buzzing noises.

I hoped he wasn't planning to frisk me in the parking lot—a great man-bites-dog story, criminal frisks cop. He resisted the urge and nodded toward a man down on the beach. ''Mr. McMaster wants to talk with you.''

''Gideon McMaster?'' I asked. ''Or is it old Caleb?''

He gave me another dirty look and said, ''Good to see a man in your position can keep his sense of humor. I doubt I could.''

I let him have the last word and walked down the beach to talk with Mr. McMaster. Maybe Mister was his first name.

''Good afternoon, Chief Yamasaki,'' he said. His pronunciation was precise and his voice very cultured. It was the kind of voice that you get by shipping buckets of money to an institution back east. There was no doubt in my mind that he was in command. The chairman really had been out of town, I thought to myself bitterly. ''I have trouble believing that that is allowed.''

As he said it he was looking over the chain link fence at the construction in progress on the resort side of the beach. The developers had come in during the early sixties and bought a big chunk of beachfront property from the Harshaws and built a resort on it. A large amount of beach had suddenly become off-limits for locals, but on the other hand the resort employed lots of local folks too. It was a tradeoff. They had left a portion of the beachfront vacant where it met the state park, but they had never promised that they would leave it undeveloped forever. Now they were building condominiums for rich people from the mainland—people who don't like sharing beaches with the lower classes.

"When the white man first arrived," I told him, "all the land in the islands was owned by the royal family. From the low low-tide line to the tops of the mountains, one giant estate. They owned it, but they really didn't, because it all really belonged to the gods: Pele and Maui and their kin. But the white man came along and told them they did own it, and asked them to give it away. Which they did. Just goes to show ya, brothers and sisters shouldn't marry.

"They gave a third to the government, a third to the missionaries and they kept a third. Of the third they kept, they tended to give large amounts away. They gave most of this part of the Big Island to a cowboy named Harshaw in return for him rounding up all the wild cattle. Most places that would be considered quite a bargain.

"The Harshaws sold this part of the shore to the developers and now they're building condos so rich assholes from the mainland can have a house to visit once a year. The low low-tide line, Mr. McMaster, the furthest out the water ever recedes. You won't even be able to wade near here except two or three times a year."

"That would not be allowed in Utah and I cannot believe that it is allowed here. Is there any land left for the native Polynesians?"

"One small island: don't bother going there, you wouldn't be welcome. By the way, if you intend to leave this island alive, it would be a very good idea to give Eiko back."

"My, but that sounded like a threat, and I do not believe that you are in any position to be threatening me."

I conjured up everything I could remember from the senior play and made threatening moves in his direction. I flared my nostrils and squinted and held my breath till I turned red and the veins popped out in my forehead. "Let me rephrase that, then. If you expect to leave this beach alive, you better give Eiko back. I may not be in a position to threaten anybody, but that's not gonna be much comfort to your widow."

He held up one hand. If I was intimidating him, he hid it well, because his expression hadn't change one iota. "Rest assured that we we do not intend to harm the poor girl. We are keeping her"—he paused and rolled the phrase over in his head to see if it was appropriate—"in protective custody. It is only through necessity that we hold her at all. It is obvious that the poor child is in need of immediate medical assistance, to wean her from her substance dependence." He looked at me accusingly. "A dependence that I fear you are fostering in the poor child for purposes of carnal debauchery."

I put on a guilty expression—it took a lot less effort than rage. I wrung my hands, figuratively, and started making excuses. I was weak; I loved the girl; only looking out for her best interests; did it to protect her; and on and on *ad nauseam*. God, if I hadn't known I was lying it would have made me barf. McMaster just nodded his head and tut-tutted and said it was only human. What a hypocritical son of a bitch.

He let me run out of steam and then turned to watch the waves roll in. "Of course," he said, "you must make amends. Especially if you want the girl returned to you for help instead of to a state detoxification center."

"Anything," I said, "just don't hurt Eiko." I thought about actually wringing my hands, but decided nothing could possibly be worth that. It was a public beach, after all. Somebody might see me.

"Your ex-associate Mr. Stine informed us that you are smuggling heroin. Perhaps you will tell me about it, now."

I looked up at the heavens and thought a silent apology to Betty. "I was in love with this girl, we were just children. Her father was opposed, I was a half-breed from a bad family. Not nearly good enough for his daughter. He sent her away, she died—he killed her, really." I choked up; it was the easiest acting of all. "I enlisted in the Marine Corps and asked to be transferred to Vietnam. I wanted to kill things, I wanted to kill and kill and not stop killing until I was dead. But I didn't die.

"I came home, and became a police officer. And then one day the girl's mother came to me and asked me for help. Her youngest daughter had gone to Honolulu to attend the University. She fell in with the wrong crowd, a bad crowd. She had never forgiven her father for the death of her older sister and this was her way of getting back at him."

I snuck a peek at McMaster; he was eating it up. You have to believe that the country's been ruined by television. He probably thought my story was better than his favorite soap opera.

"She dropped out of school and moved in to an apartment in downtown Honolulu, on Kuhio Street." I looked up at McMaster to see if he had a clue as to what that meant. It didn't look like he did. "Kuhio Street is where the prostitutes hang out. Good girls don't live there.

"She wouldn't answer any of their letters and her phone number was unlisted. Her father was wild, he went to Honolulu to drag her back. Mrs. Ohira told me that he came back the next day with a black eye and wouldn't tell her what had happened. He just sat in his office and drank whiskey and wouldn't talk to her."

"Why on earth would he want the girl back?" McMaster asked. I gathered that he wouldn't. White people can be such assholes. I could just hear him, *I haff no datter named Eiko*.

"You wouldn't understand," I told him.

"I told Mrs. Ohira that I was sorry to hear it, but there was nothing I could do. Honolulu was out of my jurisdiction and Eiko was of age. I couldn't just go to Honolulu and drag her back. And then she showed me her picture: it was Betty, it was as if she had stayed young while I got older and older. I was trapped, I had to go.

"Vice in Honolulu is sewn up by the *yakuza* gangs, there aren't any free-lance operators. I found Eiko's pimp, he was a Korean named Jong-ok. He told me Eiko was valuable property and if I fucked with his property he'd cut my dick off and make me eat it. I believed him, but I had to have her. I sold myself, I sold myself to the *yakuza* gangs for a girl. All they wanted was for me to transship a few packages for them, and keep this island quiet. It wasn't that much to ask."

He ate it up, I could tell. It was all that repressed sex drive coming out. The best part was that even though it was a complete lie, it would all sound true to Eiko. She'd never known the real story either. All she knew was that one day old Jong-ok had flown out to the Big Island with her. He'd had direct orders from his boss and had died shortly after arriving. She had seen him die. Eiko could verify the whole story, and cheerfully would too. Just be five minutes late with her injection.

"These *yakuza* gangs, they are the Japanese Mafia?"

"Sort of," I told him. "They've been around in one form or another even longer than the Italian Mafia, only they make the Italians look like a high school glee club. When *yakuza* gang members screw up, they like to show how sorry they really are. They used to cut off fingers, but that's too much like advertising; these days they use a branding iron where police and immigration officers can't see it. You're not thinking of messing with them, are you? They'll hunt you to the ends of the earth if you cross them."

"I find it very difficult to work myself into a lather over gangsters," he told me, showing what an idiot he really was. "I think it is time that someone showed these people that they cannot with impunity send their vile poisons into the United States."

I had been thinking that he was going to say something like that. I had wondered why they hadn't gotten it over with and murdered me. McMaster had just explained it. He was trying to score points with his superiors. His organization had taken a pounding and he was going to deal the vile drug smugglers a telling blow to make up for it. Shit, what an asshole.

I could just see the report he was planning to write when it was all finished. It would probably say MOST CLASSIFIED or PROPHET'S EYES ONLY across the top, and it would read like a Robert Ludlum thriller. "See how the forces of evil have fallen under the hammer of God's wrath. Of course there were martyrs, as there will be in any just cause." It would then go on to detail all the folks I'd murdered. I didn't see it ending that James Yamasaki is alive and well and still chief of police in paradise.

He was in for a real surprise if things worked out the way I was planning. He was going to have a tough time explaining things when it was all over, or at least I hoped he would. Presuming, of course, that he was still alive when it was all over.

"You don't know what you're getting into," I told him. "You don't fuck with a *yakuza* gang. They'll kill us all. They'll kill me. They'll kill Eiko. They won't stop until we're all dead."

"We can protect Eiko; you will have to take your chances."

He watched me, seeing how I was taking my death sentence. I took it like a man. I stared off into the distance and squared my jaw and wondered how stupid he could possibly be. Pretty fucking stupid, as it turned out.

"There are a few other matters we must clear up," he continued. "Where exactly does the heroin originate?"

I turned back from the ocean and blinked at him, refocusing. "Why, Thailand, of course," I replied. "Where did you think it comes from?"

CHAPTER THIRTEEN

□

HAWAII

The present

"From Thailand?" McMaster asked. "Is it not strange how Southeast Asia continues to pop up in your life story, Mr. Yamasaki? Goes to Laos to help interdict the heroin trade—disappears for four months and then mysteriously reappears in Bangkok. And now it turns out that he's in the business himself. Tell me, Chief"—he didn't put the usual amount of respect that most people put into my title—"how much did they pay you to betray those Green Berets?"

McMaster stood there, waiting for the truth. I doubted he believed that I'd been in the heroin-importing business before my second trip to Laos. But he was getting uncomfortably close to the truth. I wanted him to think that I was just a tool of the *yakuza* gangs, not that I was working directly with the Thais.

"We got caught in an ambush and I bugged out. You didn't really expect that I would stick my neck out for a bunch of GI Joes, did you? They died like real heroes, with their guts spread all over the countryside for the birds to peck at. I was in Bangkok for two months before turning myself in. It took me that long to make sure there hadn't been any survivors. I didn't know shit about heroin until Mr. Yoshima told me what I had to do to get Eiko."

"The B-52's didn't kill anyone but Laotian bandits then, did they?" he asked.

"Not even them, they cleared out and left nothing but peasants behind. But killing peasants doesn't weigh that heavily on your collective conscience, does it?"

"You disgust me, Sheriff. You may have been a man once, but now you're the most despicable thing I've ever met. It sickens me that we belong to the same species."

That was better. It sounded like I'd convinced him that I was nothing but a yellow-bellied coward. Too weak-willed to fight against my destiny and easily manipulated. That was half the battle. All that was left to do was to convince him that he was God's right-hand man—in charge of the divine retribution department. But, as it turned out, I didn't even have to do that. He was already convinced.

"Sheriff's a fag politician in Hilo. What do you want from me?"

"Mr. Stine is dead. The Los Angeles police are at this moment arresting hundreds of his associates. Your smuggling route is blown. You will have to arrange a meeting with your masters to decide upon a new one. Betraying them to us shouldn't be a problem for you. We also want your distribution channels on the mainland and the names of your masters in Japan."

"And after I give you all that," I asked him, "how long do I live? It'll be a race between the *yakuza* and motorcycle gangs, the Navy, probably the CIA, the state Visitors' Bureau and you people to see who can kill me first. After I have Eiko back and get a two-week start, you get the names. They won't be going anywhere."

"And why will you be so forthcoming with names if you have a two-week head start?"

"Don't be a sap. If you kill all of my ex-associates I only have to worry about you people, and I know a place where you'll never find me."

"You are truly the most disgusting worm I have ever met. How did you ever obtain the Navy Cross?"

"It was a case of mistaken identity," I told him. I used the tone of voice that punks have been using on me for years. I wasn't worried about him making me enlist in the Army, though. I'm too old. "I'll arrange a meeting with my boss; it'll be in the hills. I'll tell them that you're a meat packer from Utah and you'll be using steer carcasses to smuggle the goods. He'll want to meet you."

"Very well, I'll contact you in three days. Arrange the meeting for Saturday morning. One slipup, though, and the girl goes to a sanitarium and you'll find yourself in a crematorium. Do we understand each other?"

"Only too well. Three days won't be enough time to fly Yoshima in from Tokyo, though. You'll have to make it a week, Monday at the earliest."

"Monday, then," he said. "We'll be watching you."

He turned and walked away. I wondered if he had any concept of what it would mean to murder the boss of a *yakuza* gang—probably not. I wondered if he had a family.

I drove home and called Tokyo. I got right through to Mr. Yoshima—we had known each other for years. His clan had tried to muscle in on the heroin trade and had paid a high price in men without ever realizing a dime. His biggest problem had been a lack of local support. I was offering to alleviate that problem.

He wanted to know why I suddenly needed a partner. But I was ready for him. I had the Mormons. I explained that a new organization was taking over west coast heroin distribution and they were trying to squeeze me out of the picture. He seemed to be properly sympathetic about all the bikers who'd been arrested. He'd heard about it, of course. I told him I needed outside muscle because my own organization had gotten soft over the years due to its bloated profit margins.

He didn't think there was anything odd about the Mormons being involved in organized crime; he'd dealt with religious mafias for years. How was he supposed to know that the Mormons were different from the Amida Buddhists? As for my organization getting soft, he was only too ready to believe it. A mongrel gang in a mongrel state led by a mongrel outlaw. He probably thought we lacked Japanese discipline.

The deal I offered Yoshima was that in return for him putting a little fear of God into McMaster, I would deal exclusively with him for Asian heroin. It was a good deal, but I knew he thought he could get a better one from McMaster. Everybody always tries to cut out the middleman. He was more than willing to meet McMaster.

I was planning a hot time on the volcano when they all got together. McMaster was planning to pump Yoshima for information and then exact God's vengeance. Yoshima was planning to pump McMaster and propose an alliance to get me. He's a bastard and a predictable bastard at that. If they managed to talk for even five minutes they'd probably figure out what was going on. But they weren't going to get five minutes. I mean really, what use is there in having a police department if you don't use it? I arranged the meeting for Monday, five days away.

After talking to Yoshima I went to a phone booth and called the French Indochina Rubber Company's office in Bangkok. Actually they only have one office these days, but it is in Bangkok. I told the secretary that there was going to be a stockholders' meeting on Monday. I suggested that the chairman might like to attend.

Just for kicks I closed out my account at Hawaiian Savings and transferred the money to a stockbroker in Los Angeles. I was sure the Mormons would be watching. I booked two seats to L.A. for Tuesday, and then another two under a different name for Monday night. I could just see McMaster chuckling at my naïve little plans. I figured I had to do something, though. If I just sat on my ass he'd be suspicious.

I took the weekend off and went fishing. I had to buy a new pole; I'd left my old one on the beach and someone had walked off with it. It was a nice pole too. Joel Feigenbaum found me down on the beach Saturday afternoon.

I've often thought that *haoles* could be divided into two broad categories: *haoles* who wear hats in the tropics, and *haoles* who don't. The ones who don't are, generally speaking, excitable, mentally unstable and not to be depended on in tight situations. The Evans brothers, for instance, had never worn hats. *Haoles* who do wear hats, on the other hand, are upright conservative pillars of the establishment, who can generally be depended on to be able to string together more than one thought at a time without having to lie down. I've never seen Joel without a hat.

He'd come to the islands, like so many in his generation, courtesy of the United States Navy, and had never felt any desire to return to Iowa. He had been a correspondent in the Navy and had used the money he'd saved during the war to found the *Times-Dispatch,* currently a division of Stine Enterprises. Marty had bought the paper a number of years back and, as part of the deal, had kept Joel on as editor. Marty had made it quite clear that he was just the publisher and would never dream of setting editorial policy.

Joel was looking considerably older than his sixty-six years.

"What's up?" I asked him.

He thought for a moment, not sure what to tell me. Finally he worked up the courage to ask, "What's going on, Chief? Something's happening, I can feel it and something's not right."

"You're the news hound," I told him, "you tell me."

"There's a lot of strangers in town."

I laughed. "Tell me there, guy, when was the last time there weren't a lot of strangers in town? If there weren't any strangers in town you'd have a real story: 'Local Economy Collapses.' "

"It's not the tourists, Chief. It's different strangers, way different. There's a party of Japanese at the Beachcomber, twenty of them. They have an entire floor and they haven't moved out of it since they got here. The desk clerk says that some of them are missing fingers." He paused there, expecting I'd have something to say about Japanese tourists with missing fingers.

"So they're clumsy and hate beaches, so what?"

He got the hint—I could tell by the look he gave me. But he kept asking questions anyway. He was like a coon dog who had the scent. He knew there was a story someplace, and even if he couldn't print it he wanted to hear it.

"There was a man down at the paper three weeks ago digging through back issues. He wanted to know about the marijuana growers and why none of them ever seem to get arrested. He was quite insistent."

"Probably doing a feature for *Sixty Minutes*."

"I thought of something like that, but he wasn't a reporter. I could tell." He paused, waiting for me to say something, but I didn't have anything to say.

"That's a new rod and reel you've got there, isn't it? Charlie Nianga's got a new one too. Says he found it down on the beach. Says he doesn't think the owner's going to come back for it." I turned my back on him and cast into the surf. "You heard about the big shipment of pot that was impounded in Los Angeles Thursday, didn't you? And about the bikers?"

"Yeah," I said. "I bet they're singing the blues over in Maui right now. Clever idea, though, wasn't it?"

"I thought so when Dave Bellamy told me about it. Chief, don't jerk me around, please. Nobody's seen Dave for a month, and now Marty's missing."

I sighed and turned around. He was begging me, he had to know. It occurred to me his grandson had worked for Marty on occasion.

"Gee, Joel, remember that girl who died in the power-boat accident? The one with the big teeth marks in her? How come you didn't want to know about that? Or how about those two little native kids who went into the rain forest looking for mangoes and found a land mine instead? Why wasn't that news? Big fishing tournament didn't leave any room?

"And how about that tourist? The one who thought he could sleep on the beach, only he picked the wrong beach? Tourists getting beaten to death ain't news though, is it? Wouldn't want to scare any of those suckers off by telling what's likely to happen to them if they stray away from their hotels at night."

He couldn't think of anything to say. Ordinarily I don't believe in torturing helpless old people, but Joel and all the other "town fathers" had been looking the other way too long. It was time to pay the piper.

"So what's the occasion now?" I asked him. "You suddenly decided you're not too old to win a Pulitzer after all?"

His hands flapped at his sides; he turned left and right and looked for the right thing to say. He saw the AK-47 leaning against the rocks, and with that he knew.

"Marty's dead, isn't he? Everything's falling apart." He was just an old white man. He'd been here a long time, pretending that nothing was going on but the workings of the free-enterprise system churning out goods and services for the common good. He had known it was a lie, of course. Marty had gotten very, very rich playing the capitalist game by his own rules—which didn't fit in very well with what Thomas Jefferson intended. But Marty had paid an awful lot of money for that newspaper, so what the fuck.

"Go home, Joel," I told him. "And send that grandson of yours to Tahiti for a week. You can afford it."

He started to walk away, a tired old man. He turned at the tree line and looked back at me. "Marty told me once that he'd left his entire fortune to the Trust for Hawaiian Land."

I looked back over my shoulder. "So I'll make sure they find the body."

I think he may have been about to cry, but he turned too fast for me to be sure.

I called McMaster that night and told him he had an appointment for six A.M. on Monday up in the foothills of the volcano. I figured that was early enough so that I could set up an ambush, plus take care of the ambushes that the Mormons and *yakuza* would be setting up. I certainly didn't want to see the underlings banging into each other up in the hills before their bosses killed each other.

"The man you want to talk to is about five foot six and weighs near three hundred pounds," I told him. "Rumor has it that he once boiled his own son alive for fucking up. Sure you still want to go through with this?" He said that he did and was understanding when I told him that I would be unable to attend personally.

Monday morning found me typing away at the desk where our secretary used to sit. I was alone. I'd sent the dispatcher home because I was expecting company. It felt funny sitting there with the phone off the hook; almost like betraying a trust.

Mr. McMaster came in at eight o'clock. It was a big disappointment.

"Aren't you supposed to be doing the Lord's work up in the hills?" I asked him.

"I have the utmost confidence in my subordinates," he responded.

"Well founded, no doubt." I went back to my typing. McMaster watched me with bright eyes. He was probably looking forward to springing some bad news on me. Either Eiko was dead or the FBI was arriving at noon.

"What are you typing, Chief? Your life story?"

"Maybe. You wanna buy a copy?"

He said not really, so I went back to typing.

"Actually it's my resignation," I told him. "Life story comes later."

"How noble of you to save the town council the trouble of firing you for deserting them and leaving all that pot in your home."

I looked up at him over the typewriter. "You weren't actually going to let me run, were you? I mean, how would that look in your report?"

For the first time I saw uncertainty around his eyes. He squinted at me and his voice lowered a half octave. "What are you talking about?"

"Well," I said, "my guess is that you aren't really interested in the mainland heroin network. I mean that's not really a Mormon problem, now is it? Even if you were interested, I doubt you'd be interested in it enough to let me get away. I'm the one you know about. I'm the last one alive who knew about your missionaries. It just doesn't seem reasonable that you would just let me get away to spend the rest of my days living in splendor with my Oriental whore and my ill-gotten millions."

He started moving his hand toward his coat pocket.

"Mine's already out," I said in a voice totally devoid of emotion. A voice devoid of emotion is much more intimidating than a voice lowered a half octave. It was a trick I'd learned from Han—only with him it's no trick. I leaned back in my chair so he could see the cannon the council had bought me in case the town ever became infested with wild elephants.

"Now bearing in mind that I haven't been laid since you kidnapped my girlfriend, which has made me a tad jumpy, why don't you reach into that pocket and take out what's in there." He was very careful; he thought he still had a lot of troops on the island who were going to come to his rescue. He didn't want to take any chances.

I had him walk over to an empty cell and put his hands through the bars. I cuffed his hands together and then frisked him. His driver's license said Uriah McMaster, very cute.

"Now," I said, "as I was saying. I don't think your superiors would be too happy about you letting the chief sinner get away. Especially since he turns out to be a coward and a traitor on top of being a fornicator and drug runner. My thought is that you're probably going to give Eiko an amazing overdose and then arrange it to look like I killed myself out of sorrow. You know what they say about it running in families and everything."

He didn't have anything to say so I went back to my typing. Finally he had to know.

"What's going on in the hills?"

I stopped typing and looked over at him.

"Tragedy," I said. "That's why I have to resign, you see. I've just lost half my department in a blazing gun battle between two warring drug gangs, one Japanese and I believe the other one is from Utah." He clenched his fists and stared at me with blazing eyes. Oh well, sticks and stones.

"Don't think for a second you're going to get away with this," he said. "They may not have a death penalty in this state, but you'll be going to prison, oh yes you will. People will spit when they hear your name."

It just amazes me the dream worlds people live in. What the fuck did he think I cared what people thought about me? People have always loathed me. Well, not everyone, but it had seemed that way when I was a kid.

"Oh?" I said. "Perhaps you're going to testify against me? Perhaps you're going to tell the world about the heroin and about Eiko? I don't think so. If you keep your wits about you the world will never know that you Mormons were the kingpins in the transpacific heroin industry. There's no heroin up in the hills, and I don't think any of the surviving *yakuza* will mention it if you don't. It's supposed to look like a disagreement in the marijuana import-export business.

"Now admittedly it's not going to do your Mormon squeaky-clean image any good to be mixed up in pot, but imagine what it would do to it if word gets out about heroin and kidnapping young girls."

"What's happened to my men?"

"Well, most of them should be dead by now, along with most of the Japanese and about half of my police department. There should also be a few bent DEA agents. I sold you the *yakuza* gang just the way you wanted it, but I decided that I wanted to live long enough to collect my pension, so I'm afraid your boys got it too."

McMaster looked like he hated me pretty good. The tricky part was coming up. The story I wanted the Mormons to believe, the one they would eventually report to the DEA, was that I was the sole source of Asian heroin. Hopefully, with me dead, they would figure the organization was finished. Or at least that it wasn't worth their while to investigate it any further.

"I told my boss that your group was the new mainland contact. Then I had my boys go out there in plain clothes to arrest everybody, and finally, I tipped off the DEA this morning. Now of course nobody trusts anybody else, so it was just a matter of having a couple of guys up in the hills with rifles to get everyone shooting at each other."

"The truth is bound to come out," he said. "There'll be survivors on all sides."

"Sure, two or three on all sides, and of course there's you. But I don't see any of them gabbing. It's a matter of principle for the *yakuza*. My men will just know that they tried to arrest drug traffickers and your people aren't going to want to give the church a bad name. It's doubtful that anyone other than you and me will ever know the whole truth, and we won't be talking. Now will we?"

"You're insane," he said. "You can't possibly get away with this."

"Well, ordinarily you'd be right. But since I'm not trying to get out of it alive, I think I will get away with it. It's only one *yakuza* gang, and they'll only really be interested in me. Your superiors are the same way. Sure, it's a matter of principle, but once I'm gone they're not going to be looking for any more trouble. You're going to prison so you're no problem, and I'm afraid your organization is about to become defunct. Some nerve, portraying yourselves as missionaries and all the while importing Hawaiian pot onto the mainland. And in conjunction with a motorcycle gang, no less. You should be ashamed of yourself."

"So how are you planning to fake your death?" he asked bitterly. Of course McMaster would never believe I was dead—but it didn't matter.

"It's a beauty of a plan, but if I told you it would spoil things." I got my hat and slung the AK over my shoulder. "Now remember, not a word about heroin; it's for the good of the church."

He played his last card. "You'll never see Eiko again."

I sighed and walked over to him. "Would you like to hear the Eiko Ohira story? Remember I told you about her father's trip to bring her back? He found her in a Korean bar down by the airport. She was working. He confronted her pimp and told him he had better give back his daughter or he'd be on the next plane back to Korea. Old Jong-ok thought that was great. He had the judge tied to a chair and gave him a blowjob on the house. Guess who he picked to do it."

"So how did you get her back?"

"Why, I picked up the telephone and had old Jong-ok's boss send her, along with Jong-ok. His boss and I worked for the same organization so it wasn't much of a problem. And besides, that's how I've kept old straight-as-a-ruler in line all these years. Beautiful super-eights of him slitting Jong-ok's throat."

"You were involved long before then, weren't you?" He was slow, but he was getting it. I had been afraid for a while there that I was going to have to explain it to him. It was much better that he figured it out for himself. He'd be less likely to question it later.

"What the fuck did you think I was doing in Bangkok for two months, working in a massage parlor?" I gave a nasty laugh. "Oh well, the heroin business been berry, berry good to me. But now I think it's time to move on to greener pastures. Say good-bye to Eiko for me." I headed for the door.

"You don't give a shit about her, do you? You don't give a shit about anyone." Vulgarity, I must have really been getting to him.

I turned in the door. "I do care about Eiko. I care so much that if I knew where she was, I'd go kill her myself." He looked at me, he was speechless. "She's a heroin addict, McMaster, and you've just put her source out of business. There won't be anyone else on the island to take care of her. They'll probably be shipping the heroin through Toronto from now on. When you let her go, she'll head straight back to Kuhio Street. You'd be doing her a favor if you killed her." I left him there.

He hated me, I knew that. Maybe he hated me enough to send her back to Kuhio Street. It would be stupid, but maybe he'd do it. If he did, Pierre would take care of her. It was my best shot; if it didn't work, well, I had tried. God grant me that, I had tried.

CHAPTER FOURTEEN

□

HAWAII

The present

I'm putting a lot of faith in McMaster. He can probably get off if he hangs tight and produces ten or so character witnesses who can testify to what a wonderful upright law-abiding Mormon he is. I don't think he'll do that, though. I think he's going to plead guilty to avoid a trial and all the nasty publicity.

He's sure as hell going to look guilty. There's the photographs of him talking to me down on the beach. There's the mysterious organization he ran, which his church is going to be busily disassociating itself from. There'll be plenty of bikers who'll cheerfully implicate him as the kingpin of the organization in return for lighter sentences. That's way out of character for bikers, but what the fuck, no story is perfect.

All in all there's more than enough evidence. The only way McMaster is going to get out of it is to drag the church into the mess. But he would never do it. I'm confident that he would be willing to roast in hell for eternity if he thought it was in the best interests of his church.

There's loads of circumstantial evidence tying him to the dead men in the hills and to the nearest of the marijuana caches as well. If that's not enough, I had some physical evidence planted in his hotel room as well. When he sees the way the tide's running, I'm counting on him to completely disassociate himself from the church. He'll probably tell the judge that he personally is an atheist and that he's only been using the MPS as a cover—gulling the honest Mormon folk. It's possible that faced with a long prison sentence some of his people might have been weaker, but I've taken care of that for him.

Of course he'll file a confidential report with his superiors. He'll report that I faked my death and suggest that they should track me down. I don't think they'll come looking, though: everybody will be better off if I stay dead. If they do decide to search for me they'll probably look in places like L.A. or BoraBora, not Hawaii. I have a feeling that the MPS, or more likely the organization that replaces it, will think for a long time before coming back to the Big Island. The Mormons won't be a problem for whoever takes my place.

McMaster will try to put the best face possible on his report. He'll say at least they totally destroyed a major heroin-importing network. That probably won't impress his bosses much; heroin isn't a Mormon problem. It isn't likely that they'll send anyone to check to see if it's true.

The *yakuza* gangs aren't likely to be much of a problem either. It's ironic that McMaster was so willing to believe in them—he probably thought of them as the Yellow Peril. I mean, they certainly exist but they aren't a factor in Hawaii. The Japanese who came to Hawaii were honest working people, not the dregs of the English debtor prisons.

The *yakuza* gangs had never been able to make inroads into the Japanese community and had gotten their noses bloodied when they tried to mess with the Chinese. Ironically they did make millions in the hotel business, though it must have really rankled to pay protection to the Tongs.

The Tiger Clan's surviving members are likely to be a little bent out of shape, what with Mr. Yoshima blown into little pieces and everything. But I doubt they'll ever figure out what happened. They'll suspect me, but I don't plan to be around. It'll just be another case of not learning one's lesson. The other gangs will have a good laugh at their expense. They won't be vacationing in paradise anytime soon either.

The only other problem I had seen looming on the horizon was the DEA. They were certain to hear rumblings about heroin, and there was going to be lots of pot lying around. The last thing I wanted was a major sting operation aimed at Hawaii. But, after helping organized crime waste half of the local police department—not the kind of interagency cooperation that the Justice Department's been talking about for the last decade—I'm sure that they'll be keeping a low profile.

Of course the politicians are going to have to do something about the state's number one agricultural product. That had been inevitable since the Mormons found out about the *Dirksen*. My feeling is that it's going to a rough couple of years for farmers. But soon enough the politicians will miss the campaign contributions. And their constituents are going to start complaining about unemployment, and their sons-in-law with the Porsche dealerships are going to start going bankrupt. I figure in two years they'll be selling the state police's helicopters to pay for meals for the elderly or some such shit.

All in all, my organization is going to come out of the entire disaster relatively unscathed. It'll need a new leader, and it's going to miss Stine Enterprises. But it looks pretty much like it's going to be business as usual.

I took a last drive around town. It was very quiet; there didn't even seem to be many tourists spilling ice cream all over themselves.

Han had been wrong about one thing, I reflected as I tooled around town. There was more than enough blood on this poor tired planet. I didn't hate anyone anymore, and I had had enough of killing. I was just tired, and I wanted it to be over.

So how does a police officer become corrupt? If you've made it this far in my life story you're probably wondering about that. But it isn't police officers who become corrupt, it's people. I wish I could remember when it was that I realized that I wasn't an idealist anymore.

It bothers me how my life turned out. I never intended to become a crime czar—it wasn't one of my boyhood aspirations. Things just turned out that way.

The Marines had been real good about granting me hardship leave, and even better about terminal leave. I had gone to visit Dr. Chang in Honolulu. Pascal had indeed sent sufficient money to see Pierre through Punahou, along with three or four hundred other boys; he had sent two million dollars.

I got the hint. Dr. Chang gave me the names and addresses of some other Chinese businessmen that I might like to talk to. They lived in places like Las Vegas and San Francisco and Seattle. They sent me to places like Detroit and Chicago and New York. I was very busy for a few months.

Perhaps I was too young to command much respect from the Tong leaders, but my stay with Pascal had put permanent wrinkles around my eyes, and not unlike Pascal, I could smell the stench of death all around me. And they were all willing to listen, it was such an intriguing proposition.

The heroin came back with soldiers returning from Vietnam. There were a lot of soldiers and heroin isn't very bulky. They would stop in Hawaii and my men would relieve them of their packages. Flights leave Honolulu every day for every major city in the country, especially the cold ones, like Chicago and Cleveland and New York.

The Kona grass war nearly screwed everything up. If it had gone on much longer I would have been forced to import some muscle and end it in one giant paroxysm of violence. I didn't want to do that: it would have caused talk. But Marty, poor Marty, came along and solved my problem for me. I would have been perfectly content to keep on being an "honest" law enforcement agent after that, but Pascal had other ideas.

"James," he told me, "this is a wonderful opportunity. You cannot keep using tourists as a distribution network forever. Perhaps after the first is caught it will mean nothing. But the second will draw every agent of the

United States government down upon you. But this, it is classic. Who would look for heroin in bales of marijuana?"

Besides, I think it ran against Pascal's grain to leave an economic resource undeveloped. My share of Stine Enterprises was never very significant, a few million a year. But every little bit helped; eventually I was planning to make the Harshaws an offer they couldn't refuse.

Poor Marty. He tripped over his feet he was so anxious to do me favors. Except for Orville, his organization didn't have any muscle to speak of. After I took care of the Honolulu gangs for him it was self-evident that I had killers to spare. Marty was always such a realist. He had been calling me boss for a long time.

The Tongs were perfectly content to buy heroin from me. The price was reasonable—I only marked it up 300 percent—and deliveries were always on time. I became a very important man to the Tongs. Eventually, of course, they decided they could do without me. They wanted to deal directly with the source. It was a very bad business decision.

In the early seventies the Honolulu Tongs decided to replace me with someone they could trust, somebody Chinese. It was probably killing them to see a Eurasian making all that lovely money. They decided that presented with a *fait accompli,* Mr. Han would still do business with them. They were surprised when I refused to be killed. And then they were panic-stricken when their members began to die like flies.

I had a dream. I would buy the Big Island back. It was hopeless, I knew, but that was all right. And anyway, I didn't really want the whole thing. I sort of figured that Hilo and Kailua would dry up and blow away after we killed the tourist industry. And it was OK by me that the federal government owned the volcanoes; I've never met a Park Ranger that I didn't like.

By the time the Tongs decided they could do without me, I had decided that I could do without them. The native Hawaiians outnumber the Chinese three to one, and I had lots of money to recruit an army. Although in truth it didn't take much money, because my dream became theirs.

It didn't take the Tongs very long to figure out who was behind the sudden rash of killings. The Hawaiian killing spear is a pretty distinctive weapon and I'd told my men to leave them in the bodies. The Tong leaders were willing to call for a truce, and after only ten or eleven more deaths, they were willing to surrender. I let them leave; after all, their cousins—the ones in Cleveland and New York and Chicago—were still my best customers. Presented with a *fait accompli,* they still were willing to do business with me.

That's how I came to control vice in Honolulu. The Korean bars pay off. The prostitutes pay off. The dope dealers pay off. That's why it was so easy to get Eiko back: she worked for me.

We squeeze legitimate businesses too, although in truth not very hard, and besides, most of them are anxious to have friends in high places, in case they ever need help.

And where does all the money go? Obviously not to lavish parties. My soldiers know I live in a dump and haven't had a vacation in ten years. They know I'm not planning on retiring in Switzerland. They know I'll die on Hawaii. I know I'll die on Hawaii. I can see the hero worship in their eyes. Duty and hatred, except somewhere I'd lost the hatred, and only duty was left.

So where does the money go? Dig hard enough and you'll find that I founded the Trust for Hawaiian Land, although I'm much too modest to take credit for it. As for its finances, the Trust is a Hawaiian sacred cow. Nobody asks where the money comes from; they just want to make sure every cent gets spent on land. Which it does. Volunteers do all the paper work and businesses donate office space.

Not one thin dime has ever been spent on anything but land, and strangely enough, no one has ever tried to gouge on prices either. They're only too willing to sell for what the Trust offers. Well, there was one guy, but he quickly saw the error of his ways and sold out for even less than the Trust had originally offered. The Trust isn't very noticeable because it never buys land on Oahu.

That was my organization, the Trust. That was the reason I killed all those people over the years. I'd known from the start that people, perhaps innocent people, would have to die, because the organization came first.

Murder, murder was easy for Han—he wouldn't admit people were any different from rocks. It never even occurred to him to lose sleep over it. Killing wasn't much harder for Marty. It was all a high-stakes poker game to him. If you got yourself killed, well, them's the breaks and you should try to be a good sport about it. Pascal didn't have any problems with killing either. He'd overloaded on death young and a few more bodies didn't mean anything to him, especially strangers'. And the Mormons? They had the best excuse of all. They were killing for God. Like ten million crusaders before them, they thought killing in the name of the Prince of Peace was perfectly acceptable.

And me? It's always been hard for me. It's not a game and I don't think there's a Big Man upstairs blessing my trigger finger. When I first arrived in Vietnam I was like Marty. It was a new game with exciting stakes. In the village I fought for the villagers, and it was worth it. But in Hawaii I was killing for an abstraction, for an idea. It wasn't enough, it was getting harder and harder to kill for real estate. I can't do it anymore. But I can't stop. I can't betray my soldiers.

Kamehameha, Kam for short, was waiting on my *lanai*. For a change, someone too polite to barge in and sit in my favorite chair. He's a mountain of a man. Pure Polynesian and built like a brick shithouse. He makes me feel tiny. I said hello and went inside to get beers.

We finished the first one before anyone spoke; it's traditional.

"Madam Pele is erupting," he said. "Perhaps all the blood on her slopes has awoken her."

"Don't count on it."

"No," he said, "perhaps not. The news reports say that up to twenty men were killed on the volcano."

"What's your opinion?"

"Based on the strength of the eruption, I would guess closer to thirty. Many of them looked like police officers in plain clothes."

"I didn't want anyone answering embarrassing questions in return for immunity," I told him. "And besides, the organization's moving on and I figured the least I could do is leave the town with a fairly honest police force. It may be the only one in the United States."

"If so," he said, "it will not stay that way long. There were Japanese too, as well as your Mormons."

"Any trouble with the helicopters?"

"No. The Japanese actually managed to shoot one of them down. That drew most of the DEA's attention. The fat man was not with them, by the way, or at least I did not see him."

"Shit," I said. "That's too bad." Well, maybe it wasn't. Yoshima's pretty stupid. We're probably better off with him left in command.

"He hasn't left the island yet. We can still get him."

"Not without telling the whole world that the organization isn't dead, you can't. Let him go, but keep an eye out for his men. They may decide that they can't live with this shame. Probably not, though; they're just bandits."

"Everyone will be coming for you now," he said.

"It can't be helped."

"Come to Niihau. You will be honored there, and no *haole* or Buddhahead will find you."

"But I'm a *haole*, and Japanese."

"No, you are a brother to Maui. He lives within you."

"This is my home, I will not leave it."

He was silent beyond that. I had made my decision and he respected it. We sat there through the long afternoon drinking beers. The phone began to ring continuously around three o'clock, but no one came by. I had the AK propped against the railing in case somebody did.

Eventually the limousine arrived. The driver got out and

opened the rear door. He had to help the old man out. He was old, and wearing a large straw hat with a faded green ribbon for a band. He motioned the driver to get back into the car, and then hobbled up the walkway leaning heavily on his cane.

"Good evening, James," he said. "And have you betrayed me as well?"

"What for, Pascal? You're almost dead already."

He straightened up and gave me a grin that would have looked right at home on Lucifer. He twirled his cane once around and pointed it at me. "I like you," he said. "You are a very funny fellow." He bounced up the steps, much to Kam's amazement, and sat down. He was past ninety but a spry old goat. It must be all those long walks he used to take.

"I am so glad," he said. "Earlier today I was worried that you had decided to take care of all your loose ends. I was never sure if you had forgiven me for what occurred in Tiehereaux."

"Don't sweat it; they were just Army assholes."

He laughed. "That was not what I was referring to. Well, I am happy, and there are young girls all over the world who should be happy too, although they do not as yet know why." He laughed again and then looked expectantly at Kam, waiting to be introduced.

"This is Kamehameha, my second-in-command."

"The honor is mine," Pascal told him. "I regret that I did not bring *my* second-in-command, although no doubt you know him."

"I have met Pierre," Kam replied. "A true gentleman."

'Well, James, for whom are we waiting?"

"A gentleman named Orville. He owns a macadamia plantation. I believe that he will only be too happy to help us with the import-export business."

"Yes?"

"Macadamia nut brittle," I told him. "Sticks to the teeth, nasty stuff. Orville cans it and ships it to all fifty states."

"How intriguing. And you, Mr. Kamehameha, you have

no moral qualms about shipping this confection to ruin teeth all over the United States?"

Kam is a good man, but not much for beating around the bush; that's why he needs Pierre so badly. "The *haoles* brought us mosquitoes, gonorrhea and Christianity. Heroin is a blessing in comparison."

Pascal laughed and launched into the story of how we had first met. I glanced at my watch: Orville was late. I sure hoped that I wouldn't have to send someone to find him—there was probably a planeload of FBI agents on the way to Hawaii right now.

He was half an hour late. He showed up driving a station wagon with a child protection seat in the back; he looked very nervous. It was hard to believe that he had once been used to scare young Vietnamese children into behaving. "Mind your manners or the Magill will come get you." He stood at the edge of the porch, not wanting to come up.

"You asked me to come by, Chief?"

"It was an order, Orville; if I'd have asked, you'd never have come."

"Sorry, Chief, but you know I've retired. I've been strictly legitimate for five years."

"Sorry, Orville," I told him. "But I'm retired; you're going back to work."

"I can't do that, Chief. I have a family, and a business. I can't get mixed up in that stuff."

I was almost through with my speech before I realized my voice had gone flat, that there was no emotion in it. Pascal was giving me a very odd look.

"Sorry, Orville, you're mortgaged to the hilt and you've expanded way too fast. If you suddenly had labor problems you'd be out of business in three months. Then what would you do? Go back to raising pot? Think again, Orville, because no one's going to be raising pot on this island for a long time to come. Maybe you could get a job dishing out ice cream to tourists."

Manipulating Orville made me sick—we had been friends once. Pascal had told me long ago that you were dangerous only as long as you had nothing to lose. Mad Dog had a lot to lose.

He was in agony, but what could he do?

"What do you want?"

"Not much. You'll be shipping some cans of brittle to some friends of mine on the mainland. Kam will give you the addresses." His eyes lit up. "Kam will even give you the cans." His eyes dimmed again. Orville was no bigger fool than Marty had been. "You better get out of here, Orville," I told him. "You probably don't want to be seen talking to me, you being a legitimate family man and everything." He practically ran down the walk. It was really sad.

"You realize," Pascal told me, "that this has the same drawbacks as using the tourists. These cans will point a blazing arrow at Hawaii should even one be confiscated."

"It's only temporary. We're abandoning the Big Island. We'll only use Orville until Kam can get Kauai into full-scale operation. I doubt Orville's nerves will hold up for more than a year anyway."

"Speaking of not being seen in bad company," Pascal said, "I do not think it wise for Kam to stay here. Too many people know of you now, James."

Kam would have said something foolish, but I didn't let him. "He's right, Kam; you should be going."

"Aloha, James," he said, and with that he was gone.

Pascal and I sat on the porch and watched the sun set. It was very beautiful.

"You really shouldn't stay either," I told him.

"It does not matter. I am old and obviously filthy rich. No one is going to hold me very long and it is unlikely that I can be connected to the bright young Honolulu lawyer Pierre Arnaud."

"Does Pierre mind losing your name?"

"Well, it could be a problem for him if he ever goes to France and is mistaken for a Private Arnaud who deserted from the French Army in 1918. But that is not very likely, that Arnaud was much better looking."

I laughed. "And how is his lovely mother and his swarm of younger siblings?"

"They are all very fine, thank you. Mei Ling has had yet another son. I insisted that she name him James."

"Why, thank you," I said. I almost asked him about the Laotian girl I had slept with so many years before. Funny that it had never occurred to me before. In the end I decided that I was better off not knowing. "How is Mr. Han?"

"Fated to live forever and not enjoy one minute of it. He is minister of defense in the new cabinet. Life, it is very strange sometimes."

As the last of the sun disappeared over the horizon Pascal got up to leave. He turned at the walk and looked back at me. "James," he said, and paused. "That night in Tiehereaux, when I came back to find you gnawing at the rope like a giant rat . . ."

"Yes?"

"I had come back to kill you, James. I do not like to leave loose ends not tied up." He paused, waiting to see if I had anything to say. I didn't. "I thought you should know this, James. Good-bye."

"See you soon," I replied.

He laughed. "I hope not. There are so many young girls who have never met me." With that he turned and walked to his car. The driver got out and opened the door for him.

After he was gone it occurred to me that I should have asked him about Horus. Whether or not he had really set up Lucas and his men for an ambush so he'd have an excuse to bomb Tiehereaux. Pascal had once told me that he and his men had been in the village for more than a month waiting for the North Vietnamese to leave. The Vietnamese had known he had a huge sum of money. It was very convenient how they'd died. We were long gone before any of the other North Vietnamese troops in the area could have known the money hadn't gone up with the village. White phosphorus doesn't leave much in the way of embers.

But I hadn't asked. And I had never settled the score

with Horus. It didn't matter. I had bigger regrets to take into the great void.

I went inside and got my fishing pole. I decided to sleep on the beach. There were probably going to be lots of people anxious to talk to me in the morning and I wanted to avoid them for as long as possible.

CHAPTER FIFTEEN

□

HAWAII

The present

I slept on the beach at Kiholo Bay. It was safe for me. Actually Kiholo would be safe for anyone, but you'd certainly be arrested for sleeping there. No one bothered me, though. I understood from the radio reports that most of the local police department had died in a tragic case of mistaken identity. Killed by the DEA, which had thought they were drug runners. The governor had pledged that heads would roll.

I woke before dawn and made my first cast by moonlight. The AK was awkward, but I didn't feel like leaving it on the shore. The eruption was clearly visible from the beach, molten lava jetting a thousand feet into the air above the vent. The lava would cool and fall all around the island, Pele's tears. I doubt the goddess was crying for me, though. Maybe she was crying for her islands. Every new building is a knife in her heart and the people are like lice on her flanks, more of them every day.

Just before first light I heard the roar of the National Guard helicopters heading for the rain forest intent, no doubt, on exterminating the murderous pot growers. I didn't let it bother me. The beach was very beautiful. I felt at peace; the roar of the surf was like a lullaby and the sands looked pure and white in the moonlight.

They would all be coming to get me now. The *yakuza*, the Mormons, the Tongs, the bikers and even the Navy, probably. It didn't bother me. When I'd first started, the deaths had seemed regrettable but necessary. It just wasn't the same anymore. I had wanted to quit for years, nothing could be worth what I was doing.

And in the end, what was I really doing? The world is really just one big island. If people didn't come here they'd just fuck up some other part of it. I couldn't change that. I'd been naïve even to try. But I was trapped. Han had been right, I was trapped by my duty. I couldn't abandon my soldiers.

The beach was deserted, the way I like it. I figured I had two hours before the first tourist showed up.

AUTHOR'S NOTE

Chapters Two and Three of this book are based on a true story related by F.J. West in his classic work, *The Village*. West tells of a Marine Corps combined-action platoon that was stationed in a small Vietnamese fishing village during the early stages of the American involvement in Indochina. The selfless actions and devotion to duty of those Marines make up one of the more glorious chapters in the history of the United States Marine Corps. *The Village* is available in paperback from the University of Wisconsin Press.

TOP-SPEED THRILLERS WITH UNFORGETTABLE IMPACT FROM AVON BOOKS

TASS IS AUTHORIZED TO ANNOUNCE... Julian Semyonov
70569-9/$4.50US/$5.95Can
From Russia's bestselling author, the unique spy thriller that tells it from the other point of view.

RUN BEFORE THE WIND Stuart Woods
70507-9/$3.95US/$4.95Can
"The book has everything—love, sex, violence, adventure, beautiful women and power-hungry men, terrorists and intrigue."
The Washington Post

COLD RAIN Vic Tapner 75483-5/$3.95US/$4.95Can
A stunning thriller of cold-blooded espionage and desperate betrayal!

DEEP LIE Stuart Woods 70266-5/$4.50US/$6.50Can
The new Soviet-sub superthriller..."Almost too plausible...one of the most readable espionage novels since *The Hunt for the Red October!*"
Atlanta Journal & Constitution

MAJENDIE'S CAT Frank Fowlkes 70408-0/$3.95
Swindler against con man compete in a plan to bring the US to its knees and wreak global economy for good!

THE GRAY EAGLES Duane Unkefer 70279-7/$4.50
Thirty-one years after WW II, the Luftwaffe seeks revenge...and one more chance at glory.

THE FLYING CROSS Jack D. Hunter
75355-3/$3.95US/$4.95Can
From the author of *The Blue Max*, a riveting, suspense-packed flying adventure in the war-torn skies over Europe.

Buy these books at your local bookstore or use this coupon for ordering:

Avon Books, Dept BP, Box 767, Rte 2, Dresden, TN 38225
Please send me the book(s) I have checked above. I am enclosing $__________
(please add $1.00 to cover postage and handling for each book ordered to a maximum of three dollars). ***Send check or money order***—**no cash or C.O.D.'s please. Prices and numbers are subject to change without notice. Please allow six to eight weeks for delivery.**

Name ____________________

Address ____________________

City __________ **State/Zip** __________

Thrillers 1/88